EDGE OF
ETERNITY

FIRST EDITION

EDGE OF ETERNITY

JASON STEVENS

TATE PUBLISHING
AND ENTERPRISES, LLC

Edge of Eternity
Copyright © 2014 by Jason Stevens. All rights reserved.

The opinions expressed by the author are not necessarily those of Tate Publishing, LLC.

Published by Tate Publishing & Enterprises, LLC
127 E. Trade Center Terrace | Mustang, Oklahoma 73064 USA
1.888.361.9473 | www.tatepublishing.com

Tate Publishing is committed to excellence in the publishing industry. The company reflects the philosophy established by the founders, based on Psalm 68:11,
"The Lord gave the word and great was the company of those who published it."

Published in the United States of America

ISBN: 978-1-63122-721-9
1. Fiction / Christian / Romance
2. Fiction / Christian / Fantasy
14.06.05

The one thing I have loved more than anything else in this world is being a dad. With that in mind, my first dedication goes out to my son Cody because everything I do, I do with him in mind. In life, just about anything we embark on is only going to be as good as the people around us. God has blessed me with parents that have been married and best friends for over 40 years. I have also had tremendous Christians around me that have been nothing short of blessings from God. Most of my friends and family are continuously surprised at the experiences I have. Because of the great friends I have, things happen to me and for me in such a way that I have to continuously thank God for those blessings.

My friend Joe Allen provided me the opportunity and quiet spot to sit and write this book. Friends Allison Perkins, Sarah Hernandez, Stephanie Shraml, Eric Butler & Eljeana Quebedeaux gave me tons of encouragement and gave me great advice when I needed it in finalizing decisions about this book. A special thanks to Bill Windish who utilized his professional expertise to put this book in print ready format for my publisher. I am so grateful for his willingness to help!

End-Time events fascinate me! For me and my walk with God, they make Him even more real, and more present to me. As I mature as a Christian I am blessed to hear God more and more… His direction in my life is becoming clearer and clearer. I love that. I basically wrote a book that I would like to read. I also dedicate this book to you, the reader, in the hopes that you find this story encouraging and in some small way I hope it gives you something to look forward to and helps you to see God in a more real way in your own relationship with Him.

CHAPTER 1

James sat in "their" loft with his head in his hands, face puffy and eyes swollen. The thought crossed his mind that he cried more in the last 12 hours than he had in his entire life. His mind went back and forth between now and past memories. There were so many memories that James had running through his mind, of times spent with his wife Rachel. James and Rachel enjoyed hearing time and again how "unreal" their relationship was. Now James was wondering how he was going to go on. Just over 12 hours had passed since he received the call letting him know she was gone. At this point, he took little solace in knowing that one day he would see her again in Heaven, for now he felt her loss. He tried to focus on the fact that she was with Jesus, and for a half of a second this would ease his pain. He was not sad for her sake. He was simply missing her and realizing a life without her was what lay ahead.

James is a man of prayer and a Christian. As a result, he spent most of the time since this terrible news arrived, praying to the Lord for strength. Sadly, he realized he had to start calling people to tell them. How could he repeat this terrible tragedy to many different people? He could not even bring himself to say aloud to their golden retriever, Rock, that "mommy" was not coming home. Rock, who is one of the friendliest full of energy dogs one could ever meet knew something was wrong….and sheepishly stayed on his mat, looking as sad as James.

James and Rachel had been married for eight years. They met and married in college at Arizona State University. They were both sophomores, and met at a rock climbing club on campus. Rachel was one of only 3 girls in the whole club. Rachel had the attention of every guy the second she walked in. She had that rare combination of being athletic while maintaining the most beautiful femininity. Even with a pony tail, and no makeup she was a knockout. Rachel knew most eyes were on her, but her eyes were already on James.

With guys tripping over themselves to be around her, she had no reservations about approaching James. She pretended to need some help with some of her equipment, but in truth, she was probably the best rock climber in the gym. She just wanted an excuse to talk to James. While they were climbing and making small talk with each other, James was recalling a list he had made describing his ideal girl. In 10 minutes he was astonished to already know that she had six of the 11 qualities he listed. Of the five remaining, they were all possible she would fit those as well.

As the night was wrapping up, James knew he was not going to let her get away without asking her out on a date. James, normally fairly reserved when it came to meeting girls, had no issues at all when it came to asking her out. His interest in her felt as natural as could be. In fact, he never gave a thought to her saying no. Of course she did not hesitate and they agreed to meet two days later at a restaurant near campus.

She mentioned during rock climbing her love of Italian food. James figured Oregano's would be a fun tasty place to go. Knowing how small the restaurant is, and how busy it gets, he figured he should get there early. As calm and comfortable as he was around her rock climbing; two days of focusing on nothing but their upcoming date had him very nervous. Now he was terribly concerned that they would not be able to talk to each other very easily. He was concerned that if there was a long wait for a table, he might look foolish if they had to stand around talking for an hour waiting for a table. The fact is, he had absolutely nothing to worry about. Not only did they have tremendous chemistry; their interests were amazingly compatible with each other.

James was already sitting at their table 27 minutes before she was expected to arrive. He sent her a text message telling her where he was seated. She replied back making fun of him for being early and letting him know she was running about 10 minutes late. Two minutes later, the most beautiful woman James ever saw walked towards him with a huge smile on her face. All he could think of to say was "Ten minutes late huh?" She laughed, and said "I thought I was the only dork who arrived a half hour early for a date! I was going to wait in the car until it was closer to seven to come in but I didn't want to appear to be too eager. But since you were clearly more eager than me, you let me off the hook!"

James was surprised that she looked even prettier than

she did in the rock climbing gym. He told friends about her and described her as being better than a "10". In his opinion he was sitting in front of a 25 on a scale to 10. Before they even began any real in-depth conversations, they each felt as though they had known each other their entire lives. Both felt like it had never been easier to talk to anyone before. James was terrified to ask her one question though.

James had been a Christian as long as he could remember. Nothing ranked as high on his list than her being a Christian. He was so adamant about this that he was not even willing to date a girl if she was not already a Christian hoping that she would become one. However, as James sat there completely enamored with this sweet girl, he caught himself waffling a bit in his mind thinking that she seemed so sweet, that perhaps if she was not already a Christian maybe she would be open-minded to learning about God. Quickly he scolded himself in his head, knowing that if God brought this beautiful girl into his life, she would have to be a Christian if she was at all part of Gods plan in his life.

As they chatted over many topics, he was thinking about how to bring it up. He was disappointed in himself, because he was avoiding it. He was afraid that her answer would be something he did not want to hear. Just when he was about to ask her; she said "James, can I ask you a pretty forward question?" He replied "sure". For the first time since he met her, she kind of stuttered and stammered over her choice of words. She was obviously nervous. She apologized and said "I am sorry, I am little nervous asking you this, because I don't want to offend you or send you running for the hills... but I was wondering if you would be my date this Sunday to an event I am very much looking forward to?" James replied "I would love to be your date just about anywhere! Where are we going?" She said "Well, my niece is getting baptized at church, afterwards there is a party at my parent's house for her. I thought it might be fun if you were there with me, if that type of thing does not make you uncomfortable. What do you have planned for Sunday, are you available to go with me?" James was blown away! He let her know that his plans were to go to church! Their conversation turned to faith, what churches they go to. They were so excited to find out that the church James attends is the parent church of the one Rachel goes to. Their Pastors were good friends, and worked together for years. Both were non-denominational churches. James was thankful to God for matching him with a girl that appeared to be so perfect for him! Rachel also had been a Christian for much of her life.

James knew deep down that God brought them together. James thought to himself "Wow that makes seven out of eleven so far…and most importantly, she is a Christian!" He did not tell her, but his plans for the evening included them going to the local comedy club. However, as he sat there, laughing with Rachel, learning all he could about her; he could care less about the tickets in his pocket. The last thing he wanted to do was go somewhere where his attention would be away from her! All he wanted to do was keep talking with her, hear her voice, admire her beautiful face, and interact with her as much as possible. James had no idea that Rachel was feeling very much the same things.

Later in their relationship when the topic of how they met and how their relationship developed would come up, neither wanted to over dramatize it. They did not want to admit they fell in love with each other that first night. They thought it seemed too dramatic to say that, but they truly did. They would discuss the immediate connection they had, and how much they enjoyed each other, and how silly Rachel was, and how James energy and passion attracted her to him. When they parted ways late that evening just before midnight, James leaned forward and kissed Rachel on her cheek. They both drove away convinced they just met the person they were going to marry.

James was absolutely heartbroken now, the one true love of his life was gone. He was exhausted early that morning, he might have slept an hour the whole night. The night before James had a surprise for Rachel. He was not sure if she realized it was exactly nine years ago that he had proposed to her. He knew she was going to stop on her way home to workout. James used that time to create a very romantic scene for her. He had more candles in their loft than should be allowed by law! He prepared her favorite meal and a tasty dessert for her to enjoy. When he was finished setting the mood, he waited for her.

Everyone in their life made fun of them because hardly an hour would pass without them calling each other. So when she was a half hour late, especially after he had told her they had dinner plans, he naturally worried. He knew something was wrong because this was not just unusual for her; it was not her at all! He kept calling her cell phone but, it went straight to her voice mail. He knew that she had not returned to the car from her workout. He went from worried, to deeply concerned after she was an hour late. For Rachel, a typical workout was running up and down Squaw Peak Mountain twice. She could make it up in 19 minutes, and down in 12 minutes. She would go up and down the mountain twice in a single workout. She had this same routine even five years before she met James. James jumped in the car, and headed to the mountain hoping he would not find her car there.

As James took the windy road from the residential neighborhood towards the mountain near where the cars parked, he caught some flashing lights ahead for a brief second. His worst fears were starting to become more real. As he took the last part of the winding road to the parking lot she normally parked in, he could see Fire Trucks, Ambulances, and Police Cars. His phone rang, and a person identifying himself as a Phoenix Fireman, asked if he was her Husband. James could not even say yes, he just started to cry; and all the Fireman could utter was "I am sorry". James told the Fireman he just arrived at the parking lot, and the Fireman approached him. He was told of the news of what they guessed was a freak accident. Some climbers had found her. She apparently tripped and hit her head and fell 20 feet. The way she landed, they said she had died instantly.

He was stunned. He saw her body, and except for a few minor cuts and scrapes, she looked like she was sleeping. He begged her to wake up. He begged God to allow her to live. He cried so hard, and so loud, that grown men, tough city serviceman; police officers and fireman had to wipe away their tears. James pain was so intense that everyone in the area was truly sad. He just held on to her, and prayed. He then knelt over, and said aloud "Lord, I know she is already with you, and as much as this hurts, I pray her soul to you, and am thankful that she is home, with you, her Savior. Please tell her I love her, and I will look forward every day to seeing her again. In Jesus' name I pray, Amen"

With that, he stood up and left. Some who witnessed this thought he was some sort of a freak; others, few as they were, completely understood, and quickly said a prayer of their own.

So now, James, sitting with a phone in his hand, trying to figure out how in the world to he is going to call her parents and tell them. Rachel's Dad, is a man whom James respected from the first day he met him. James often said he could not have been blessed with a more perfect Father in Law. Through the years, he has come to be James mentor. James has said he has learned more about God, and his maturing faith through John (Rachel's Dad), than any other person. Johns Wife, Rebecca is the epitome of class. Everyone thought of her as sweet, refined, and lights up a room with her presence. Her faith is off the charts, and the women of her Bible study just love her leadership.

After sitting for nearly 20 minutes trying to figure out what words to say to her parents, he decided it was only appropriate to tell them in person. During the 25 minute car ride over, James did call some of their friends to tell them. He called his best friend and his wife, who Rachel had become very good friends with over the last three years. Of course, they were heartbroken and stunned. They wanted to keep James on the phone, and make sure he was alright, and get more details about what had happened. They just did not feel like they should let him be alone. He insisted that he should keep the phone calls short. He knew if he stayed on too long with anyone he would lose it on the phone and break down. He also said it was important that he call others to tell them too. He called his boss as well as Rachel's boss, who was also one of her best friends. Rachel told James that it was just a matter of time before her boss was going to make her a partner in the law firm. Rachel was so much more than just one of the lawyers to her boss.

James arrived at Rachel's parents. John and Rebecca were outside doing some yard work. They lit up when they saw James car pull up. As James exited the car, Rebecca said "Where is Raech…." Then she saw his face. In an instant Rachel's mom knew the look on his face was bigger than regular bad news, she knew this was not something silly like an argument between James and Rachel. She knew she would never see her daughter alive again, and she just fell to her knees and bawled. James saw a look in Rachel's dad's eyes that he had never seen before. This confident, intelligent, man of God suddenly looked like a zombie. Neighbors heard Rebecca crying and came out. John helped his wife to her feet, and the three of them went into the house. James fell into a chair, and John helped Rebecca to the couch, where he held her. Her sobbing calmed to crying, and not a word was said for nearly five minutes. Finally John looked up from his devastated wife, and looked toward James. He asked "what's happened to my baby girl?"

James had hoped by telling a few people on the way over that it would make it easier to say it to her parents. But as he told them "she had an accident during her workout on the mountain", he just lost it. He started crying. Rachel's parents instinctively moved towards James and held on to him. The three of them held each other crying, for what seemed like hours. After they stopped crying, John's dad insisted they pray together. They did. They confessed that even though there is no way in this world they could ever understand this part of Gods plan, they would do their best to focus on the fact that she is in Heaven with Jesus.

As they were praying, Rachel's brother walked in. David is Rachel's big brother, older by almost three years. James hit it off with him when they first met at Rachel's church, for her niece's baptism. They have become very good friends, playing in basketball and softball leagues together. Like everyone else, David was absolutely crushed. He could not believe his little sister was gone. David lives right up the road from his parents; and when he saw James and Rachel's car out front, he thought he would come by and see his sister. David happily came to visit his sister. Little did he know the bad news he was walking into. .

After a while, James stood to leave, and Rebecca asked that he stay for a bit. She fixed him some food, and insisted that he use the guest room to lie down for a little while. James lay down figuring he would leave in an hour or so. He slept through the entire day, and did not even stir until about 3 a.m. He woke up, contemplated heading home, but just laid their thinking. He recalled a dream he had that night.

He dreamt about seeing Rachel at a waterfall. He remembered the water being so loud they had to yell to talk to each other. He could not remember anything they said in their conversations though. He also remembered one other dream that he had. This dream was more like a memory he had of when he and Rachel played each other in a basketball game. She guarded him so closely that it tickled him, and he lost his coordination. He felt like a limp noodle playing against her and she whipped him 11 to four. She never let him live that down. He dreamt every single moment of that memory, like it just happened. He also vaguely remembered what felt like God or an Angel telling him to be faithful and everything will work out.

He thought long and hard about this, but the details

were so sketchy. He felt like he was sort of remembering someone else's dream. He began to pray. First he asked, if this was a dream or real. Then he asked if this was God, or an Angel. He did not feel like God was talking to him at all concerning this. As he kept praying, earnestly asking what this was, as he fell back asleep.

The Sun finally woke him up just after 10:00 a.m. He could only see the bright of the light coming in through the blinds. When his eyes focused on the guest room he had been sleeping in; it all rushed into his head like flooding waters. He quickly remembered, and knew, that Rachel was indeed gone, and sadly, it was not just a bad dream he would awake from and things would return to "normal".

He took a quick shower, and changed into some of the athletic clothes that he left at her parent's house, in case a pick up basketball or football game was started during a family gathering. He walked into the family room to see Rachel's parents sitting in silence. John asked him how he was doing. Rachel's parents surprisingly apologized to James for "his" loss. James was caught off guard by their sympathy, for him. Rachel was every bit "daddy's little girl" and mommy's little girl too! He knew how much this wounded their hearts. He knew that things would never be the same, for them either without her. Once again, they showed James how compassionate they are. James was impressed, and felt a little guilty that they were able put aside their own pain to worry about him.

He had a few stops he needed to make, but remembered that Rock needed to be let out and was probably starving by now. As James went in the house, the silence was deafening. Rachel was one of those girls that never are quiet! However, when you put James and Rachel together, it was nonstop talking. James could not recall a Saturday that he was home without Rachel. Although he knew their had to be occasions that she would run an errand, or have something going on with a girlfriend; in his pain, it seemed like this was the first Saturday in their entire married life that he was home without her.

James was used to thinking about Rachel. He estimated he thought about her just about every minute of every day. While apart, he wondered how his successes would impress her. He worked out every bit as hard as she did, to give her his very best physically. They even discussed that as healthy as they were, they were sure to either live to a ripe old age together, or until Jesus came back for his children to take them to Heaven. Either way they thought they were covered. James realized the irony of that. She was so determined to be in top physical shape, to avoid any unexpected health issues; it was this very drive that ended her beautiful life so prematurely. Now it was glaringly apparent though that thinking about her every minute would not bring out feelings of optimism and excitement; because now, thinking about her every minute was a reminder of what he had lost.

James knew he had many calls to make. As much as this pained him, he did not want people to hear this terrible news through the grapevine. He felt like he owed it to Rachel to tell everyone himself. He spent that afternoon calling people. Most calls were short, and sad. Some calls would lead to reminiscing about how exceptional she was and how much they will miss her. With a few people, like James sister Stephanie, she brought up a memory that James had not thought about in years. When Rachel turned 21, all everyone did was ask her if she was excited that she could legally drink. Rachel could care less about drinking. She was not opposed drinking; in fact, there were plenty of nights that Rachel and James would sip a glass of wine on the patio of their loft looking at their scenic view. Rachel heard about a costume party that was being thrown on campus the very night of her birthday. She dressed as a bottle of tequila, and made James dress as a six pack of beer. Then to be silly, as only Rachel could, she declared that she and James only drink Root Beer that night! Of course James sister who was only 19 at the time, dressed as a playboy bunny and was chastised by James many times over the years for drinking something much stronger than Root Beer that night!

James wondered if he could ever bring himself to go to a costume party again, or Rock Climbing, or sipping wine looking at "their" view. Common sense told him he would have to engage in life again. For now, he could not imagine that, and felt common sense or not, there are just too many things he will never be able to do again; not without her.

James was grateful for all the kind sentiments from his family and friends. He was so appreciative of how obvious it was that everyone who knew Rachel, truly loved her, and thought she was as special as he did. He also thought it was truly special and realized how blessed he is to have so many people willing to drop everything they are doing to come be with him, or make a meal, or for those who do not cook to bring him some takeout. He told everyone the same thing; "thank you, thank you so much, but that is not necessary, and I have so much to do, and really; I need to be alone right now to gather myself". Of course hearing him indicate this just gave them more cause for concern. Most believed that he needed to be around people, and not be alone. They tried to encourage him to accept some company.

As he sat, in the dark, after 9:00 p.m. on the floor, with Rock in his lap, he was simply crushed. He had a million thoughts running through his head, and none, at the same time. He could not believe two nights had already gone by since "that night". He was pained to think that in the blink of an eye, he would be realizing "I can't believe it's been a month" since she passed away. Of course he envisioned that each minute going forward would be as painful as this one. Despite the efforts of family and friends, to tell him it will get easier, he did not believe that; he did not want to hear that! As his phone was ringing, he thought "another dear friend to tell me it's going to be okay". He appreciated their intentions, but he did not believe things were going to be all right.

He pushed the dog off of his lap and leaned back to grab

the phone. This was not the phone call he was expecting. He figured it would be a friend or his sister checking on him; it was Rachel's mom. She did, in fact, ask him "Are you hanging in there sweetie?" James replied "you know mom, it's so hard, just like I am sure it is for you, everyone means well, but I think my heart is just going to stop, you know?" She attempted some soothing words, then spoke of something that he was not expecting, at all. Rebecca said "James, we have to plan the funeral" James exclaimed "Whoa! Funeral?" He was thinking to himself "That's for dead people right?"

Obviously this was a natural part of this devastating situation, but James had not even neared the thought of a funeral. He did not know how to respond. After about 10 seconds of silence Rebecca inquired "James?" He responded "yeah, I am here…I am sorry. I just…I just didn't even think about that. Wow, a funeral for Rachel. Those words just don't make sense. Is that what we do? We have a funeral, put her to rest, and then move on? Oh my gosh, that hurts to think about." Rebecca in her most sympathetic voice said "Honey, I know, don't you think I know? A mom is not supposed to burry her child. But Rachel deserves this! Everyone deserves this; everyone needs an opportunity to celebrate her life….

and say goodbye."

James, realizing he may have hurt her feelings let her know that was not his intention at all "oh, Rebecca, I know that. Please, know I know that. I am not trying to be selfish; I know you and John are as heartbroken as me. I know that. Please know, when I say what I say, I am not trying to take away from your pain, or monopolize all the grief. That's not it at all. I am lost. I mean, she was my world, you know that. I have only had one death to experience in my life before this. My grandfather died at eighty two. That wasn't so shocking or sad. I didn't have to plan anything, you know? I mean, I am just lost, and sad, and confused. I mean, do I call a mortuary? Do I call the Hospital, the church? Mom, I don't even know where her body is right now."

Rebecca reassured James telling him "Hon, there is little you can say right now that is going to hurt my feelings, so don't you worry about that. I know you are hurting and believe me; you are constantly in my prayers. I can only imagine what you are feeling right now. Truth is...I didn't want to step on your toes with all of this. I know she is your wife, and I know how seriously you take the responsibility to honor, and protect her. James, if it's okay with you, I'd be perfectly fine handling all of the arrangements; is that okay with you?" James said "absolutely, please! Thank you. Oh my goodness, how pathetic, I am grateful that someone is handling the details of my wife's funeral. There is something gravely wrong about this."

Again, Rebecca reassured James "I know honey, I know. You are so right. Maybe we all put her on a pedestal. Listen, is there anything you want to request, or make sure that is included in the arrangements?" "I haven't even been to a real funeral, so I don't even know what I don't know. All I know, is that I want a chance to speak...is that okay?" Rachel's mom replied back "of course, not only okay, but I'd have to say, as tough as it will be, quite expected. Listen you go to sleep sweetie, get some rest, and just lean on the Lord right now. I know you probably feel like He took her from you, we all do to an extent. But God loves you, so much, we all do. God can, and will provide you strength through this if you rely on him. Trust Him James; okay?" James was quick to say "I do, I promise you I do. I have no doubt that God brought Rachel and me together. How could I be bitter towards Him now? I mean, even if I only had a week with her, I wouldn't trade it for anything. He allowed eight years of what I have to describe as an absolutely perfect marriage. I mean how many marriages even last eight years? Let alone, a truly happy eight plus years together."

Rebecca had to hold back her tears as she said "James you are so right. My baby was so lucky to have you in her life. When she was a little girl, we talked about the kind of man we wanted for her, and I prayed with her for the right Christian man to come into her life. It was you. I love you James. We all do, and you will always be part of our family, I hope you know that!" James was now crying a little too when he said "oh I hope you know, that you and John and the rest of the family are so important to me. Not just because of Rachel, but I love you all so much."

"I wouldn't be the man I am today if not for all of you, sincerely I mean that. Thank you! Thank you for calling, I am going to bed now. I feel like I really need to be in prayer right now." "Okay sweetie, I hope you have comforting dreams tonight" Rebecca said. James quickly replied "Oh, one more thing, is there like a gathering afterwards where we meet for drinks and snacks or whatever? You know, like a reception?" Rebecca Chuckled "Yes dear, it's not called a reception, but yes, we will all get together after the funeral."

James asked "Can you make sure the only drink available is Root Beer?"

CHAPTER 2

The next morning James woke up closer to his usual wakeup time of 7:30 a.m. He felt like he had slept well, but his dreams seemed heavy. He knew he spent the entire night dreaming, but could not remember any details. However, he felt very strongly he had been visited by an Angel or God again. He tried to recall, but could not remember. The only thing he could figure out was that God was somehow comforting him in his sleep. This gave James somewhat of a sense of peace; however, being the details guy that he is, he wanted to know what was going on.

As he showered and shaved, he wondered if he could make himself go to Church on this day. The last time James went to Church without Rachel, she was sick. This was only about seven months ago. She was convinced she was having morning sickness. Turns out it was food poisoning. They never actively tried to have a baby, but recently started saying it was time to. He never regretted putting that off, until now. As much as he would not want to raise a child without her; he sure wished he had a piece of her to watch grow up. Now he was going to go to church without his best friend, the only women he ever loved. He knew that there would be 30 to 40 people there that had heard the terrible news, the ones he personally called. He also knew that word had surely spread, and church would be about her this morning. James appreciated this, but it only made him sadder. Deep down, James thought he should have the answers, but in truth, nobody expected him to.

He had no idea how hard it was going to be. The instant he walked away from his car, friends greeted him in the parking lot. He received what felt like a million hugs. James completely broke down. He was overwhelmed. All the way into church, he was showered with sympathies. He sat down, and the Worship team started the music. Of course, by pure coincidence the second song they sang was Rachel's favorite song for the last year. After the singing, the

Pastor walked up to the pulpit.

He began his sermon "Friends! Many of you know we have lost a dear, dear sister. Rachel Mahody passed away this past week. For those of you who knew her, she was a wife of eight years, an accomplished attorney, a rock climbing enthusiast, and loved nothing more than being active. She died doing something she loved to do. I have to tell you, I have known Rachel, way before she was a Mahody, back when she was a Miller. I baptized her when she was 11 years old. Normal procedure is to stand up here and say nice things about people that have passed on. In Rachel's case, it is all true. Heart, energy and passion. Beauty, wit, and drive. She had it all!"

"When she married James, I thought wow, what a lucky guy. As I have come to know James, I realize she was equally blessed. James, John and Rebecca Miller, and other family members, I am so deeply sorry for your loss. Selfishly, we all want her here, no doubt about that. But knowing her heart, the way I have come to know it over these last 13 years….Our loss is her gain. We have all suffered a profound loss by her passing on. But Heaven, under Gods will, and wonderfully divine plan, is absolutely a better place as of now. Rachel had so much to give, but for reasons only God understands, her passing serves a greater purpose. I hope we are witnesses to that greater purpose while we are still here."

Church was more unbearable than he thought it would be. He even questioned if this would be easier if she were not so likeable to everyone! Of course he knew this was ridiculous to even think; but it was quite the extreme to go from planning a nice romantic celebration of an anniversary, to dealing with his wife's death, right in her prime. This made no sense. He could not reconcile it. And, tomorrow morning at 9:30 a.m. would be the funeral for Rachel Mahody. This would be worse than Church. On top of that, after the funeral, he would be expected to resume his real life responsibilities again.

James wondered how that could be possible. For James, Real life had been rock climbing with Rachel. To him it was endless conversing. Cuddling up on the couch to watch their favorite movie for the hundredth time together was real life to him. As James thought about it; he realized that nearly one hundred percent of his planning for the last nine years involved her. He did not even eat a meal without her mind. When they met, James thought she could play any sport she wanted to. James thought Rachel was the most athletically gifted girl he had ever met. However, she loathed golf. She said many times in their first year together "golf is a sport for fat men who can't move their legs". He laughed at her, and told her "if you only knew!" The closer they grew together, the more she realized how silly it was for him to go golfing, with two or three strangers, when she could be with him doing something he enjoyed. She decided to learn how to golf. Like everything else in her life, she was very good at it. Not before a few tantrums that were the result of her competitive spirit! She did become very good. She beat James six out of 10 times they would play.

So how was he to "move on"? How could he do that, when his entire life was spent with her? They prayed together, worshiped together, and went to church together, dreamed together. Often they felt like God was telling them the same things. In Bible study the other couples would laugh at them, because they would trip over each saying the same things. They marveled at how they even felt like they grew in the Lord at the same pace. Of course this delighted them. They loved each other, and cared for each other very much! That said, they always put God first in their relationship. They truly had a special union.

James recalled a conversation they had together one night in which Rachel asked "do you think God delights in our relationship?" James remembered being puzzled by the question, but said to her "I know that God delights in all praise towards Him. I know he delights in the fact that you have given your heart to Him, as have I. We put Him first in all we do, probably why we are pretty much always on the same page, that, and you know I am always right!" Rachel shot back "shush! I am being serious!" He said "I know, I am teasing…but seriously, individually we have strong faith, and love God with all our hearts. Our marriage is built on a foundation of our trust and faith in the Lord, and sincerely we seek him as a married a couple. So yes, I would think he does delight in our relationship. Friends of ours use us an example of what they want to be; so that means we are a good witness! So yes, to answer your question!" Smirking Rachel said "Good man, such a way with words, now I remember why I married you!"

Now James was questioning his answer to her on that night. Did God truly delight in their relationship? If He did, why would he end it? Why would He let her fall or trip, or whatever happened. Why did she have to die? If they were such a blessing to others, such a glorifying witness, how could her death serve a greater purpose? Maybe their marriage was not such a glorifying witness; he started to question everything. Then he popped himself in the forehead, and reminded himself not to rewrite the past because something bad has happened. Deep down he knew they were a delight to the Lord, they loved Him, and put Him first; but James still had that lingering question, of why God allowed her to die.

James woke up and reached to Rachel's side of the bed; but felt nothing. As he rubbed his eyes, dreading the funeral, he was terribly confused. He just had the most vivid dream of his life. Every detail and conversation was crystal clear. Some of it made sense, and some was terribly confusing. He dreamt that he and Rachel were walking through a forest. James was holding her hand as they walked. She asked him "babe how much do you love me?" As James started to answer she said "no, I want to feel it....you know, like the song, "it's in his kiss" He took her by the hand, stepping towards her. She backed up slightly, up against a tree. He brushed her hair away, and leaned forward to kiss her. Like the millions of times before, they passionately embraced, kissing a kiss that was more than a kiss. He felt so connected to her. This kiss told volumes. He kissed her like he had not seen her in years.

They started walking again. She said with a huge smile on her face "wow, I am really loved!" He asked her "did you really question that?" With his normal smirk when he is being sarcastic. She then said "no not at all, but I don't want you to forget….will you still love me, even after I fall?" James was struck at how out of place this question was, but then all at once, he felt like he was in the moment, and the memories of her death flooded in. As he looked up, she was gone, but in the distance was a man in a white robe, chiseled features, long beard, with a walking stick. He simply said "James, have faith, Trust in the Lord your God, with all of your heart, mind and soul" That is was when James woke up.

What in the world could this dream mean? The dream was so real, so vivid! As he dressed for the funeral, he prayed, and asked God repeatedly to reveal to him what this means. Was his mind just going crazy searching for answers? Was God telling him something? He already knew to trust in the Lord with all his mind, body and soul. So if he already knows this, James thought perhaps his mind was using his own knowledge to make sense of this. James was hurting, terribly confused. He could not fathom God speaking to him in this manner. He never had dreams like this before; nothing even close!

As James was seated waiting for the Pastor to come up and begin, he looked around at all the pictures of Rachel that had been placed all over the room. He could not help but think that the pictures appeared more like a photo shoot for a model, than for a funeral. There were about 25 pictures properly placed for all to see. Most of the pictures were Rachel by herself. There were also a few family pictures mixed in. One was an impromptu photo take by a friend in a restaurant with a bunch of friends. The picture, more than any captured the beauty, passion and essence of Rachel. She was so laid back, huge smile, comfortable being around people she enjoyed. James had seen this picture before. Rachel even teased him about it. Everyone in the group was talking to someone else in the group. Except James, he was sitting off to the side staring at Rachel.

He reflected on what this day meant, and said a quick

silent prayer to himself. He could not believe why all these people were here. Rachel was known for getting groups of people together; the thought never even crossed his mind that so many of her friends and family would gather for such a sad event. As far as funerals go, it was a nice presentation. As sad as people were, most of people who did speak, like her brother, and parents, kept it very positive and upbeat. They spoke of how special she was, how she impacted them, but seemingly avoided speaking of how much they will miss her.

James was the last to speak. He felt lethargic and wiped out walking up to the podium. James had not thought of much else since it happened, but he could not bring himself to sit down and write down any thoughts. He simply walked up, and said what came to his mind. He stood behind the microphone, nobody stirred. There was not a sound in the building. If asked, James would never want this to be about him. He did not want this to be about what he was going through. However, everyone in that room was acutely aware of what he lost, and there was a tremendous sadness for him. He cleared his throat, and began to speak "Wow…look at all of you here. Thank you for coming. Man this sucks. I have to tell you, as much as I already miss her, I can't help but reflect on how blessed I have been. Many of you know me well; is there a more perfect girl for me? I already miss her terribly, and am truly stunned she is gone. But I feel like I really want you to know her the way I knew her. I really want you to leave here knowing how truly special she was. Anyone could tell by looking at her how incredibly beautiful she was. We all knew from minute one she was a terrific athlete, funny, and fully of energy. But she was so weird too! I mean weird in a fantastic way!"

James paused, kind of chuckled then went on "One time, she woke me up with a loud noise; I looked around, and saw a trail of paper leading out of our room. I followed the trail, until I was standing in front of our pool. The trail led to the drain. As I bent down to open the drain, she flew from around the corner, launched at me, and tackled me into the pool! I asked why she did that, and she responded "because I really wanted you to go swimming with me!" I asked her "couldn't you have just asked?" She said "of course! But what fun would that have been?" Everyone who came to say their goodbyes laughed at his story. This just gave them a little more insight into what they already knew about

Rachel. James went on to ask "What kind of girl does that? That's how she was. She made everything a memory. I feel like I remember just about everything we ever did, because she never let it be small. She never did anything exactly like you expected it."

"Many of you have heard and know the details of when I proposed to her. What most of you do not know is what Rachel did the following night. I came home from work, and she was hiding in my apartment. As soon I shut the door, she screamed Freeze! She told me to not say a word, and to put my hands up, and turn around. She blindfolded me, and walked me outside, through the street, and into the community pool area. She had the pool area all lit up. There was a table with candles, and a nice dinner waiting for me. She visited the manager of my apartment complex, and reserved the pool area for two hours. Before dinner, she sat next to me, and explained how excited she was that I asked her to be my wife. She informed me that she needed to ask me a question. She wanted to ask me if I would be her husband, and if I would promise to be her best friend forever! She wanted to know if I would continue to trust that God brought us together. She also wanted to make sure that we would always seek Him as a couple. She continued by pulling out a ring and asking if I would wear her ring forever. I was floored. After I had proposed to her, she proposed to me. That is how she was. In our relationship, she wanted everything to be equal. She never presented it as a one up type thing. She just wanted me to feel how she felt."

With James voice trembling he said "and that is how I felt. I love her so much, so completely, so deeply, but she made me feel the exact same way." James paused, reflecting on his own words "I have to add one more thing. To some, the worst thing about Rachel was her devotion to God. Of course there are always going to be some that think she, or any believer in Jesus takes it too far. There are some people, even to her last day, she prayed for you to come to know the Lord. I know Rachel would want me to convey this to you at least one more time. We will miss her. But let it be known, Rachel is alive. She is alive and well. She is in Heaven, with our Savior, Jesus Christ. Please, if you have not accepted Him as your Savior, especially if you have been putting it off, please don't delay anymore! Rachel is a perfect example of how fragile and unexpected the end of life on this planet can be. Nobody in a million years woke up last Thursday thinking that Rachel would not survive the day."

"I have tried and tried to reconcile her loss. I have asked God repeatedly why He let her die. The only thing I know to be true is that God has a plan. The Bible says what man intends for bad, God can use for good. I have to believe that there are some of you in here today that will come to accept Jesus as your savior because of Rachel's death. For those of you that have listened to her, heard her, and hopefully were considering what she had said; I ask you prayerfully to consider the words she told you. You are not guaranteed to make it home safe today. Even Rachel, seemingly as perfect as they come had sin in her life. Like us, she still had the need of a Savior, to pay the price for those sins, so she could go to Heaven. She is there now. Believe me, she is! The only thing that could help lessen the pain of this tragedy would be for someone here today to accept Jesus as a result of what Rachel has said many times before. Eternal life is only assured by accepting the gift that God gave us. His Son Jesus Christ who paid the price, once and for all for our sins. I urge you today; assure yourself of an eternity in Heaven with your creator who loves you, and the added bonus of being able to see Rachel again someday."

As James looked across the room, he could see looks of both agreement, and others thinking he was one of those crazy "bible thumpers." James finished by saying "Look, I know this makes some of you uncomfortable. However, if you really knew Rachel, then you know how important your soul is to her. Rachel loved with her whole heart, and many of you were the recipients of that compassion and heartfelt interest in you. Just know that there is a Heaven and Hell, and Rachel is in Heaven, for only one reason; her faith in Jesus as her Savior. I looked forward each day to what adventures Rachel would bring into my life. I know how blessed I was to have her for the nine years that I had her in my life."

"Rachel, I love you with all of my heart, and that will never, ever stop. You were absolutely the best friend, and wife I could have ever dreamed of. I will continue to see you in my dreams, and look forward to seeing you in Heaven. Please wait for me by the Eastern Gate; I love you!"

After the funeral family and friends went to John and Rebecca's to gather and have a chance for a more personal goodbye in sharing memories together. James sister walked up to give him a hug, and could not help laughing about the Root Beer. This was probably the first time in four days that

James genuinely laughed. There were tons of shared stories, some that James had not even heard. Rachel's childhood best friend, April, came to pay her respects. Rachel and April were best friends until college. April went away to Syracuse. They promised they would stay in touch and talk every day, it just did not happen. When James and Rachel married, April was in Europe taking part in an internship. This was the first time James met her in person.

As sad as he was, he enjoyed hearing the many stories of Rachel as a little girl from April's perspective. Not surprisingly Rachel was no different in many ways as a child. April told of her twelfth birthday. April called Rachel the night before crying because her dad had some problem with one of his properties in another state. Her parents were to leave first thing in the morning to go deal with it, and would be gone for four days, and promised to celebrate her birthday when they returned. Rachel felt so sad for April that she gathered some things, and snuck out of her house. She had spent half the night going around their neighborhood hiding things and drawing a map. Despite staying awake most of the night, she showed up at April's house bright and early, with balloons and a birthday hat. She sang April Happy

Birthday and told her to get ready. They spent most of the day searching the neighborhood for clues, having all kinds of fun. The 'prize' at the end of the map, was a strip mall nearby where their favorite Ice Cream shop was.

While enjoying some Birthday ice cream, little did either of them know that April's parents never did leave town, and their original birthday plans were to go on as planned. They were trying to surprise April. While Rachel and April enjoyed their reward for finding the "X" on the map, April's parents were searching the neighborhood for her. The two had unknowingly caused a great deal of anxiety and panic, including a call to the police! However, in the end, it ended up being April's favorite birthday ever!

After saying goodbyes and shedding a few more tears, James headed home. He recalled the past four days in his head. He thought to himself "that's it, it's done?"....then interrupted his own thoughts and said aloud "it's not done! Just because we had a dang funeral doesn't make it over!" James was heartbroken. Was he expected to just return to the way he lived his life before, but without Rachel? He could not understand how he was going to start living his life again, when the biggest part of his life was gone? Real life, he knew, would never be the same again.

CHAPTER 3

James lay in bed that night with his eyes wide open thinking about things. He could hear Rock laying next to the bed whimpering in his sleep. He wondered if Rock was having a bad dream, missing Rachel like he was. While in the midst of praying that God would lessen his pain, he fell asleep. James experienced another vivid dream. This time he was sitting on the edge of a lake looking at the water. He could see Rachel about 50 yards down the coastline standing looking out over the water. Her hair was being blown straight back, she looked almost angelic. He knew it was her. He could not speak to her though. As he was staring at her off in the distance, someone came up from behind him, putting his hand on James shoulder. James tried to turn to look, but the grip on his shoulder tightened, and would not allow him rotate at all. He heard the man in a deep but soothing voice say to him "Beloved, do not fear, nor be sad, for she is Home. Stay faithful and you will hold her once again"

After hearing this, James literally launched out of bed from a deep sleep, in the middle of the night. Rock started barking extremely aggressively; James scared him into thinking something was wrong. Never before had James experienced dreams quite as vivid as this. He thought long and hard about this dream as he stared out the window, acutely aware that this had been "their" view that he was staring at. He lay back down, and could see Rock sitting, staring at him. Rock knew the bed was off limits to him, but James made an exception and asked "you want up? You want to sleep with…." and before he could finish asking if Rock wanted to sleep in his bed, Rock launched up into bed. Rock moved up against James, and fell asleep almost immediately. James realized that even poor Rock was affected by Rachel's death. As James contemplated the meaning of the dream, he soundly fell asleep.

James awoke and readied himself to go into the office. All morning as he went about his normal routine for work he thought about how different things already were. He recalled how he and Rachel had breakfast together at their house the morning of the day she passed away. James spent the previous night working on his computer until late in the evening. He recalled how slow he was getting around that morning. Rachel made breakfast for them, to enjoy together. They had very nice intimate conversation that morning, and James did all he could to not mention that it was the anniversary of his proposal to her. He did not want to give any hint of the plans he made. He started to question himself regarding his plan to surprise her versus letting her know up front. He questioned that if she had known his plans, perhaps she might have skipped her workout. He wondered if perhaps she was anticipating a night alone with him, she would not have been on the mountain by herself.

James deliberated on these thoughts for a few minutes in his head. Then he realized how ridiculous these ideas were. Rachel and James both went to extremes planning surprises for each other. Why would James have on this one occasion not surprised her? Of course hindsight gave him an excellent reason; but logic said that just did not make sense. Additionally even though James did not understand, he knew

God has a plan. James knew very well, that if it was her time in Gods plan, whether she was running up and down a mountain, or having dinner with him, she would still be gone right now. As much as he missed her, rewriting the history of their relationship was not going to change anything.

James arrived at work, and went into his office and closed the door. The second he walked into the building he could tell people were quieting themselves. They were surprised to see him at work so soon. Various coworkers who also considered James a friend, wanted to console him. There were others whom barely knew Rachel, or had only seen her a few times and were not sure how to react or to approach him. In these instances, they just kind of paused and watched James walk into his office and close the door.

James sat down at his desk. He exhaled and worked his mouse until he was in the inbox of his email account. James saw that he had 177 emails. His eyes became blurry as he had no interest in reading any of them. He sat back in his chair and wondered what he was doing there. He realized at that moment that work was the furthest thing from his mind. That morning while getting ready he tried to trick himself into believing that working would help take his mind off of the greatest loss in his life. As he was contemplating what he would do next, one of the managing partners of his firm walked in asked "James, what are you doing here?" James looked up, and said "Tony, I really don't know. I thought it was time to go back to work, and try to take my mind off of things, but I just don't know. Now that I am here, I don't want to be here, and I don't think I can do this. To be honest, I just don't care about working right now." Tony replied "James, go home. You need to have time to mourn. You'll know when it's time to come back. Just go home, take care of yourself; okay James?"

James informed Tony "I am going to take two weeks off if that is okay…I have no idea what I am going to do, but I have to get away. I never realized before, but as much as I love my job, my sense of purpose was Rachel. Even in my efforts here at work. More than the accolades, or the money, all I cared about was what Rachel thought of me. I need to figure out how to live for me now I guess." Tony was sad hearing the obvious pain that James was in. There was no doubt in his mind that James was a vital asset to the company; but right now, all he wanted was for his friend to stop hurting. He told James "I think you are right buddy.

You aren't helping yourself going through the motions. Do what you have to do, and if you need an ear, you know I am here for you! One more thing, if you need longer than two weeks, take it, okay?"

James pulled into his driveway right next to Rachel's car. This made him sad. He knew that Rebecca must have arranged for Rachel's car to be delivered. He realized he was very blessed to have such a kind and helpful Mother in Law, and briefly thought how different things would have been the last few days without her. James went into the house and sat down on the couch. He threw his head back in despair, and cried. As his crying subsided he began to pray aloud "Lord, what do I do? I love you, you know I do. I know your word tells me that you would never put more on my plate that I can handle, but I am questioning that right now. I am not sure I can handle this. I confess to You, I have no idea why you allowed this. I have no idea why this is part of your plan. I have no idea what to do. I need you right now. I beg you Lord, heal my broken heart. Please give me comfort, and please, please show me what you want me to do."

James jumped up, changed out of his work clothes into some exercise clothes. He grabbed some bottled water, and the dog leash. Rock jumped up, ran to the door wagging his tail so hard it thumped against the wall. James wondered if Rock was excited to get out, or if he thought they were going to see Rachel. James questioned himself as he drove that winding neighborhood road towards the parking lots at the base of the mountain. He wondered if he was torturing himself by going to the mountain, or if this would have some sort of redeeming healing aspect to it. James parked, and let Rock out of the car. He looked towards the mountain peak, and just stared. He wondered if he had the energy to do this. All he had wanted to do for the last few days was lie around and sleep. He stared up at the mountain wondering if he had the energy for this kind of exercise. Rock started barking at him, making clear he was ready to go!

The two worked their way up the mountain. Rock was excited, James was sad. He did not know the spot that Rachel tripped and fell, and did not want to know. When they reached the top, he sat and eventually lay down on a very familiar spot. On the occasions that he accompanied Rachel, they would stop at the top, and sit on this spot. The rock was long and very flat which was considerably more comfortable than the jagged points that made up the peak. Now he sat with Rock, on the smooth rock, instead of his beloved Rachel. He took out his water, and let rock drink some as he lay back and let his mind wander.

James was surprised to see a man in a long robe, white hair and a walking stick arrive at the top of the mountain. He could not see the man's face because of the glare of the Sun. As James sat up, and started to speak, the man said "Silence!" His voice seemed to boom and echo through the mountains. After a pause, he said, "Dear child, your prayers are being answered even as you sit in this very moment" James awoke to Rock barking loudly. A hawk had flown by and Rock wanted to let him know who was boss! James sat up suddenly, and calmed down his fearless four legged friend. They began to make the trek back down the mountain. James was starting to believe this was not a simple, ordinary dream. He found comfort as well as anxiety in these dreams.

Who was the man in the Robe? James wondered, "Could that be Jesus?" Something inside told him it was not. He wondered if it was an Angel, or a prophet. Why was God speaking to him in this manner? James recalled that in his entire life his dreams have never been this vivid, or meaningful. James often boasted of being a left brained person. He considered himself analytical, and logical, not the creative type. He thought to himself "I am just not creative enough to invent dreams like this. This has to be some sort of message!" James had been an avid reader. He had read many Christian books. He could not recall any that did not date back to B.C.in which people had visions or dreams of visits from Angels. Could this be happening? James reasoned "God is all powerful, He can do whatever he wants!"

James wondered to himself "Why me?" Why would He take the time to give him these dreams or visions? Then he reasoned, that God does answer prayers. Maybe it is as simple as that. Perhaps God's heart ached for James. Rachel was persuasive; maybe she talked God into comforting him. He laughed out loud at this thought knowing that nobody can talk God into doing anything he does not want to do. James drove home, wanting to open his Bible and see if he could find any answers.

James could not find anything in his Bible that could support what he was experiencing. He knew he wanted, if not needed to find the meaning and understanding of these dreams. James called his church, hoping to find the Pastor available. He asked his Pastor what he thought this meant. Pastor McFarland had few answers for James as well. He explained "that nothing in the Bible definitively speaks of what you are experiencing. I know you are familiar with Acts 2:17 'And it shall come to pass after that I will pour out My Spirit on all flesh; your sons and daughters shall prophecy, your old men shall dream dreams, your young men shall see visions.' These are in fact the 'last days' that the Bible refers to. But there are debates as to whether these verses are talking about before, during, or after the rapture."

After a sizeable pause, Pastor McFarland went on to say "That being said James, here is what I think. Use this as an opportunity to draw even closer to God. Be very still, very quiet, and hear what He has to say. God is the creator of all things. Just because I haven't experienced what you are experiencing or know of others who have, doesn't mean that God can't do whatever He chooses to do! He may have a wonderful plan for you my brother. So listen! Hear Him, and do what he tells you to do. We know that prophecy is happening right before our very eyes all over the world right now. You may be a preview of bigger things to come from our amazing Lord! I am sorry I am not giving you the solid answers you are looking for; but it seems to me that God is trying to get your attention. There is nothing more special than that! You said yourself at Rachel's funeral that 'God has a plan, and what man intends for bad, God can use for good'. Perhaps he is about to do something miraculous with your painful experience."

James was probably more confused now than before he called his Pastor. James said to his Pastor "I feel that. I know these dreams are bigger than me. I know I am not creative enough for my brain to make this up. It's just so strange how something so seemingly profound could offer such little detail!" Pastor McFarland chuckled and said "I know what you mean! Although I have no definitive answers, you have to understand that if God poured out all of His knowledge or things revealed to us at once, we would be overwhelmed; especially while we are still here on Earth. If God is doing something incredible in your life; clearly this is something that you haven't even remotely come close to experiencing. Maybe he is preparing you. Giving you little glimpses and little insights so that when he reveals His plan to you, you can actually handle it! James, all I can do for you is to love you, and pray for you."

James thanked his Pastor and briefly spoke of what a crazy week this had been. Pastor McFarland had one final thought for James, saying "I am a bit jealous James. As a Pastor it's easy to see God working in other people's life. Sometimes it's more challenging to see Him working in my own life. Right now, I see God obviously working in your life, in a mightier way than most. Will you touch base with me from time to time to let me know what's going on?" James said "of course! You should know that if this is just the beginning, I am going to have more questions for you. I am confused and scared too." The Pastor ended their phone conversation by saying "All you can do is pray, use this to draw closer to the Lord, and do what He says! You are going to be just fine! Goodbye for now James."

James decided to make some dinner. Rock was so exhausted from getting his first exercise in over a week that he plopped down in the middle of the kitchen and James had to step over him as he prepared his meal. As James cooked he mused at his own thoughts that he was having. He wanted to sleep as much as possible right now so he could have more "dreams". He wondered aloud "Is God just giving me something else to think about instead of thinking about Rachel all of the time?" At least by asking this question out loud Rock woke up and trotted off into the other room. James quickly ate his stir fry, and jumped in the car.

As he drove off he had no idea where he was going. He started driving shortly before dark, and 45 minutes later, it was completely dark out. He worked his way to his office building and went to the top floor. James often went up there to think, and a few times he took Rachel up there to see the view. The last time James was up there he gave Rachel her Birthday present. He took her up there, a few days before her Birthday. They were sitting in comfy chairs sharing a nice conversation. She told him she was in the mood to have a quiet Birthday this year, just the two of them. He surprised her with a brochure showing her where they were going for her Birthday. He made reservations at a remote bed and breakfast in Prescott Pines North of Phoenix. They marveled at how they were always on the same page, even when they did not plan the details together.

James thought how he would give anything to spend one more weekend with her, anywhere! He could not believe it was already approaching a week since her passing. He could not remember the last time he spent this much time apart from her. Sadly he knew this was just the beginning of being apart for a long time. He consoled himself knowing he would see her again in Heaven, but life as he knew it was forever different. James decided that he needed to get out of town. He needed to leave for a week or so, and hopefully get away from so much that reminded him of Rachel. He wanted to go somewhere they'd never gone together. He needed to clear his head, and give himself a chance to get on with his life, even though he did not want to.

James hopped in the SUV, and headed towards Rachel's parents house. They were happy to see him, and invited him in. They were very concerned with how he was coping. James said "I am very sad, and very confused, but I am hanging in there" Rebecca jumped up and gave him a hug. She loved James like her own son! He also had a special place in her heart because of how happy he had made her daughter. He told them "I have been having some pretty wild dreams lately!" John asked "What kind of dreams?" James said "I have had the most vivid dreams of my life involving Rachel; and others where I have been visited by an Angel or something promising me everything will be okay. In one of them I was told I would hold her again. I am really confused as to what all of this means."

"Listen, I have to get away for a little while. I need to get way from every single thing that reminds me of Rachel, and just keeps me sad, and in a funk. I need to go somewhere, and deal with my pain without all the reminders. Maybe the reminders will make me happy again some day, but for now it just hurts too badly." Rebecca stood up and put her arm around James and asked "Are you sure getting away is the best thing? I am worried about you, and wonder if you should just stay with us for a while until you get your bearings straight?" James said "I really appreciate that! But I just want to leave for a little bit, and clear my head on my own. You know my life has completely revolved around Rachel and I as a couple. I have to learn how to be on my own again. I have to learn how to live for me right now."

John said "Whatever you think is best; but we are here for you! I am not terribly excited about you traveling around right now if you are in a funk like you say. We don't want to lose you too James!" James clarified "I am in a mental fog from the pain, but I haven't lost my common sense. I am not going to do anything that would put me in danger. I just need to work through this, in my own way I guess."

Rebecca asked "Is there anything we can do for you?" James said "Actually, I was going to ask; do you mind if I bring Rock over to stay with you while I am gone?" John said "Of course! Anytime!"

They asked "Where are you going?" He said "At this point, I really don't know. I plan to bring Rock over a little later, but not sure if I will leave tomorrow, or the day after, and don't even know the details yet. I am not even sure how long I will be gone. Right now my mind is wrapped around all of the sadness. I am hoping getting away helps so I can come back and hopefully appreciate the reminders and memories more, rather than them making me more depressed with each thought." He assured them he will be fine. James had come to know John very well. He knew John had to be wondering if he was losing his mind. He explained to John that he was not doing anything drastic or crazy. Rebecca asked "may I pack some travel food for you? I assume you are driving?" James said "that would be great!" She told him "I will pack you a couple of day's worth of food and drinks in a cooler, just promise to be safe, okay?"

CHAPTER 4

He went home to scoop up Rock. He wanted to drop him off that night. James was not sure when he was leaving, but he wanted to feel free to leave when he felt it was time. James again assured them he will be all right. He added "Thank you so much for everything! You really have always done so much for me! I hope you know how much I appreciate it!" Time was getting away, so James headed home again. No Rachel and now no Rock in the house and the silence was deafening as James walked into their home. James logged on to his computer, to surf the internet for some ideas on where he could go.

He knew he was going to drive. He figured he would end up covering a lot of territory but he still did not know where he would end up going. James being the planner he is, figured he would plan his entire itinerary but he did not know where he was going first. After an hour or so, the only thing he knew for sure, was that he was going to head to the coast. He figured some time around the ocean might be a nice escape. He laid back on his couch thinking to himself, whether he should head towards San Diego, or further north up the coast. As he was sifting through these ideas, he fell asleep.

James found himself standing in a forest. When he looked straight up he could see the sky, bluer than he had ever seen it before. He watched a squirrel run by, and he followed his movement until it ran out of sight. As James whirled back around and took a step, he plowed right into someone. When James walked into the man, he immediately fell to the ground. As his eyes focused he could see that it was the same man in the white robe, beard and walking stick that James had dreamt about on the mountain peak. This man may have been walking with a walking stick and looked at least 75 years old, but he was as solid as a wall!

As James was picking himself off the ground he apologized and the man replied "My dear brother, I have been sent by the one who loves you most to soothe your wounded heart and to prepare you to work on His behalf." James was stunned, and asked "Who are you?" and the man quickly retorted "Silence! Who I am is of no importance! Have I not delivered a message unto you from the Creator of all things? Further, have I not explained that He cares deeply for your pain, and that He is going to perform good works through you for the fulfillment of His will?" James was embarrassed and could barely utter a "yes" in response to his rhetorical questions.

The man went on to say "Our Lord and Savior knows your pain, and wants to provide measures of relief. Your continued faith and trust is necessary, and you must be still and await further instruction. Your prayers are being answered in this very moment in time!" James awoke to a crash as he rolled off the couch and landed on the floor. He laid there staring at the ceiling through the glass of the coffee table. In a gasp of desperation James said aloud "What is happening to me!" James continued to lay there thinking about what he was just told. At this point he was able to feel a little solace in knowing that his pain will be lessened. In his heart, he knew the only thing that would truly lesson his pain was for

Rachel to be with him. He also knew that was not going to happen.

James finally gathered himself; after getting to his feet, he went into the kitchen to get some bottled water. When he opened the refrigerator he noticed the light did not come on. He bent down to get a better look; he tapped the light bulb and the light came back on. James had a strange sensation and could not make himself stand up straight. He found himself captivated by the light, and it kept getting brighter and brighter. The light was so bright; it seemed to fill his entire line of sight. He could see a person in the distance seemingly miles away, but felt too paralyzed to approach. He then heard a voice declare "Go to the new port, and find the 316th dwelling." Immediately the light dimmed, and returned to a normal refrigerator light, and James was able to move.

James was stunned! He could not believe what was happening to him. This was the first time he had a dream, or now what he was considering to be a vision without falling asleep. He was so caught off guard by this, that as he settled in a chair to ponder what had just happened, he realized he forgot to grab the bottled water that he went to the refrigerator for. He wondered, "What is the new port?" Despite the seriousness of what was happening, he could not help but joke aloud "I don't even know any old ports!"

James ran to his computer and did a search for old and new ports in America. The results did not shed any light on where he was to go. Then it occurred to him, that if this is truly of God, perhaps he is to go to Israel, or somewhere in the Middle East. He modified his search to find new and old ports in Biblical places as well as some specific spots that he could think of. Still, nothing made any sense. How was he to go when he had no clue where to go? James already decided to head to the West coast, but now he wasn't sure. This simply made no sense to him.

James dropped to his knees and prayed fervently "Lord I am really at a loss now. Now my confusion extends to even more than losing the love of my life. I must first pray that your hand is upon me! I want to serve you, and I don't want to be led astray, or follow anything that is not of You. If these dreams and visions are of You, I beg You; please give me confirmation of this. And if indeed they are from You, Thank You! Thank you for caring about me and loving me. Thank you for taking an interest in my broken heart, and letting me know that you will lessen my pain. I must admit, the visions alone are distracting me enough that I feel a sense of hope. I feel like you are pulling me, I just have no idea where. Lord please help me with this. Please show me clearly what you want me to do, and where you want me to go. I was told that you are going to use me in fulfilling Your will. I am honored, and truly ready for this. Wherever you tell me to go, I will go! I love you Lord, Amen"

James immediately went to bed; because he was tired and hoping for another dream to tell him what to do. Seemingly five minutes after he fell asleep, he awoke to the sound of landscapers working on his neighbor's lawn. He could not believe it was already 10:00 a.m. He felt well rested but was disappointed that he did not have any more dreams or instruction. He was no closer to having any answers than he was the night before. He was also surprised at how rested he felt.

As James was getting around that morning, preparing for the day, he made a decision to head toward the coast; figuring that if God does clarify specifically where he was to go, he could adjust and go anywhere he was led, even if it was in the opposite direction. He felt as if he had more energy and alertness than he had since he received the terrible news of Rachel's accident. In fact he started to feel a bit guilty for having a renewed sense of excitement. James spoke aloud as he was showering wondering "Am I already forgetting about her? I can't forget about her, I love her too much for that to happen. The man said he would lessen my pain, but I don't want to carry on as if her passing is okay, or no big deal."

James was conflicted, but also had a sense of peace about this. He suddenly felt as if Rachel were in his presence. He knew she was not but he felt something. He felt as if he were part of something much bigger than himself. He also had a belief that even though Rachel was not with him, she was very much apart of this. As James stood in his closet, he was deep in thought and used the towel to finish drying his hair. As he was rubbing the towel through his hair, he had an incredible sensation. He felt as though he was receiving the most satisfying head massage, and he let his head kind of fall back, as if he were allowing himself to fall asleep. He then heard a powerful voice declare "And it shall come to pass after that I will pour out My Spirit on all flesh; your sons and daughters shall prophecy, your old men shall dream dreams, your young men shall see visions"....after a pause, the voice declared "James, the Hand of the Lord is upon you! Trust, and go! The Lords plan is being revealed to you. Go James! Your creator is about to complete a good work through you. Go!"

With that James was very much back to being alert and in control. He was actually starting to get used to this, and a little less apprehensive. He thought to himself "this is incredible! I heard the voice talk about what I am experiencing, in relation to the end days. Is God going to use me to usher in his return? This is too awesome! How does Rachel factor in? Why me? How does my pain and sadness have anything to do with this? Go? Go where?" These and a million other thoughts ran through his head. James gathered his things, and jumped in the car to head over to Rachel's parents to say goodbye and pick up his travel food. As soon as he walked in Rock nearly tackled him! He was very excited to see James, and did his best to follow James around the entire time he was there. John and Rebecca were just sitting down to lunch, and invited him to join them.

James could tell John and Rebecca had something on their minds and were very concerned about him. When James was about to offer some reassurance to them John spoke up. "James…son, we are concerned about you; and we wonder if perhaps we could persuade you to stay with us for a couple of weeks, instead of going off on your own. Maybe you need to be around family right now, and get your mind right before you embark on a big trip across the country" James broke in at that point to reassure them things will be fine. He was not sure how much he should tell them, but he tried to help them feel better about his own state of mind. He worried the truth would make them think he was crazy! "Listen, I have to tell you some things. I appreciate what you are saying; but please know, and believe, I am okay. I don't mean that I am okay with what happened to Rachel, but I am healing. Faster than you could possibly imagine. I have to tell you something, but I don't know how to say it." Rebecca quickly interjected "Honey, you can tell us anything, you know that!" James had a sheepish smile on his face when he said "well, I know I can, but this isn't anything like what you are thinking. I also worry you might think I am going crazy for real, but I am not! I promise!"

"I have prayed so much for God to help me get through this; I know you have been praying for me too. God is answering those prayers. I have had more dreams, and um, visions." John questioned "Visions? What kind of visions?" James did not want to go into too much detail so he said "I don't even know. All I know is I have a great sense of peace about it. I feel like God has been trying to reassure me. In one, it felt like an Angel told me that God cares about my pain, and will help me. I know this sounds crazy, but I believe God is indeed telling me something, and for whatever reason, I believe that God has a plan, and that He is going to work things out for me!" John sat back in his chair and said to James "you thought we think this would sound crazy? James, we believe in the same powerful God that you do! This very conversation is an answer to our prayers as well. I don't know what God is telling you, but I have no doubt that He is with you! Trust Him James! Trust Him! You are a very level headed man, and if you believe what you are hearing is from God, then I believe you! Just be safe, but follow God!"

James was a little surprised. Not at their faith, he had always known Rebecca and John to be two of the most Christ centered people he had ever known. They so quickly changed from concern, and worry for him; to then encouraging him. It made him wonder if John had a visit from an Angel himself. "Well, I appreciate that! More than you know! It's a relief that you are less concerned for me now than you were…and also your encouragement is a confirmation to me as well! That said, I know the Lord has been speaking to me, and I feel like Rachel is a big part of this. I have no idea how she factors in. But I know at the very least, she is watching me, and rooting me on! I really think that when I come back, all of this will be reconciled. I think I will be able to move forward, and think less about my own sadness, and how I miss her so much, and be more focused on how great it must be for her in Heaven with our gracious creator! Is that bad? I mean, right now, even though I know there is not a better place in all of creation for her to be, I want her here with me!"

Rebecca put her hand on James arm, and told him "James, I am not sure that anyone ever becomes so mature in their faith…that when someone they dearly love, prematurely goes home to Heaven, they wholeheartedly rejoice. I think it is more natural for us to be selfish when it comes to losing someone we love. John and I love our children so much. Nothing has given us more joy in this life than raising some very good children and watching them grow and mature, and celebrate their successes in life. We have always wanted what is best for our children, and we have worked hard to make sure they are as prepared as possible. What is more satisfying to a parent than knowing they raised their child right? That is especially true when it comes to knowing they have the faith and assurance of being with God in Heaven. However, despite the satisfaction of knowing that she is in heaven; we want her here with us too. We do not want to wait years, or even a day before we see her again. So no, you are not out of line for thinking that. You are a devoted husband who expected to stay hand and in hand with your wife for a long, long time."

James had tears running down his face. He realized he had not shed any tears in the last couple of days. Despite feeling sadness once again, reflecting on his loss; he felt relieved that he had not so quickly managed to move past her death. James wiped his tears away, stood up, and said "I better get going. There is still enough time for me to reach the coast while the sun is still out. I'd rather not be driving after dark." Rebecca asked him what he was going to do in California. James replied "I really don't know, I just feel like that is where I am supposed to go. I hope the answers are provided as I go along."

As Rebecca was putting his travel food and drinks together, she had a request for James "Just promise me one thing honey; if you see Rachel in one of your dreams, or know she is part of what you are going through, please tell her how much we love and miss her." James was expecting her to ask him to check in from the road, and to be safe; not to so quickly be on board and encouraging him in what was happening! He wondered to himself "what makes her think that I would see Rachel or have any means to give her a message?" This was incredibly exciting and scary for James. What was to come on his journey? He had such a feeling of anxiety, but it was similar to how one feels the night before Christmas. His fears had changed from the unknown, to simply hoping he could honor God in this. He desperately wanted be the man who God apparently knows him to be.

James went into the bathroom to wash and clean up as he was readying to leave. While he was in the bathroom he felt a bit dizzy, so he sat down. He noticed in the magazine rack, the announcement for his engagement to Rachel. On the announcement was a note from Rachel that she wrote herself. James began to read the words "My dear family and friends please come join me in celebrating my marriage to the man that I have been praying for, for so long. He is truly my best friend….." As James was reading these words, he found himself getting very, very dizzy. As he looked up to gain focus, he found himself standing on a beach.

The waves were crashing against nearby rock formations that jutted out of the water. The waves seemed much louder than he could remember the last time he was at the ocean. There was no one around. He walked, and walked. He could see footprints in the sand, so he followed them. He felt like he walked for over a mile. Then the footprints just suddenly ended. James sat down feeling very confused. He leaned forward, so that his head was between his knees. As he was sitting there, trying to figure out what he was supposed to do, he felt a hand on his shoulder. He looked up to see what he thought was a warrior. The man James saw looked like he was well over 6 ft tall. He had very broad shoulders and very toned muscle definition. He carried a shield, and had a sword on his hip.

In the deepest, strongest voice James had ever heard, the man asked "James, my brother, are you prepared to battle for the Lord of Hosts?" James stood to his feet, and responded "I am, but I am not trained to fight in the battle field. Will you help me?" The man replied "You and I are to fight very different battles. I fight forces and principalities that you cannot see. I fight warriors not only with strength, but indeed, by the power of the Lord. You indeed must be prepared to battle. However, you will not be fighting with a sword. The Lord has blessed me with strength, and the heart of a warrior. I will go to the depths of hell, to fight for my Lord. This is not expected of you. You my brother are to be prepared to fight, to win hearts for your Savior. I fight to protect the kingdom of heaven. You must fight to build the kingdom of heaven!

"My mission is simple; to fight and destroy all demons and forces that work against the perfect will of the Creator of the Most High! Your mission is to have faith, and trust in what you are told, and to help win the hearts and minds of the people of this Earth, so that they may believe in the Messiah, Jesus Christ, the Savior of this world. You must win souls, and prepare others to do the same, so that the true Word of God will reach the ends of the Earth. You must be prepared to fight daily, to spread the Good News, the message of the Gospels, Gods divinely inspired word. You must work tirelessly to spread this message, so that the evil one; when he rises will be defeated, once and for all. We fight different battles in the same war, but our missions, and goals are the same."

"You will be ridiculed, harassed, and some will attempt to obstruct you in your efforts. But fight on! You have experienced great pain; a pain in fact, that was so deep, that even Gods own heart was burdened by it. He felt your loss, and your sadness. And like you, took joy in your love, faith, and actions that you experienced prior to this loss. I don't know of such a loss. I have fought by myself, for no one other than the Lord, for my entire existence. I have been joined to my Lord, since the beginning of my creation, and have been blessed with the use of Gods supernatural power and strength to fight these intense battles. You have not been blessed with such dependence."

"You will be blessed. Blessed indeed for your works on this Earth! You are about to embark on a journey, that will forever be written into the annals of history. Prophets and, great men of God from past and future will one day partake in great dinner feasts prepared by the Lord, in the eternal kingdom of Heaven, and your adventures and successes will be enjoyed by all. Angels will sing commemorating all of the great men, actions, and successes of those that fought for the God of Creation, and His perfect Kingdom in Heaven. Brother, your blessings will not just be in heaven, for you are to receive special blessings, even on this day, before you are ever close to going Home to your Father in Heaven, who loves you!"

James was stunned, as much as he thought he understood every word that was being said; he was also confused as usual, and wondered if he could possibly retain this incredible message. He started to ask a question when the man cut him off declaring "Silence! My message to you is clear, and complete. You are being told, all that you need to be told. Anything I do not reveal to you at this time, you are not supposed to know! You will be visited by me, and by others created by the Father, just like me, who will instruct you. Some you will be permitted to talk to, and discuss things with, others, and you will be instructed to simply listen. I will be with you, at all times, fighting forces and principalities that are working against you, that you cannot see. I will be the force behind your victories. When you have a victory, know that I am there too, celebrating the sweet successes you experience by the grace and love of our Father. When you struggle, know that the victory has already been won for the Lord, and that we will emerge victorious through every challenge we face. The outcome has already been determined. I merely fight the fights that God wants me to win. Know that the hand of the Lord is upon you!"

"I have one final message to impart to you before I resume the good fight. You have been chosen for a unique quest. You are experiencing things that most of the Lords creation will never experience. The specific nature of your visions and dreams, are to remain between you, the Lord, and the ones who visit you. Clarification and details will be provided at the appointed times. For now, trusts in the Lord with all your heart, in all your ways acknowledge him, and Lord of all will make your paths straight, and clear!"

As he was focusing on the message being delivered he quickly realized he was alone again staring at the words on the piece of paper in his hands. He was no longer sitting on the beach, hearing the words of a great angel warrior. This had gone past the point of amazement to shock. James had prayed for years, as his faith grew, to experience God on a deeper level. This was indeed happening. He wanted so badly to know what kind of blessings he would receive while still here on Earth. Were these the kinds of blessings that were the result of witnessing Gods miracles? Or, did God have plans to bless James with certain gifts or privileges while fighting this battle? He realized his task at hand was to witness for the Lord; he had to wonder how prepared he was for such a task!

James walked out of the bathroom and back to the kitchen where Rebecca and John were. Rebecca was still making his sandwiches and fitting everything neatly into the cooler. James felt like he had been "gone" for an hour, but John and Rebecca did not act like he had been in the bathroom for any extended period of time. He asked them "Um, how long was I in the bathroom?" Rebecca laughed, and John replied, "30 seconds, maybe 45. Did you lose track of time?" James laughed it off. Rebecca quickly turned the subject back to their previous conversation and asked James "why, did you have another vision? Did you see Rachel? How is she?" James could not help but laugh, this was starting to become fun now. James said "whoa, whoa, whoa. No, well yes. I definitely had another vision, but I can't talk about it, specifically. No, I didn't see Rachel.

John was more than a little curious. "James, why can't you talk about it? Sounds like you are experiencing something really powerful, please, share the details with us!" James told them "I would love to! I have been told I can't. I know that sounds weird, but those are my instructions. I promise, as I figure this out, and when I know what is okay, and what isn't, I will share with you, I promise!" John wanted to press him, but he knew better. "Well, son, we are all sad, but through you, we are all gaining a sense of peace, and optimism in the midst of something tragic. Thank you! May I pray for you before you leave?"

After a beautiful heart felt prayer for James, and some whimpering from Rock, James was in the car, moving along on I-10 heading towards the Arizona-California Border. He wanted to make a call before he was too far out in the middle of nowhere and had to worry about cell phone reception; he called Pastor McFarland. The Pastor was not in his office, so James had to leave him a voice mail message "Pastor McFarland, I wanted to ask you to please keep me in your prayers. I have had more of what I told you before. I am heading out of town as we speak, and I believe big things are ahead. Please pray for me. Pray as often as you think about it. As soon as I have any details I am able to pass on, I will. Take care!"

James mind was racing. He felt like he was heading towards a treasure chest, with no idea what the treasure is. He kept reminding himself, if this treasure is from God, how fantastic it must be! The words of the warrior Angel were running through his head. He kept thinking about the Angels promise that he would receive blessings not only in Heaven, but here on Earth as well. What kind of blessings on Earth? James was getting so excited at the prospects of what was in store. He wondered about the possible details of Gods plan that he would use James to accomplish and that would would earn him such favor. The possibilities were endless.

As James drove, still about 50 miles from the California border, thinking all these things, he started to get a little sad. James missed Rachel terribly. He knew something like this would have excited her so much! She dreamed of these very things. In fact, James recalled a night just a year ago, when the two of them went to a park that is known for its huge fountain that shoots into the air. They laid side-by-side on a blanket in the grass dreaming together. He remembered how Rachel would just jump from topic to topic. She started out all excited about the prospects of becoming a partner in her company, to what Christmas was going to be like that year, to eventually having children, to making up stories of the two of them working together to accomplish Gods will.

Sometimes Rachel simply spoke about the two of them getting involved in some sort of marriage ministry that they could counsel other couples. Other dreams involved the two of them going to the college and attempting to reach out to students who wanted to know the truth about God. The stories she was most passionate about were the ones that James would tease her the most about. She would get so excited and so creative in bringing up these adventure type crusades the two of them would go on together, winning Souls for Christ. Her stories made James out to be some sort of an Indiana Jones and she was like Lara Croft the Tomb Raider traveling around the world finding treasures and helping people to know Christ.

James would just laugh and laugh at her, as she would get so frustrated with him but they always had fun in these exchanges. James figured she intentionally embellished the details in her stories, just to see how much she could surprise him. And the more she would, the more he would make fun of her for being so far "out there"! Suddenly, he felt like her stories were not too far off, but instead of them going together, James was on a solo mission. Again, he was quickly saddened.

He improved his own mood by day dreaming of a journey that he and Rachel could go on together. He recalled one of her stories where the two of them ended up on an island on an exploration trip. As she was setting up the background to the story, which included running from island head hunters, James would interject teasing her "But they would never cut off your head, your entirely too beautiful, for even they know the curse that would be befall them if they wasted such beauty!" She would retort back "Do you want me to continue this story? .I could stop right now if you like, and you will never find out about the adventure we experience, and the people that will be so grateful to us in Heaven for sharing the good news! So, should I stop?" Of course he did not want her to stop and she knew that too. But James would answer back sarcastically "oh please, by all means, continue! I desperately want to know how many people make it to heaven because of us!"

The thought of the details of her story lifted his spirits. Even though he had not seen her in over a week, just thinking about her telling the story made him feel like she was right there with him, telling the story. Even better, he was so entrenched in the memory he felt like he was with her living it out. Arriving at the border snapped him out of his happy relief. He crossed the border after a short delay. The border patrol asked each driver if they had anything in the car that they should not have. As James crossed into California, he was now focusing on a previous message from the man with the white hair and walking stick.

James was a couple hundred miles away from home, and he still had no idea where he was going. His mind was now focused on the message about the new port, and the going to the 316th dwelling. For all he knew he was heading to Los Angeles to catch a plane to somewhere in the Middle East. He truly had no idea where he was going. In his mind he kept thinking "316th dwelling.....316th dwelling.... dwelling...is that a house? A dwelling is a house, right? We don't call houses dwelling, so maybe it is in a foreign land I am heading." Then it occurred to him about 3:16, John 3:16 is the most famous Bible verse there is. He reached for his Bible, to check it out. He knew reading the Bible as he drove down the freeway probably was not the safest thing, but then again, if he was on a mission from God, surely God would protect him at this point!

Nothing in or around John 3:16 shed any light on where he was supposed to go. James hoped that as he neared the coast, the details would become clearer as to where he was going, and what he was supposed to do. However, that was not happening, in fact, he was becoming more confused. As he thought about things, and possible areas in California he should be going, he could not think of any ports or costal cities that would be considered new. The more he thought about it, he could not think of any that would be considered old either. Suddenly, James had an overwhelming sense of peace that the details of what was to happen would work itself out.

This is very ironic for an analytical thinker like James! James prided himself in being a planner, and precise in his thinking. James did not argue very often, because most of his opinions were based on facts and statistics. But here he was, "Mr. Left Brain" as Rachel used to tease him; driving hundreds of miles away, no clue of where he was going, just a belief he will figure it out! Then he chuckled once again and thought "if this is not of God, then I don't know what is!"

CHAPTER 5

When approaching Palm Springs, he decided to pull off, get some gas, and stretch his legs. As his car was filling with Gas, he could see something shiny reflecting in the desert behind the gas station. He was curious, and figured this was as good a way as any to stretch his legs. As he walked about a hundred yards towards the shiny object, he could not see it anymore. He walked around a little more, day dreaming some more, missing Rachel. He was reflecting that this was the first time in nearly 10 years he went on any sort of a trip without her. Aside from getting to the coast before the Sun went down, he was not in any hurry to get going.

As he was feeling sad that Rachel was not with him he suddenly felt very lethargic. He saw a big rock formation and sat in its shade to rest a bit. He had to laugh at himself; he had been sitting for a nearly two hundred miles and now he walked out into the middle of the desert to sit down, so he could rest. As he was sitting, Rachel was firmly on his mind. He missed her terribly. He felt like he was already forgetting what it was like to be with her. It was scaring him to realize that despite so clearly seeing her face in his mind; he felt like he already forgot what it felt like to touch her. He wanted so badly to touch her again.

As he sat in the shade he was thinking about a few weeks back when he came home from work and they had planned to have a quiet dinner together at home. He remembered walking in the door and being struck by how cute she was. Rachel was beautiful by anyone's standard. Everyone thought she was a pretty girl. James friends teased him about how sexy she was, especially when she played a sport or climbing a mountain. But on this occasion when he walked in the door, she was just simply cute. She seemed so innocent and fresh. She was excited to see James that night too. They always enjoyed their time together, and missed each other when they were apart. Something just felt different that night.

He remembered setting his brief case down and cupping her face in his hands as he kissed her. James was surprised that the memory could be so vivid and yet, he could not remember the actual feel of her face in his hands. He remembered how right her touch felt. He remembered how her face fit perfectly in the cup of his hands. However, he could not remember the actual feel of her skin. He could remember vividly the conversation they had that night. She wanted the two of them to take a trip together. She was in the mood to get away. She said she wanted to get away for a week or so, order room service, hang out together, and spend most of their time in the room away from people. Very much like their honeymoon. They had an amazing time on their honeymoon. They had about 40 things planned, but spent five of their seven days in their room. It was special and spontaneous. Even though they did not accomplish 90% of their plan, the fact that they just ignored months of planning, and went with the flow, totally focused on each other, was something neither would ever forget. They often spoke of repeating that honeymoon sometime.

These thoughts gave James some much needed comfort. Even though he was sad she was not with him, he felt like he stayed connected to her by thinking of these wonderful memories. As James stood up to head back to the car, he looked up at the sky, and the brightness of the sun left him feeling paralyzed. As vivid as if he was there, he could see himself holding Rachel's face as he kissed her. He felt like he was a fly on the wall. He was there, but he was not really there. Rachel was speaking about going away together, and how much it would mean to her. Then she looked away from James in the vision, and in the direction that he was viewing them, and spoke as if she were speaking right to him at that very moment and said "James, your still my best friend, meet me there! We need a second Honeymoon! Sweetie, have faith, meet me there; Go!"

With that, James snapped back to reality and was already approaching the car. He could not remember standing up from the rock he was sitting on and walking back to the car. Seemingly he just stood up a second ago. Suddenly he was near the car. James felt like he was completely out of sorts. He put the gas pump away, and put the gas cap back on and was back on the road. He could not believe how vivid that "dream" was. Even minutes removed from it, he felt like she had been right there. He could see her eyes plain as day as she looked at him. He felt her eyes penetrating him. That literally melted his heart. He missed those eyes staring deep into him. He wanted that again. Why would she say what she said though? "Meet me there!" That was so out of character for both them. They went everywhere together. They certainly would not go on a trip together, without going together.

In his mind, he kept running through the words "meet me there". He was wondering "meet her where?" The thought occurred to him that she looked at him, at him in the vision, not the James in the memory. He wondered aloud "Was Rachel really talking to me?" "Is it possible I might actually see her again?" Then reality set in, and the thought "no. You are punishing yourself thinking like that. She died, and I will see here again, but not in this life. Not on this planet" Then he recalled the words of the Warrior and the white haired man, "Have faith!" "Go!" What did this mean? She said to meet her there. Again, James wondered "where is there?" As he tried to piece it together, he recalled she was speaking about their honeymoon. She was recalling how special their honeymoon was, and to repeat it, and to meet her there.

Then like a lightning bolt, the answer was clear. "No way!" He could not believe it, it was right in front him. Suddenly tears flew down his face and he started to believe he was hours from seeing his wife again. He did not want to get carried away by this thought, because it defied all logic, and all reason. Things like this do not happen in real life. Then he recalled the warrior Angel declaring that he will receive blessings, on this very day. Did he mean, literally, to-day? James thought more, and more about his honeymoon. Their honeymoon was spent in Newport Beach, California. With tears flowing down his face he said "Newport Beach; the new port. Unbelievable! Lord, thank you! Thank you so much! If this is what I think it means."

James and Rachel spent their honeymoon in Newport Beach, at the Hyatt Regency Hotel. They had many plans in and around Newport Beach, but they spent most of the trip inside the 11 story Hotel. Instinctively he believed that he was to return to the Hotel where they spent their honeymoon, and request room 316. He wanted to call her parents, and everyone else he could think of, but he was told not to share these experiences. He was about one hundred miles from the Newport Beach area and was literally astounded at the idea that he could see Rachel again; whose funeral was just days ago!

Despite his excitement he began to think about what this could mean in the grand scheme of things. James wondered aloud, speaking to God "Lord, does that mean that your return is close at hand? Are these the times that the Bible refers to when we hear about the "last days"? What are you going to have me do? Am I the right man for this?" He knew he was getting ahead of himself. For all he knew, that hotel room simply had another vision or dream awaiting him. Maybe the next instruction would be there. Common sense said he would not see Rachel again anytime soon unless he himself had an accident too. Maybe the blessings he was promised were in the form of the Angels that had visited him. After all, a blessing is a supernatural act of God. What the warrior promised James does not have to mean that it is specifically something for James to personally enjoy.

As James was flying down the freeway, he was so excited, he felt like he was literally sitting beside himself. Life was forever changed the night he found out about Rachel, and in a short time after that, it was changing on a whole new scale! He decided even if he did not get to see her again before he goes to heaven, he will be nothing but grateful to God for what was happening. He realized that regardless, already his pain was lessened. Just knowing that God is working in his life the way he is, was proof that God cared about what he had experienced and what he had lost. And if she gets to be a part of this with him, all the better!

James was so excited as he arrived in the Newport Beach area that he was afraid he might steer his car right into someone! He just wanted to safely arrive at the hotel, and find out where this was going. This reminded him of the day he was driving to the church to marry Rachel. Two different friends called him to make sure he was not too nervous, and wanted to back out of his wedding with Rachel. They were not calling to reassure him, they were hoping he would back out, so they would have a chance to date Rachel! He remembered how excited and anxious he was driving down the street to the church. He believed that Rachel was completely out of his league. At the same time he had no reservations or concerns about her love for him. As he pulled into the church, he knew he had more than an hour before he could see her; he felt like he was about to view an angel.

James reflected on the irony in that! He could remember

like it was yesterday looking forward to seeing her beautiful smile in her wedding dress. He was so excited to hold her hand, and profess in front of their friends and family that he would love her forever. He could not help but wonder what it would be like to make love to her for the first time. Now, as he was approaching the hotel he wondered "Is there any chance I might actually get to look into her pretty eyes again, and perhaps, just maybe, be able to hold her hand?" He wondered if he did get to see her again, would should be an idea or vision in his head, or his wife to physically hold.

James walked into the hotel more nervous than he had ever been. He was surprised at how many people were in line to check in, which just added to his anxiety. When he reached the front of the line, he said he would like to check in, and requested room 316. The lady at the counter checked her computer, then informed him room 316 was occupied. This confused James a little. He quickly realized there must be a key waiting for him. He then asked if there was anything waiting for James Mahody. The lady looked and said no. He then inquired if there was anything for or from a Rachel Mahody. The lady sensing James sadness shrugged her shoulders and apologized.

James walked away, very confused. He sat down in the lobby, thinking of his options and going over the instructions in his head. He thought to himself all of the instructions in the visions… "Meet me there…dwelling 316… have faith… you will be blessed on this day… new port…" He could not think of anything else to do at this point. He realized that even though these obstacles confused him, he still felt a sense of peace. He did not have it figured out yet, but he had the desire to keep going for answers. Despite the road block, he felt like he was where he was supposed to be.

James stood up from his seat in the lobby and took his place in line again. The same lady that tried to assist him before asked "How may I help you?" James asked her for the name of the occupants of room 316. She apologized, but said "I am not aloud to give out that kind of information about our guests". James was so desperate he leaned forward and whispered "I'll pay you!" She responded "I would love to help you, but I really cannot." James was more confused and losing a little hope. He felt he was out of options. He did not know what else to do. He knew he could not leave either.

James went into the hotel restaurant and decided to

have dinner and ponder his next move. He hoped he would stumble upon some answers. Maybe he would have a vision staring at his steak or something. He laughed at his own silliness. He glanced around the restaurant noticing several families. He saw a little girl that reminded him of a picture he had seen of Rachel when she was a little girl. He wondered what it would have been like to have babies with her. He wanted a daughter with her. Now he was just sitting there alone, finishing up his dinner, having no idea what he was going to do next. He could hear some children at a nearby booth starting to get a little rambunctious. He was not paying close attention to them but they kept getting louder.

He noticed that the little boy, about 11 years old, was picking on his younger sister, who was probably about nine years old. She kept saying "stop it!" Their parents were too preoccupied with their dinner company to help settle the kids down. The little boy persisted in picking on his sister, and she yelled out "Get away from me!" Again, he kept annoying her, and she yelled out "Go away! Go, Go, Go!" And James felt like he was hit by a ton of bricks! The words "Go, Go, Go!" felt like they were blasted on a loudspeaker directly in his ear. He was told in his visions to "Go!" As soon as the thought entered his mind and words barely escaped his lips "Go where?" He knew where he was to go, he already had the answer. Five minutes later after paying for his dinner and taking the elevator to the third floor, he was walking down the hallway in search of room 316.

His heart was pounding, his legs felt heavy as he walked the hallway. He had a million ideas racing through his head at the same time, thinking about what he was about to encounter. And yet, the deeper he thought about it, the more he had blankness in his head. Of course, doubt set in as he wondered to himself "What if nobody is in the room, or what if somebody is in the room? And they aren't there for me?" As he approached the room, he could see there was something attached to the door. He stood in front of the door, absolutely stunned by what he saw.

There was an envelope taped to the door, with his name on it. What was even more stunning was that the handwriting was unmistakably Rachel's. He took the envelope from the door, and found the door card swiper inside. He opened the door; it was dark inside. He could tell the patio door to the balcony was open. He started slowly, towards the balcony. A voice from the balcony, called him "James, my brother, please join me" The voice was that of an elderly man. He had a very soft voice, but protective as well. The voice was very reminiscent of the cadence of the way his Grandpa would speak. James moved the drapes aside as he stepped out onto the balcony.

The elderly gentleman introduced himself as Kaleb. He explained to James that he was there to prepare him, for what was to come. He explained "like the visions you have encountered to this point, I am also a brother in Christ, and your friend. Unlike the men you have previously been visited by, I am not a warrior, and I myself do not know what tomorrow holds…however, I do know what the next step is in your journey. I am a guide that you may actually speak to, and ask questions of. I am patient, and I will help you in anyway I can, but please do not ask me any questions that you already know the answers to." James interjected and asked "are you real, or are you a vision?" Kaleb chuckled and said "I am as real as you are! Do I not look real? I may have been created many thousands of years ago, but I am still very real!" James was embarrassed, and clarified "I mean, are you here physically or are you a vision in my head?" Kaleb held his hand out for James, and the two shook hands.

This was all so surreal. He felt like he was living someone else's life. He wondered "How could this be happening?" Kaleb responded I will be glad to explain how and why this is happening. James quickly shot back "You can read my mind?" Kaleb laughed, and said no, I am afraid not. However, God speaks directly to my heart, and the Lord of all creation informed me that you questioned how this could be happening. I would like to explain that to you. "James, my dear brother in Christ, I know you have had many questions about what has been happening over the last three days, 10,147 thoughts to be exact! And truly, I say to you, the Lord is showing you special favor."

"The day of the Lord is upon us. Soon the Savior Jesus Christ will return for his children, and take them directly to heaven to spare them the wrath and judgments of God." James asked "How soon?" Kaleb responded, "My dear friend, no one but the Lord knows that, you know that! Not even I know the day or the hour of our Lords return. Soon! That is all we know. We know we are in the end days. In your measurements of time, this could be tomorrow, or this could be in the decades to come." With a wink, Kaleb went on to say "I think since the Lord has an incredible plan for you to serve his purposes, it's safe to assume that Messiah is at least a week or two away before he returns." James laughed at his own naive question.

Kaleb asked James "Shall I continue? Or is there something else you need to know first?" James sat down on a patio chair, and begged him "please continue!" Kaleb explained "There is a great deal of work to do to prepare the hearts of the unbelievers as well as future teachers of the faith. Much work must be done to build Gods eternal kingdom. Additionally, work must be done in advance of the rise to power of the one known as the "anti-Christ". You are going to be given a series of tasks. In some instances you will be expected to spread the good news to people who do not yet believe. In other cases you will be used by God to thwart evil plans of those who oppose God."

Needless to say, this is not what James was expecting when he arrived at the hotel. James inquired "Am I really the guy for this task? I must say, as strong as my faith is, I have always been somewhat disappointed at the infrequency of the witnessing opportunities I have had. I surely don't want to mess up some ones chance to receive salvation, and I don't want to mess up Gods plans!" At this point, Kaleb was more than chuckling when he said "James, surely you know that faith is of God's grace, not by your own doing. Don't you know better than to foolishly suggest that you, all by yourself, could spoil the plans of the Creator of all things? God made the heavens, and the Earth; he made the mountains and the oceans. He made you! Your inclusion in the fulfillment of His will is more of a blessing and reward to you, than any sort of necessity for Him! Make no mistake, Gods will be done. That said you must take your assignments very seriously."

James inquired about how and when he will be given his assignments. Kaleb informed him "You will continue to have dreams and see visions. I will visit you on occasion, and as well as others like me that may have already visited you. You may even have a new visitor or two speak to you. Additionally you will be assigned a helper." James was quick to ask "Who will my helper be, and when will he get here?" "Kaleb answered "in due time my friend! Your partner in this journey will arrive shortly after I depart you this evening." Your helper has been prepared for the tasks at hand, and will be a valuable assistant to you. You will know where to go, and what to do at all time. I would be remiss though if I did not inform you, you are still susceptible to the elements. Although your partner will not be."

This confused James. He inquired "Do you mean I could get sick? Stuff like that?" Kaleb responded by reminding James he is still human "James, you are merely a mortal man, with an Earthly body. Do not make the mistake of thinking you can jump off mountains, and escape evil doers harm without being smart. You will have protection, and plenty of help, but if you test God in irresponsible ways, you will pay the price. Your helper will be able to offer you insights, but do not think that bullets and heavy machinery cannot hurt you. They could hurt you yesterday, and will just the same today and tomorrow."

"James, my time with you this evening is drawing to a close. I must leave, so you can begin your journey; however, there is one more thing I am to discuss with you. The Lord has chosen you for this for a variety of reasons. Some you may understand now, some you won't understand until well into eternity. Our God is merciful, and compassionate. He loves you, and he loves when his children love Him, worship him, and obey him. You and your wife often asked the question if God delighted in your relationship. The answer to that question is, emphatically yes! The Lord enjoyed a great deal of delight from the relationship you two shared. And indeed, as painful as it was, the passing of our sister Rachel, was part of his perfect will, and will have far reaching benefits for Gods eternal kingdom; again, you will not even begin to understand the reasons why until well into eternity."

"You and Rachel shared a life of love, and obedience. You were selfless towards each other, and lived a very transparent marriage, that others looked at, with a studying eye. Few people on this Earth have ever been able to truly master loving God first, and allowing that love, and obedience to trickle down into every area of their life, including their marriage, family, and occupation. This was natural for both of you. God blessed you two greatly. Individually your faith and obedience to Christ has been very good, but together, you were even better. You became one. You truly were under Gods arms as a couple. Our Lord delighted in your relationship, and very much like you, has been saddened that it does not continue."

"You have been chosen, my brother James, because of your faith, commitment to Christ, and because you truly have brought honor and glory to God. If you continue these good works to the end, you are sure to receive many rewards in heaven, and indeed, many rewards here on Earth before you go to Heaven. You must have faith my by brother! Your faith will be tested. You must have complete faith and trust in all that God sends to help you! All of those assigned to prepare you for your tasks are paramount to achieving the success that our Lord knows you will achieve. You are about to begin, and be part of a mission that will usher in the return of our Savior for his faithful children, the rise and defeat of the Antichrist, and the millennial kingdom, as well as eternity in Heaven with our creator."

"My dear James, you are but of a privileged few that will be part of the most fantastic climax of this age. You are but of a privileged few who will truly get his instructions from the Lord, and the Lords host of Angels. You are but of a privileged few who will fight the good fight, and know that every day, you are truly in Gods perfect will. There are people all over the world that will fight the fight, simply on the basis of hope and faith. Faith is paramount, but you can be faithful knowing that every battle you fight, every person you speak to, is instrumental in Gods ultimate plan! Amen!"

"My brother, and fellow crusader for the cause of Christ;

the Lord indeed has a gift for you tonight. You are about to be blessed in a nearly unimaginable way. First, please look up towards that building over there and into the sky above. Look at the star shining brighter than all others." James was looking and awaiting further instruction. Finally James said, "Okay, I see it." There was no response. He whirled around to find he was alone on the roof. James yelled out "Kaleb!" "Kaleb!" Still nothing. He looked around, even looked over the edge of the balcony. Once again he blurted out "Kaleb! Where are you?"

CHAPTER 6

From inside the room, he heard a familiar voice whisper back, "He's gone." James had chills run down his back, he could feel the little hairs on the back of his neck hairs stand as high as they could! Could it be? The soft voice vaguely sounded like Rachel, but he could not be sure. He wanted to run inside, but he was scared to know the truth. What if it was not? What if it was! He wanted nothing more than to see his beautiful wife again, but how do you react to meeting the love of your life that has been dead for nearly two weeks? Very slowly, James turned to walk into the room.

As James moved the drapes out of the way, and entered the room, he had no idea what to expect. Standing near the foot of the bed, was Rachel! She had tears streaming down her face, and all James could say was "is that really you?" Rachel did not whisper this time, she replied "yes babe, it's really me!" James ran to her, and they held on to each other so tightly, for several minutes, neither saying a word, both crying. James had to see her face, so he gently pulled back. He reached towards her face, to wipe her tears away telling her "I have craved to feel the touch of your soft skin" She could hardly speak. Through her sobbing she was barely able to say "in heaven, there are no tears, nobody warned me I would make up for it when we received this gift!"

With that, James asked her, "How is this happening? Why is this happening?" Rachel replied "James, you have no idea, no idea at all. I cannot put into words, to describe to you, the love that God has for us, for all of his children. I asked you so many times, if God delighted in our relationship. James, he let me see our relationship through his eyes. It was absolutely beautiful. And sweetie, I have always thought I knew how much you love me, but wow, I truly had no idea. God is amazing, so loving, and so perfect; there are not words available to convey to you how perfectly perfect He is!" James was astonished this was happening.

He had to ask her, even though the answer frightened

him; "Raech, when do you have to go back? How much time do we have together? At first, the look on her face scared him, and she really started in with the tears again, and then she said "James, I am your helper, I am the one God assigned to you for this journey. I am your gift, and you are my gift; but I am your assigned helper!" James could not believe what he was hearing. He responded by asking "Do you mean, all of these tasks, and crusades for Christ that I am to go on; you will be going with me? Rachel said "James, I am yours, again! I am here, we are together, again!

James was elated! He couldn't help but ask "Are you serious? Is there a catch?" Rachel did not waste any time making fun of him replying "Well yes, there is a catch, if you spill water on me, or if I get wet, I will melt, and disappear!" James' expression quickly changed, and began to question how that works when Rachel playfully slapped him and said "I am kidding you goof! You really think God has a catch to things? Look sweetie, there is no catch, but there are some rules I should tell you about. James said he was ready to hear them, but nervous too.

Rachel had to hug him before she could begin; she was so excited to see him again. James was always amazed that whether it was their first hug of the day, or their fifteenth, he could always feel how special and loved he was by her. Rachel backed up a step, and said "okay, first all of the great news! I am yours babe, I am back; we are husband and wife. We are married, and a couple, and together. We may even make love again if you are lucky" James shot back "If I am lucky! Hey I have been single now for a couple of weeks, I am not ready to just give myself up to the first girl that comes along, I may play hard to get!" Rachel responded "yeah, play, hard, to get, that's all you can do is play; you could never resist me! Anyway, silly guy, I am your helper. With what God has shown me I will be a tremendous asset to you as we do Gods work. We will work together, and God and his Angels in heaven will constantly convey anything that you should know, that you don't already know. We are going to have some serious work to do, and there may even be some danger along the way, but with Gods help, we will, I should say He, will be victorious! I will be with you every step of the way!"

This all sounded like good news to James but he asked "What is the bad news?" Rachel said there is not any bad news per say, but again, there are rules. Nobody who knows me, or us, can know I am back. We can not tell any friends, family, or even my parents. If anyone we know sees me, we are done, and back to heaven I go. In the long run that is not bad news for me. However, you would be losing me for a second time. James, the way I see it, I get the best of both worlds! I have been to heaven, and trust me, I long to return! That said, I want to spend as long as I can with you here, doing Gods work, enjoying the best husband a girl could ask for, then go to heaven with you and be there for all eternity!"

James was quick with his response to that last item "well then, nobody will know! Because I am not losing you again! I cannot believe you are here! I do have more questions though, well at least one more question for now!" Rachel inquired "what's that?" James with a smirk on his face that Rachel could barely see asked "can we turn on the lights so I can see your beautiful face that I have been missing?" As Rachel laughed, she found the light switch and turned on the light. James gasped and said "wow, I don't know if you have ever been more beautiful. If I didn't know better, I'd think you are an Angel! Wait! Are you? I mean, technically, are you an Angel now?" Rachel bonked James on his forehead and said "DUH! You know better than that! Angels are Angels, and people are people! How long have you been going to church and reading the Bible?"

Again, James laughed at his own thoughtlessness. He then said "yeah, true, I should have known that. But that said, wow, you are stunning. Raech, I have missed you so much, you just have no idea. And to go from the pain I was feeling, to this overwhelming sense of happiness is literally off the charts. My life has completely revolved around "us" for so long, I was so lost! I did not know what to do! I knew you were gone, even before I was informed, you know?" Rachel asked "how did you know?" James told her "when you were late, and your phone was going directly to voice mail, I just knew. When the fireman called, he didn't even have to say the words. I was so devastated." Rachel grabbed him, and held on to him, and apologized for the pain he had experienced.

James told her "ah sweetie, you don't have to apologize, it wasn't your fault. I am just glad you are here now. We had a perfect marriage, didn't we? I mean, that wasn't in my head was it? I was so lost when I lost you. I was so confused, so hurt, so numb." Rachel started to cry even harder and held him even tighter. And told him "James, there wasn't a single day, or even single hour in our entire relationship that I didn't have intense love for you. There is nobody that could have given me what you have given me. You have always been my best friend. I have always said that you were my answered prayer. Well, I learned first hand, from God, who created every single thing, that indeed you were my answered prayer. So no, it wasn't in your head, and I always felt exactly the same way!"

"Rachel; what happened on the mountain?" Rachel was a little embarrassed "James, it really doesn't matter. I tripped. I dropped my stupid water bottle and tripped, next thing I knew, I was standing before the Lord." James had to ask "what is Heaven like?" Rachel was noticeably excited as she said "oh James, it's incredible" but then tempered her enthusiasm a bit when she said "Listen, even if I wanted to, I could never convey to you the wonder and spectacular nature that Heaven is. Words do not describe it. The truth is I am not able to give you any details. But know this, God is everywhere! I mean, He truly is in your entire being. He is in every word you speak. Every expression of worship you offer is full of the Lord. Everything about God is celebrated with every thought and action. Even when you are not specifically talking to or about God, its all about Him; and it just feels so incredible"

"I cannot wait to experience that with you. I can't wait to see you overflow with joy in Heaven when you experience this feeling. Oh, one thing I can say. Do you know how you have heard about the Angels in Heaven singing?" James quickly agreed. "Well, they do, for real. They sing all the time. They sing songs to the Lord, songs about the Lord, and they even sing when there is a new believer. And I am telling you; the greatest voice you have ever heard pales in comparison to the awe inspiring sounds of choirs of Angels singing in unison praising the Creator of all things! They sing about the simplest things. They sing of things that even the newest of Christians knows, and probably has experienced. And yet, while they sing of these things, in a powerfully majestic way, you can't help but to be drawn even closer to the Lord."

"What is even more amazing is that you feel like you are close as you can possibly be to God. He is right there. The love, and feelings are....well, words can not describe. But you have this feeling of wholeness, of being completely immersed in Gods love. Then suddenly, you meet someone, or the Angels sing, and that completely full feeling, grows even more! You then realize what you felt before, is now more complete than it was. Again, I can not describe it, and I am supposed to let you experience it for yourself. But James, trust me on this, knowing what I know; the greatest tragedy in the entire Universe would be, for us to do anything less than all we can, to make sure that every single person who God puts us in front of makes it to Heaven. I have no idea what hell is like, and I do not want to know. I do know how amazing and spectacular Heaven is and I am telling you, I could just cry rivers of tears at the thought of a single person missing out on being in Gods presence for all eternity."

"Babe, I do have a little more good news though. This is more on a selfish note; especially in light of what I just said." James was eager to hear, and exclaimed "tell me!" Well, I know that our first assignment is at least a couple of days away. We have some time to spend together, just us." James was very excited "That is great! I am so excited to do the Lords work, and I am even more excited that I get to do his work with you. You remember your silly stories? The ones you used to make up all the time about you and me traveling around on adventures doing Gods work?" Rachel gasped as she said "Silly huh? I thought those stories were exciting and romantic!" James backtracked a bit "Well yeah, of course they were! But you know you always embellished them to get me going!" Rachel replied "True!"

James continued "Anyway, the thing is, we are about to do those very things. We are going to go on crusades for Christ together. We are going to have the very adventures you spoke of! This is exciting! And what makes it even more exciting is that we know for a fact, we are truly doing exactly, the work Gods wants us to do. Instead of simply going out there with the best of intentions, and doing things we think God wants us to do. We know that every step we take will be of God, by God, for God. Does it get more exciting than that?" Rachel agreed "Oh sweetie, you have no idea. Our assignments will come one at a time, and I have only been given a general idea of what our tasks will actually be, but I have no doubt things are going to get very exciting. We are going to witness Gods supernatural power here on Earth. This is going to be very exciting!"

Rachel continued "but for now my sweet husband, we get some us time. Some very overdue us time. There is something I am very much in the mood for!" James broke in "wow, you don't waste any time do you? I told you, I am going to play hard to get!" Rachel countered "ha ha ha, stud! Actually, I am in the mood for Italian food! Will you take me to dinner?" James was a little surprised by her request "really? You come back from Heaven, and you have food on your mind?" Rachel said "no, my stomach has its mind on food! I must say, in heaven, you are never hungry, always satisfied. Again, no details, but needless to say, we didn't eat because we had to; we ate to celebrate! But I am starved, I feel like I haven't eaten in a couple of weeks!" James smirked and said "Very funny!"

Rachel and James left the hotel room hand in hand heading towards the elevator. As the door opened James looked at Rachel and said "Rachel, I have missed this. Just holding your hand like this is an answered prayer!" All Rachel could say is "I love you" They stepped into the elevator and pushed the number one button. As the door closed, James turned to Rachel, and pulled her close and leaned in and kissed her. They softly, passionately kissed as if they were kissing for the first time. Both of them were completely caught up in the kiss and were off in a world of their own. They were both snapped back to reality when they heard a man clear his throat. They looked up, to see the elevator doors already open and more than five people waiting to get on the elevator. They were a little embarrassed and James sheepishly said "sorry, we haven't seen each other in a while" as they exited the elevator. They could hear laughter behind them as the doors were closing.

As they walked to the car hand-in-hand, Rachel leaned towards James so their shoulders brushed against each other, and she whispered "It's nice to be with you, babe." James let her know he felt exactly the same way "I feel like I am living a dream! It is so great to be with you. I told you how I felt when you were gone, and that couple of weeks felt like months…but you have only been back an hour, and it feels like you never left. You truly make my life complete. Thank God for this amazing miracle and gift!" Rachel smiled and said "I am telling you James, you have no idea!"

They arrived at the restaurant and requested a table or booth for two with some privacy. They were seated, and immediately ordered their food. Rachel was surprised at how wonderful the food tasted. She told him "The food I ate in heaven was the best, and most satisfying I ever ate, but you never lose your appreciation for some good Italian restaurant food!" James just laughed, knowing he had no way of relating to this. Rachel had to ask something that was on her mind "James, how are my parents?" He reassured here they were doing well considering "Rachel, your parents are truly awesome. They really are. They love and miss you terribly. Despite their sadness and loss; I can not even begin to tell you how much they have done for me since you…left."

"They are truly champions of grace, and faith. Your mom has gone out of her way to make things as tolerable and easy as possible. Your funeral was incredible. Wow that is weird saying that to you! But they are great. Rock is with them right now!" Rachel had not thought of much besides James, and her parents when she said "Oh, I was not even thinking about him…Poor Rock, I miss him. What a great dog, does he miss me?" James kind of laughed "That poor dog, has been moping around, very sad actually. I don't know if he understands what happened, but he definitely knows you are not there. He's even had some bad dreams! He misses his mommy!" Rachel added "What a cool dog. I feel bad for him. At least he still has you and my parents."

James mind was racing. He could not believe his wife was sitting next to him again. This was truly prayers come true! He had so many things to ask Rachel. Yet, he knew he probably would not get answers to most of his questions. He figured it would not hurt to ask things though; Rachel would answer what she could and not answer the other questions. James asked if there were others like her and other couples like them; Rachel said "I have no idea. I would have never believed God would allow something like this, and I was never told if this is a one time occurrence, something He has been doing, or something He is starting to do. All I know is that despite the wonder and awe of heaven, I am so thankful that He has allowed me to return to you, and have this exciting history altering journey together!"

The car ride back to the hotel was surprisingly quiet. They spoke little to each other as they were driving. They would glance back and forth at each other; as if they were making sure what they were seeing was real. They would catch each other seemingly checking each other out. They had little smirks on their faces almost as if they were embarrassed to be caught by the other. James reached over and held her hand. He ran his hand from her fingers up her arm enjoying the feeling of her skin, something he had been missing. She felt the same. This was like a dream to have the love of his life back.

When they returned to their hotel room, neither said a word. As soon as they entered the room Rachel turned to him and began to kiss James. She playfully backed away, then said to James "You know, there is something I miss even more than Italian food…" James asked "and what is that?" Rachel responded "I have been enjoying the feel of your touch tonight, and wondered if you are in the mood to give me one of your world famous body massages." James had to laugh as he said "I think I could muster the thought of touching your perfect, beautiful body tonight!" Rachel responded "Great! Let me go freshen up a bit, I will be out in a few!"

James heard her in the bathroom. He felt like he had to keep listening to make sure she was still there. He hated the idea of letting her out of his site, he was afraid the bubble was going to burst! He heard her start the shower. He didn't want to leave the room feeling like he might be risking her going back; but he reasoned that Gods plans extended way past tonight and he was so safe to leave the room and decided to run down to the lobby real quick for some candles. He made it back just as she was turning off the shower. He quickly turned back the bed, lit the candles, and turned off the lights. He even managed to find her favorite flower downstairs in the lobby and was holding that in his hand to give here when she walked out of the bathroom.

She walked out of the bathroom in a big fluffy hotel robe. The robe made her look even more petite than she already is. She walked towards him; as she received the flower from him she whispered "I see you haven't lost your touch." James leaned forward to kiss the side of her neck and whispered in her ear, you have not felt anything yet!" After some soft kisses on her neck, and lips he walked her towards the bed to lie her down. She removed her robe, and much to his delight, she was not wearing anything underneath the robe.

James began by lightly caressing her skin. He missed the touch of her soft, seemingly delicate skin. He knew from enjoying so many athletic activities with her, she was anything but delicate; he always enjoyed how soft and sweet she was when she just laid there anticipating or enjoying his touch. Even though, in reality it had not been very long ago that they enjoyed each others touch, the intensity of their desire was so strong that it felt as if it were the first time they were together. After exploring most of her backside with some caresses he began to massage her neck and shoulders and Rachel completely relaxed in his hands.

He worked his way from her head all the way down to her feet. They were both completely lost in the passion of his touching her. As she rolled over, she sat up towards him, and kissed his forehead, then kissed several times softly all over his face as she rubbed her hands through his hair. She knew this relaxed him more than anything. She lightly kissed towards his ear and whispered to him "I can't wait anymore, please, make love to me" They made love off and on all night long. Despite having a love life that had always been so fun and fulfilling they connected that night like never before.

CHAPTER 7

The next morning Rachel awoke to see James eyes fixated on her. She smiled at him "how did you sleep?" His response was "Too well! I woke up from an extremely deep sleep when the sun came through the window. It was bright, and directly in my eyes. I couldn't see you right away. I got scared. But my eyes focused, and then I couldn't take my eyes off of you! You know I have always enjoyed watching you sleep, now even more! Thank you for last night!" Rachel blushed, and said "you don't have to thank me! You know that! However, thank you too sweetie; that was special!"

They decided to spend the day at the beach since they had not been there together since their honeymoon. The last time they were at the ocean together, was a few days after they became newly weds. They often reminisced during their marriage about how romantic their honeymoon was, staying in their room nearly the entire time. Although this was true; part of the reason they ended up in the room as much as they did was because within two hours of settling in at the beach, it began to rain very heavily, and showed no signs of letting up. Their extra romantic time was aided by some unexpected weather.

As much as they liked to look back fondly at that memory, especially considering the incredible night they just experienced together, they wanted to spend some time together at the beach, playing in the sun. They went out and picked up some beach supplies; an umbrella, some towels, sun tan lotion, bathing suits, a football, and some drinks. They were ready to have a fun play day. After they were settled, leaning back, soaking in the sun rays, James asked Rachel "Do you remember just over a month ago, you brought up how we needed to blow off our jobs, get away, and have some uninterrupted play time together?" Rachel remembered and James replied with a smirk "Who would have thought it would have taken you dying for this to happen?" Rachel gasped and said "Do you really think you should joke about that?" James shot back, "Hey! I don't know what else to do! Most painful time in my life, and here I am with you. This is completely unreal!"

Rachel understood exactly what he was saying. James could not hear it, but hardly a minute went by where she did not pray to God, thanking him for his incredible blessing. Even having been to Heaven, in Gods presence, literally being touched by Him, she had no idea why she was blessed with such an unbelievable experience. This was so strange for her. Heaven was so amazing! Now that she was back here, there were few words to describe what she experienced. The conflicting emotions were difficult for her to reconcile. When she was there, she had no regrets of not being here. She tried to think back to how she felt and it was strange to her, because she could not remember being sad about leaving James, or even what he was going through, but at the same time, as soon as she was informed of this miracle, and upon her arrival, those emotions and more rushed in!

Now, Heaven was almost becoming like a memory; even though she was just recently there. She could not articulate it in her head. Despite the range of emotions, she was equally excited about doing Gods work. She recalled that in Heaven, she met and heard some of the greatest people in Gods creation discussing things they'd done on Earth. The pride these people had in works that had long lasting, eternal benefits. She remembered Paul saying how amazing it was to go from a man who tormented Christians to a man who God used to bring so many more to Heaven. Paul said he felt so blessed to be part of Gods plan and to encounter so many of the people in Heaven that were only there because of the works that God did through him.

Rachel certainly never felt bad or less important or less loved in Heaven because she had not accomplished anything like the people she read about in the Bible, and so many more that were not even written about. In fact, she had a feeling of complete fullness, satisfaction and understanding she was right where she belonged. However, she had something deep inside her which yearned to please God in the greatest possible way. She had a desire to be someone who God would use to bring many, many more to his Kingdom. Heaven was perfect; but there is a longing deep in her soul that she wanted every person that God created to have that complete connection with God. She could not fathom the thought of eternal separation from God. Even though she knew, or least while safely in heaven, she thought she knew that she would no longer be part of Gods plans to bring new believers to his eternal kingdom; it still excited her to hear the Angels celebrating victories that were happening on Earth. Her joy knew no bounds to hear the Angels proclaim how near Gods final victory was. Her passion for these victories grew, even though she had no inkling of a thought that she would ever be part of a plan to return to Earth to reach more lost souls.

Now here she was, laying in the sand, on a beautiful California day, no clouds, 88 degrees, holding the hand of the love of her life. She also knew it was only a matter of time that the work God intends for them to accomplish, would be revealed. She felt like she was created for this very moment in time. Rachel had so many thoughts running through her head. She was thinking about all the adventure stories she made up with James. She knew they were just stories, but to her, they were not just stories, but true desires. Now, in a moment of clarity, she believed those desires were instilled in her by her Creator. Just thinking of this she had tears streaming down her face.

James sat up real quick. In a very concerned tone he

asked her "are you okay? What is wrong?" Rachel could not contain herself as she began to cry "James, in the blink of an eye I went from being at work, going for a workout, in heaven, and now with you again. I feel like God is revealing things to me at this very moment. I have no doubt that everything in my life, in our relationship, our marriage, even my death, was for what is about to happen. You just have no idea. When I made up all those silly stories, I embellished a lot just to get you going because you are so practical; but in truth, deep down, I craved for such adventure. And now, we are about to get it. I just feel so blessed; and to share this with you is just more than I deserve! There is nobody I would rather hang out with, let alone have a ministry with, than you!"

"Babe, we are about to do some things that might have the greatest historical importance in all creation. I think that God is going to allow us to see some things, and experience some things that are truly unimaginable. I can feel it! I just feel it! And I am overwhelmed by the sense of excitement, honor, and blessedness I am feeling. You know I think the world of you, but in the grand scheme of things, who are we? We are a couple of nobodies! I mean, outside of a hundred, maybe two hundred people, nobody even knows who we are? And yet we are being included in Gods plans; possibly one of the most important parts of His plan considering this is all about the final chapter in end of times events!"

James was mesmerized by her as she spoke. He had always enjoyed Rachel's passion and enthusiasm. He even enjoyed hearing the smallest things she spoke of, but this was different. Rachel was always the most optimistic person he had ever known. She was always coming up with ideas for things that "would be cool". However, as active and busy as she was accomplishing and doing things, her stories were always larger than life. They were things she would like to do, or could only hope to experience. But now, listening to her go on and on about what was happening. Her tone was different. She was not contemplating adventures that could be fun to do; she was getting her self ready! She was accepting Gods gift, and challenge. She was not simply dreaming; she was planning! This had James even more fired up than he already was. He was ready too! He was also falling more in love with Rachel by the minute if that was possible!

Before he heard Rachel crying, James, himself, was thinking about how incredible this was. His mindset was a little different from hers, because he had never been to heaven, and experienced God the way she had. However, he did have visits from the Angels in ways that would change anyone's thought process and outlook forever! James was beginning to feel a bit conflicted before he felt a sudden peace while working through some of his own thoughts; a peace that he knew could only come from God! As he started to worry, he instantly felt God in control.

The issue he had been deliberating on was how he could be so caught up with the return of Rachel. He realized that his love for her was growing, as well as his desire and focus on her. Yet, at the same time he was acutely aware of the tasks that were forthcoming, directly from the Creator of all things! He heard that sentiment so many times before..."The Creator of all things..." Now it felt more real, and more important than ever before. He was worried that his focus might be misdirected, or lessened by his love and affection for Rachel. He even considered that perhaps their marriage and love for each other should be even less important now. He wondered if he should completely focus on the assignments they receive to carry out for the Lord. Quickly he reasoned that if God did not want them to celebrate their love for each other, and connect the way they were, he would not have sent her back.

As James was reconciling these thoughts in his head, he had a calming sense of peace which came over him. He felt reassured loving Rachel and appreciating all that she has to offer is a gift from God. He felt he can do this while fully keeping his focus and accomplishing anything that God has for them to do. James leaned toward Rachel and wiped the tears from her face, and held her as he said "Something tells me the amazing things we have already experienced are just the beginning. And you are right, in the grand scheme of things, we are nobodies! But, so were the disciples! Fishermen? A tax collector? Even Jesus and his Earthly dad were simple carpenters. Peter wasn't exactly known for his intelligence before being filled with the Holy Spirit, and look at how boldly he proclaimed the guilty actions and motives of the Pharisees and the divinity of Jesus!"

"That said, I also wonder, why us? But I think I am pretty much finished asking why us, and ready to start doing Gods work. I am so thankful for everything that is happening. I can't help but wonder and worry about what happens when we have accomplished all that God wants us to do. I really don't want that to happen too fast because I don't want you leave again! However, when you go back to heaven this time, at least I won't be as sad and heartbroken, and I will have more optimism about everything considering what we are about to experience. How in the world will I ever go back to work after all of this? I mean, we are about do some mighty things for the Lord, and then I have to go back to sitting in my office and sifting through emails and paperwork? All of a sudden, that sounds kind of depressing!"

Rachel cut in "I think we just have to focus on the now. We need to appreciate what we have, and enjoy this time, and consider ourselves so blessed to be part of carrying out Gods plans" James became excited and said "that is exactly what I was going to say! We need to live for the moment. I am going to cherish every moment I have with you. I am going to enjoy you completely, and fully as much as I can. I am also going to relish every opportunity I have to do what I know will be exactly what God wants me to do! So, Miss Lara Croft Tomb Raider, are you ready for some fun?" Rachel laughed and said "Yes Mr. Jones, um, Indiana, yes I am ready! Let's go do the Lords work together!"

They spent the day enjoying the Sun and all the fun the

beach had to offer. They started playing catch with the football, and drew a bit of a crowd. Soon they had a big eight versus eight game going in the sand. They loved to team-up and play competitive games against others. They had done that for as long as they knew each other. This time they had a few teammates to help them out but they still felt, the "us verse them" mentality they had since they first became a couple. James loved to tease Rachel about her attractiveness. He would embarrass her by bragging that not only was she so athletic, but that she was the most beautiful as well.

James could not keep his eyes off her. She looked so casual and carefree. She looked so vibrant and full of life. Rachel seemed to have even more zest than usual. She did not act like a girl who just came back from greatest place in existence and had to leave suddenly and settle for something less. Instead she acted like a girl who just started walking again for the first time in years. She ran, seemingly gliding through the sand like she was having the time of her life. James was too, but half of his excitement came from watching her. At one point James went out to catch a ball but was watching Rachel more than he was focusing on the play, and he was surprised when the ball hit him in his side.

Of course, this gave Rachel even more reason to enjoy the moment and she let him know it!

CHAPTER 8

After the game was over they were catching their breath, relaxing and drinking some water. A few of the people they had been playing with invited them out on their boat to go out and do some scuba diving. James and Rachel jumped at the chance. Rachel always spoke of wanting to go scuba diving. Less than a year before, she convinced James to take scuba diving lessons so they could be certified. They just never made it a point to go to the ocean or even a lake to try it. They grabbed their stuff and joined their new friends on their boat. The boat, named "Still Searching" was a beautiful new red and black speedboat.

The owners of the boat were a couple about the same age as James and Rachel. Rick and Marcia had been married about four years and had recently inherited a large amount of money, so lately they were doing more playing than working. Their close friend Steve was hanging out with them for the day as well. So the five of them strapped on their gear, and explored the ocean for the next few hours. They had a fantastic time, and Rachel was sure to point out to James the benefit of already being certified for scuba diving, especially in light of the fact that James had teased Rachel over the last year for making him get certified when they had no real plans to even go scuba diving. He had such a fun time; he had to concede the point to her!

Afterwards the group decided to go to a sea food restaurant located on the sandy beach and continued their fun into the evening. They hit it off very well and were enjoying each others company. They had many similar interests, Rick and James even shared the same profession. After dinner while they were all sitting chatting enjoying the perfect California night, James asked Rick and Marcia what the name of the boat means. Rick said "actually, I am kind of glad you asked, because I was about to ask you something along those lines. I am assuming by some of things that I have heard you and Rachel say to each other today, that you are, um, church people?" James laughed, and asked "Do you mean, if we believe in God?"

Rick responded "Yeah. I already know the answer, but I was just clarifying." Rachel interjected "Yes, we are both Christians, very strong in our faith, why do you ask?" Rick was quiet, as if he was a little embarrassed and said "Well, the meaning of the name of my boat is exactly what it says. I am still searching, we, are still searching. My wife and I have gone round and round about this whole religion thing. Every time something starts to make sense, and I start to think I might be ready to lean towards a certain direction, we see something, or hear something that totally gets us going in a different direction. I guess we are more agnostic, even somewhat cynical when it comes to calling ourselves that. To be honest, it's not that we believe in a god, it's that we want to believe!"

"We both see too many things out there that make it challenging to believe. We want to. I mean, who wants to believe that after this, it is all over, and kaput, and we cease to exist?" James acknowledged that thought by saying "Yeah, that is very depressing to think of things like that isn't it?" Rick nodded and said "It definitely is. But if I am being honest with you, it just seems to me, that it makes more sense that way. Don't you agree Marcia?" Marcia added "Sometimes it does. I want to believe in Heaven. I want to believe that I blissfully live in the clouds, playing my harp or whatever, thanking God that I am still around. But there just doesn't seem to be anything that shows me otherwise"

Rick jumped in agreeing with his wife and said "It just seems like science says all this stuff, and all the religions are all messed up and self serving, and every time I get to a place in my head where I start to think that maybe God is real, something snaps me out of it. I seem to be more at ease at the thought of a god not existing than one existing. But that said; I have to tell you, if there really is a god, I want to know the truth. And that is why I am asking you about this. You two seem different. There is something about you, and for some reason, I just have this feeling you two might have some answers for us; and Marcia feels that way too! If there is any chance that someone is going to show us something we can hang our hats on; maybe it is you?"

James and Rachel looked at each other almost in amazement, and Rachel moved her eyes in a way to encourage James to respond. James replied by saying "I'd have to say, that if God is real, like Rachel and I know Him to be, and you have this feeling that we are ones who can help you with this, that perhaps the true God of all creation is already speaking to your hearts before you have even accepted his gift!" Rick responded with surprise "Gift? What gift?" James spent the next hour explaining our need of forgiveness of sins, how Jesus is the fulfillment of the law and so many prophecies. James and Rachel answered many of their questions, and learned they had assumed so many things that were simply not true; it was obvious why they were off track and questioning the very existence of God.

When James and Rachel sat in their car, Rachel had tears streaming down her face. All she could say was "Could you feel that? Could you feel that?" James knew exactly what she was speaking about "He asked her, is that how the disciples felt? I mean, the presence of God was so thick! He was not only with us, but He set that whole thing up!" Rachel turned to James practically floating off of her seat and said "That was a divine appointment! God didn't tell us where to go, he brought them to us! We just helped three people accept Christ as their personal savior! James tried to be funny by adding "I never thought a guy who tackles as hard as he did, would cry as hard as he did! I guess he needs to change the name of his boat now!"

They returned to their room elated. They felt like their feet barely touched the ground as they walked hand-in-hand through the lobby. They were exhilarated. They could not believe that even while they were just having fun, enjoying each others company and the sunny day, and before God even gave them their first assignment that He was already using them in mighty ways! As soon as they reached their room, they both dropped to their knees and thanked God for their new friends, and new brother and sister in Christ. James and Rachel prayed that they will be ready at all times to hear God, and to lean on Him for his strength and power as they are ready to be used by Him to reach as many as He wants them to.

The next morning, after being in each others arms all night, they went for some breakfast. James dropped his keys in some mud when he exited the SUV, so he excused himself to go to the bathroom to wash up. After locking the door behind him, he went to the sink and turned on the water. As he looked down at the running water, he felt himself getting sleepy, and caught up in staring at the running water.

He found the sound of the water running down the sink so soothing. Despite being aware that he was getting sleepy and drawn in by the water, in a public restroom, he could not make himself look away. He felt like he was completely falling asleep and about to fall over.

James eyes closed shut, and the next thing he knew he was surrounded by hundreds of people, mostly what he thought were media members. He could see an emblem on the wall of the building he was in, identifying it as the Los Angeles City Hall building. People were excited about the arrival of the president. He could hear some of them praising the president for his policies, and others ridiculing him and questioning how he was elected once, let alone twice. As he was turning to look around the building he felt himself knocked down, and as he looked up, he was in an alley behind a trash can.

Now terribly confused James could hear some foreign speaking coming from down the alley way. He peered out from behind the trash can, and could see what he thought looked like Arabs loading all kinds of weaponry into a storage shed. He could see assault rifles, and saw multiple crates loaded into the small room. He saw something that he guessed was some sort of missile launcher. James counted 8 men. One of them did not look like be belonged with this group at all. He was dressed in a basketball jersey, and athletic shorts, looked very American.

The American's phone rang. He mostly listened, but concluded the conversation in English saying "Yes, I understand, 5:00 p.m. We will meet after it is done." After he put his phone back in his pocket he pulled one of the men aside and told him "The president is expected to be on time, and will arrive tomorrow no later than 5:00 pm and will be leaving by 5:20 after his speech. You will have your best chance for success if you come in from the East stairwell. Your clearance has already been approved; your papers and ID's are in the envelope in the car." The Middle Eastern looking man handed him a brief case, and the American turned and walked away.

James realized he was standing in front of the running water in the sink, and proceeded to wash his hands before returning to join Rachel at their table. When he arrived at the table, he leaned down to kiss her on the cheek, and whispered in her ear "I think someone is about to assassinate the president of the United States, and it's our job to stop them." He calmly sat down, then Rachel could see James face turning white as a ghost. She asked him "What makes you think that?" James said, "I am not really hungry anymore, but let's order some food real fast, eat, and get out of here!"

15 minutes later they were in their car, heading for the freeway. Rachel asked "Where are we going?" James said "We are heading for L.A." Rachel needed details at this point "James, how do you know this?" James told her of the vision and added "It was just strange, one second I am watching all of the hoopla surrounding the arrival of the president, which I know doesn't even happen until tomorrow. Then I was watching what looked like some really bad men loading weapons into a storage shed, and talking about the president's arrival tomorrow. This is all new to me, but if these are visions from God, I have to assume that the bad guys with weapons are going after the good guy!"

James handed Rachel his cell phone and said "Do me a favor please! Call information, and get the addresses for every Surety Guard Storage facility in the Los Angeles Area." Rachel hung up the phone, and had six locations to choose from. James responded by saying "Thank God! I was terrified there were going to be over a hundred to choose from. At least six is manageable." Rachel asked James "How do you think we should stop this? Should we call the FBI or Homeland Security?" James half heartedly shook his head no and said "I have been wondering that myself. I just don't know how we even tell them about this. I mean, how do we say that we found out?"

Rachel was just as confused but added "But that is the thing, I mean, isn't that what they do? Isn't that their job to thwart terrorist activities and possible assassination attempts?" James replied "You know, I agree with that. But it seems that God came to us with this task. I just don't think He would have shown me both sides of this, to simply make a phone call to inform them what is about to happen, and let them take care of it. Besides, I read once that the FBI gets dozens of threats against the president daily. I am sure they take each one seriously, but what if they don't? What if it doesn't make sense with their other intelligence? What if they don't believe us? What if they are too late? I think we need to find the weapons before the assassins return to get them!"

Rachel asked "What are we going to do when we get

them?" James said "That's what I am trying to figure out. We could destroy them, leave them somewhere for the feds to find. I don't know. Let's get them first! Then we will worry about what to do with them! I could be wrong, but I am guessing if the attack is tomorrow, they will return either late tonight, or in the morning to retrieve their arsenal. It's going on 10:00 AM now, so I am guessing that gives us about eight hours to be able to clear out the shed, and not be too terrified about them returning while we have their guns and missile launcher in our hands! I seriously doubt they return again anytime before the Sun goes down. Just to make sure these aren't just my thoughts, would you say a prayer for us as I drive?"

Rachel closed her eyes and bowed her head and said "Father God, thank you for choosing us today for this incredible task! Lord we pray that nothing we do today is anything other than what you want us to do! Please speak to us, and protect us, and most importantly guide us. We know that if we are doing what you want us to do; everything else will fall into place! If we are doing exactly what you want us to do, then please just keep your hand on us. If our plans are not your plans, please either speak to our hearts, or send us a messenger to clarify what we are to do for You! We love you Lord, and want so desperately to serve you, and be tools for you to use to accomplish your will! Lord, we are planning to find this storage facility, and by some means, open the door, and take the weaponry out away from the terrorists who want access to it for evil plans! We hope and pray that these are indeed your plans. We submit this plan to you for your blessing! In Jesus' name, we pray to You! Amen!"

James asked "Rachel, will you please call the numbers on that list of storage facilities and ask them if they know of a billboard for Humana Health Insurance that is viewable from the alley behind the storage sheds?" James asked. Rachel responded "Sure, I take it you saw that billboard in the vision?" James confirmed, and added "I saw the Bill Board and also remember that the area had an industrial park feel to it. It didn't feel like it was right in the city, or an area that is heavily trafficked." While Rachel made her calls, James kept a lookout for a Home Depot. He knew they were going to need some supplies. As Rachel finished her last call, James was exiting the freeway. Rachel inquired "Why are we getting off the freeway?"

James responded "I saw a Home Depot and we are definitely going to need some supplies." She informed him "Of the six storage facilities only two have alleys anywhere in the area." She also asked for details about the surrounding areas. One of the storage places described the area as a family friendly area with plenty of nearby shopping and restaurants and the other as an industrial park. Neither location could recall seeing any billboards around. James hoped that Rachel's research narrowed it down to the right storage facility. They arrived at Home Depot, and their mini shopping spree began.

After about 45 minutes, they left with a tool box, bolt cutters, a power saw with blades that could cut metal, AC Adaptors for the car, a crow bar, and a few other odds and end items that James thought could come in handy at some point. James also asked for directions to the nearest sporting goods store, and much to Rachel's surprise, inquired if they sold guns. The second they finished loading up the SUV, and sat inside, Rachel asked James "Why do you want a gun?" James smiled and said "I don't!" Rachel let out a gasp of relief but before she could say anything James continued "I want guns, lots of them!" Now the look of concern was back on Rachel's face!

Before she could begin to question his thinking James tried to reassure her. He said, "Listen Raech, as far as I understand, we have Angels that are fighting the forces we do not see; and from what I understand, in some cases they are fighting those battles on our behalf! Indeed, God is using us to stop evil, especially in this instance! That said, the evil people we face are of this world, and they will hit us with real, physical objects, and shoot us with real bullets! I am guessing you can't die, or maybe you can, I don't know! But I do know getting shot doesn't help us in our efforts to be used by God!" Rachel was speechless and getting scared.

James continued "Maybe God is going to protect us completely, and step in every time we are in danger. Maybe he won't! Maybe we are going to face some seriously evil people and part of our responsibility will be to take them out!" Rachel reacted in shock "Take them out? Do you think we are real life Spies for God? I thought you were going to be more like Indiana Jones not James…James Bond!" James could not help but laugh a little as he tried to calm her down "I am not planning to go around shooting people. But if it comes down to choice between someone we are confronting that we know is evil, getting shot or killed, verses you or I getting shot or killed, I choose them! I want to be prepared for whatever we have in front of us. If it means cutting a lock, I want bolt cutters, if it means running through the desert for days, I want water, and if it means possibly having terrorists coming after us, I want to be able defend ourselves!"

"I hope we never have a life and death confrontation face to face. I hope we can have the fun kind of adventures you have always talked about. But after this latest vision, and what God wants us to do, it occurred to me that things might be really serious at times. Plus I remember Kaleb reminding me that I am not immortal. I assume he wouldn't have warned me about that unless we were likely to encounter some real danger. I sure hope we can sneak in, load the weapons, and sneak out, and everything works out like we want it to. But I guarantee you, if they find us taking their weapons, they will shoot first, and ask questions later. I trust in God, and I am sure He has an incredible plan that doesn't involve us getting shot today, but as far as how that plays out, I don't know. So let's be prepared for whatever comes our way!"

Suddenly things seemed much scarier to Rachel, and considerably less romantic, but James' logic made some sense to her. This scared her; she said "I trust God too, and I trust you! This is all happening so fast! A trip to Home Depot for some bolt cutters made sense to me, but I didn't expect you turn into Rambo in less than an hour!" James laughed and reassured her "We are going to be fine! But we will be prepared too! I love you too much to let some crazies pin us into a corner, and have no way to protect you! Now, let's get in here, and get this over with, so we can go steal some missiles and rocket launchers from terrorists!"

Rachel thought James was having way too much fun for how serious this was. James was always like that though. Everything he did, he completely put himself into, while at the same time having a carefree fun attitude about it like it was not work. Rachel usually loved that about him. However, on occasions when something was serious and important his happy go lucky behavior made her a little nervous. However, she had to admit, that James always came through. That being said, Rachel chose to bite her tongue when they walked out of the sporting good store with four hand guns, two rifles and a shotgun and some binoculars. Additionally, they had what she thought was more than enough bullets to take over a small country!

As they were leaving James noticed a Verizon Wireless in the same plaza that the sporting goods store was in. They stopped in real quick to add another cell phone line of service to James account so Rachel could have a phone. James reasoned to Rachel "Just in case we have to split up for any reason." As they were nearing the door Rachel teased "James, do you think I can get my old number back?" Of course she knew better but thought that it would be funny and lighten up the mood a bit after how concerned she had been. In truth, even though she thought James had a few more things than they could use, she was proud of him for thinking this out so well and making sure they were prepared. Even though she knew she was there to help James, and perhaps even protect him at times, his preparation and care always made her feel safe; and despite her nervousness about what was to come, she felt just as protected by him now, as she always did. Of course, now, beyond a shadow of a doubt, she also knew God was leading this adventure!

CHAPTER 9

Just after two o'clock they arrived in the area of the storage facility that they felt was the most likely location of the list of choices they had. James immediately recognized the area. When they made their way to the alley behind the storage company, they could see the billboard that he had previously spoken of. He continued down the alley past where the storage sheds were. He kept going to get a feel for which directions people would be coming and going from. The alley continued on for a few blocks, but the location of the storage room made James feel confident because there were only two ways that anyone could get in or out of there. This made James feel a little more secure in terms of keeping a watchful eye.

They continued on down the alley, and turned off until they found an area that was somewhat secluded. James loaded some of the guns, handing one to Rachel asking her 'Do you remember how to use this?" Rachel responded "of course! I just hope I won't have to!" James was prepared for a mini battle, but he hoped this was just a recovery mission. He explained to Rachel his plan "Okay Rachel, here is what I am thinking. We take one more drive down the alley to make sure nobody is around. We are going to pull up right in front of the storage unit. We will each have these two guns on us, and the rest will be sitting in the front and back seat of the Navigator, just in case they are needed."

"Now, once we are in front, I will get out and use the bolt cutter to open the lock, and get the storage door open. I will start to load the SUV with the light things and whatever I can handle by myself, and you use these binoculars to keep watch in both directions. As soon as I get all the light stuff in the car, I will call you to start helping me load the rest. If you see a car, warn me, and we will shut the door and quickly pray that it's not the assassins! If it's anyone else, they won't even think twice about seeing a car in front of a storage unit; they will probably just assume it's our unit.

So, no real reason to be nervous unless we know the bad guys show up! Does this sound good to you? Rachel silently nodded her approval. Anything you think we should do different?" Rachel said "No, I think it makes perfect sense. I am thinking what you said earlier makes the most sense, that they aren't going to show up during the middle of the day to retrieve these things. We should be able to be in and out in fifteen minutes."

James agreed with Rachel and suggested they pray again before they get started. "Lord, we truly are your humble servants, here to do what you ask of us! We are both scared, and honored that you have chosen us for this task. This is an incredible honor we have before You and even though no one knows it, a great privilege as well to represent and protect our country the way we are. We pray that you will keep the alley clear of anyone. Please Lord; make this to go as smooth as possible! In truth we are out of our league. It's fun to play soldier and act all brave and prepared; but the fact is, I am terrified. I am not trained for this, and without you this can't happen. I am also terrified of losing Rachel again; I beg you, please prevent us from any danger, I can't lose her again so fast. I know that you have blessed us to have her as my partner in all of this, and I know we will have other assignments after this. I know the victory is already Yours. But the weak part of me needs some reassurance, and needs to lean on You as much possible! Amen!"

They jumped back in the car, and made their way to the storage unit. Both of them armed with handguns, and prepared to confiscate these very scary weapons the terrorists plan to use to assassinate the president. As they were nearing the right unit; Rachel, with a smirk on her face said to James "Don't be scared honey, I have your back!" James laughed, and said "Let's do this!" After James reached the unit, he went to the back of the SUV to grab the bolt cutters. Rachel already stepped out of the car with the binoculars in hand to watch guard. All was quiet except for the sound of the metal lock breaking and falling to the ground, but not before it banged and scraped along the metal door on its way down.

Most likely, this sound could not have been heard by anyone who was not within 100 feet of the storage unit. However, to James and Rachel, it was so loud they worried it was heard all the way back in Newport Beach! As James opened the garage, they both gasped at what they saw inside. They saw at least 10 machine guns that they assumed were

M16's. They saw what looked like three rocket or missile launchers, and at least 10 crates of grenades. Rachel stood there with her mouth open staring in silence with the binoculars at her side. James cleared his throat and whispered "Babe, do you want to keep a lookout?"

Rachel immediately resumed her post looking in each direction for about five seconds at a time making sure nobody was coming. James loaded the machine guns in the car, having no clue if the guns had safeties or even where the safeties were on the guns if they had them. He was terrified he was going to shoot up everything in site just moving the guns. He quickly figured that if Rachel helped him with the rest, they could probably load the rest in less than two minutes and be on there way. Rachel tossed the binoculars in the front seat, and they quickly loaded the grenades and the rocket launchers into the vehicle. The rocket launchers were in big heavy cases that required both of them to lift them into the back hatch of the SUV.

Rachel jumped in the front seat as James closed the storage door, and quickly made his way to the driver's side door, and immediately took off after getting in the car. As they drove off there was silence between the two of them as

James navigated the SUV out of the industrial park. After a few turns and putting some distance between them and the storage facility James screamed out "Wow! Can you believe what we just did?" Rachel was as surprised as James, and said to him "No, not at all! If not for the fearing and worrying about terrorists showing up at any minute, I would almost say that was fun! But, I have to ask you a question!" James had no idea what she was going to ask and replied "What's that?" Rachel quickly asked "What are we going to do with this stuff? If you get pulled over for speeding or anything; they are going to think we are terrorists!" James was thinking that very thing! He said to her "That is so true; we have to get rid of this stuff quick!

As James was sifting through choices in his head something occurred to him. "Raech, I just thought of something we hadn't considered yet." Rachel responded very curiously "What is that?" James said "Well, most likely the bad guys will show up, freak out, and run and hide. But what if they have more weapons somewhere else? Or, what if they have another means to kill the president?" Rachel's silence indicated she had not considered that either. After a minute of both of them quietly thinking of ideas Rachel said "So we have to alert the FBI, and now. We have no choice. Plus at least we know where the bad guys are going to be; just not when."

James agreed "Right, we don't know when, but we have a window of time for FBI though. Maybe we didn't need to come here ourselves and take this stuff, maybe we could have just alerted the authorities from the beginning and let them deal with it. Maybe that is what God had in mind from the beginning." James sounded a little down, because now doubt was creeping in. Rachel's confidence was growing as she told James "Listen Honey, I think we did the right thing. We knew God wanted us to stop this, we did that. We listened. Aside from being obedient to God; you and I discussed some of these strategies. Do you remember, we had concerns about whether or not the authorities would take this serious, and actually arrive before it was too late? We made that a non issue. Assuming the bad guys don't have plan B for executing this tonight, we stopped them. The worst that happens is that they get away, and make another plan."

James was impressed with his wife's thinking "You are right. On top of that when we call the FBI we will not be speculating, we will be speaking about facts that they will have to deal with! We need to make a plan though, and fast. We need to find a place to get rid of this stuff and somehow contact the authorities and tell them what we know. Prayerfully they can act quickly, and get a team over to arrest the terrorists when they get here, and make sure the president is protected as well. Okay that said, I am terrified at the thought of the authorities knowing where this information came from. We cannot reveal our true identities! They would detain us for so long wanting to know how we received this information. With all their tools, the Patriot Act, surveillance, tips, etc they are going to wonder how a couple of Joe Shmo's foiled a plot to assassinate the president of the United States! That would also put us on the radar too! Not to mention, they can not know about your involvement at all! I was thinking that if at some point God wants to send us out of the country that could become a problem as well; but we'll worry about that later."

As James was wrapping up his point, Rachel yelled out "I've got an idea!" James was more than ready to hear something that could offer the solution he was failing to come up with. "What's that?" he asked. Rachel asked "They have pre paid phones you can buy, that don't require service, or ID or any of that, right?" James knew exactly where she was going with this idea and said "yep!" Rachel continued "So, we find a place to hide or stash this stuff. Then we go get one of those pre paid phones. While on the road we place a call to the FBI, and soon as we finish with the call we throw the phone out the window!" James was a little puzzled at the last part of the plan and asked "Why are we throwing the phone out the window?" Rachel chuckled a little, and asked "Can't they do one of those cell phone trace thingies and find out where we are?" James realized they were now in a new world and said "I have no idea! Is that real? I guess better to be safe than sorry!"

Rachel thought of something else and said "Oh, before you get too far away, we should probably find a place somewhere around here to leave this stuff." James interjected "Why is that?" Rachel countered "Because if the Feds have to check out the weapons, and show up to arrest the bad guys, probably shouldn't have the weapons in one city, and the bad guys in another. Plus, if we hide it closer to where we are going, that would just draw more attention to us and maybe give them something to tie to us. I'd just assume that if we are going back to Newport, lets leave all this stuff here, as well as the bad guys in Los Angeles and maybe when this over, it will be completely over for us as far as us being involved!"

Again James was impressed "Great idea babe! I am very impressed Lara Croft! I am glad you are on my side! You already have your mind wrapped around this spy business! Are you sure you weren't leading some sort of double life from before?" Rachel laughed and said "Ha ha funny guy! Before what? Before I…died? Is that what you were getting at? James replied back "Oh ouch! I just meant before in general. I mean, your espionage skills are so impressive!" Rachel had a smirk on her face when she said "Well, Indy, you're not so bad yourself! So far, we make a pretty good spy team!" James held her hand and said "Rachel, we have always made a very good team!"

Taking Rachel's suggestion James stayed off the freeway and was driving in another industrial area about 5 miles from the storage facility. Nothing seemed right as they drove the area. This was not like hiding a note somewhere. They did not want to be seen, and God forbid have someone find the weapons. This weaponry was bad news, and they were very nervous. As James was driving Rachel yelled out "James! Turn there!" He backed up a few feet and drove down a long cull de sac. At the end was an abandoned warehouse. James said "I think this perfect! Nobody would have any business driving down this street, unless they were specifically wanting to go to the warehouse, and I don't think anyone has wanted to go here for years! In fact, the entire cull de sac appeared to have been abandoned for quiet some time!"

The cracks in the street had weeds and grass growing up through them. There were a few broken windows which suggested vandals had been through the area, which concerned Rachel a bit. She asked James "If vandals broke these windows, do you think that means they might hang around here and that they will be back?" James said "No way to know for sure, but I doubt it. I bet if they came through before, and now there is very little left to break. I think this is a great spot for this! This warehouse should be easy to guide the FBI to as well." They drove to the end of the street and stopped in front of the warehouse. They exited their car, so they could walk around. James grabbed a handgun and held it in his hand as they walked.

At first Rachel grinned at him, and thought to herself

"He's taking this Rambo thing way too seriously!" But after a minute or two, the silence in the area was deafening. A pigeon flew away, and they could hear each individual flap of his wings. Rachel could not recall being in such an eerie place as she grabbed his arm she whispered "I am glad you brought that gun with you! I should have brought one too." James looked at her with a smirk on his face, almost in disbelief at what she just said. Rachel looked at him and said "You know, just in case!"

The area had been deserted, and it was apparent that nobody was in this building, and probably anywhere else in the area as well. The front of the building faced the street. Between the building and the street was dirt, and they noticed on one of the sides of the building were some cut outs that used to have doors, where trucks probably used to drop off deliveries. James reasoned that was perfect, and asked Rachel "Do you think the SUV can make it all the way in? Rachel said "I think so." They returned to the Navigator and James backed it in, and around to the side. Rachel hopped out, so she could help guide him in. As it turned out, it was an easy fit as James pulled the Navigator completely inside. They felt better knowing that from the street, there would be no signs of anyone inside and nobody would be able to see them dropping anything off. The only way people would know they were inside; was if they watched them go in, or if they saw them come out. So far, they felt like they had been unseen.

James noticed just inside the building off to the side of where the Navigator was parked, was a heaping trash pile of debris. The trash was stacked against the wall, in a messy pile. James immediately started moving some of the trash out that was against the wall, and Rachel asked him "What are you doing?" James said "We can hide everything in this pile. I am moving stuff out from the side closest to the wall, and we can slide the rocket launcher cases against the wall, and set the machine guns on top. The crates can go anywhere, but we can probably cover them with this trash too. That way if anyone does come in here, the last thing they will be interested in is the trash pile!

Ten minutes later after scoping out the area outside of the warehouse to make sure no one was watching, they were departing the warehouse and leaving the industrial area. Once on the freeway, both were looking for a shopping center to pick up a pre paid cell phone. Reality started to set in as they were heading down the freeway. All Rachel could do was laugh and say "James this is kind of hysterical! I would have never expected to see weapons like this, let alone steal them and driving around with them in my car!" James laughed a little as well as he said "We did good though! Obviously God is with us, but I think we put together a good plan, and we made it happen, and clearly God blessed us. We still have some work to do, but I already feel like we have saved the president! Pretty cool, huh?"

As they pulled into a shopping plaza James already had a plan in his head that he wanted to suggest to Rachel "I think you should go in and buy the phone." Rachel responded quickly with "Really?" James continued "Yes, again, I don't know how all of this works. But if there is any possible way for the FBI to try to trace the call we are about to make and put it all together; I am just thinking if they figure out where we bought the phone, and if they have any video cameras in there, it's unlikely that if they see your face, they are going to be able to track it to a girl that…." Rachel interjected "Died?" James said "Yes, it's very unlikely they are going to search through people who are dead."

"So, what do you think? Does that make sense, or do you

want to do this a different way?" Rachel answered "I think it makes perfect sense, and I agree. Even if they are able to match my face, they'll probably dismiss the idea having been dead for three weeks." James responded "Exactly! However, there is one more thing." Rachel replied "Just one more?" with a grin on her face. James responded by suggesting that she use a different name "I hate to have you lie, but if you need to give people your name in a situation where a paper trail is going to be created, I wouldn't use your real name" Rachel countered "Ohhh, I already knew that! I wasn't going to use my real name. Come on babe! What kind of spy do you take me for? Remember, I have had this secret spy life going on for years, this isn't my first rodeo!"

With that Rachel strutted away from the car teasing James. Nearly 15 minutes later she was walking back to the car with a bag in hand. When she arrived back at the car she explained to James "Well, that was easy! No different than buying a loaf of bread! I had to choose a phone, and then choose a prepaid card based on how many minutes I plan to use. There was nothing to sign, no contract, nothing; it's totally off the radar! I bought a card with plenty of minutes just in case we are on hold for any length of time. Better to be safe than sorry, right?" James was pleased and told Rachel "That is great! I feel much better about our plan! Let's get going, because we need to make this call. There is only about four hours before the sun goes down, and we need to give the FBI plenty of time to get to the storage place and be in position to arrest the terrorists."

While Rachel was in the store buying the phone, James used his own phone to look up the numbers to the FBI and Homeland security. James felt a little paranoid worrying that they could find him simply because he looked up their number. He quickly came to his senses and realized this is still a big world, and on top of that, they have the creator of it on their side! As long as they are obedient to God, everything should work out just fine! So as James and Rachel were flying down the freeway on their way back to the hotel in Newport Beach when they made the most important phone call that either of them had ever made in their lives.

James decided to call the FBI first, and hope he would not have to make a second call. An automated recording picked up, and gave multiple choices to choose from to direct his call. Much to James dismay, but not surprise because of what goes on the world; there was a choice for suspected terrorists and terror activities which proved that the FBI receives many of these calls everyday. When he was directed to the right department he guessed what was a low level agent was the first to speak to him on the phone. James said "I don't want to be disrespectful, but it's extremely important that I speak to your supervisors about a guaranteed plot to kill the president tomorrow, and where the assassins will be if they are not already there."

The person on the phone to this point was prioritizing this as he would any other possible reported threat; "low level investigative". The man responded by saying "Okay, let me start with your name" James barely let him get the words out and aggressively responded "Look, my name is not important! I don't think you understand!" The man responded by saying "There is protocol that needs to be followed. So, what is your name?" James replied "Okay, call me James, call me whatever you want" As he said this Rachel looked at him like he was crazy for giving his real name. James went on to say "Here is the thing Sir. This is real. This is very real. I know it's real, because I stole three rocket launchers, crates full of grenades, machine guns and other things today from some people that look like terrorists. I am not going to give you my real name; I am not going to tell you how I learned of this. I need you to put someone on the phone who will take this serious" James barely said the last word when the man said "Please hold"

James waited for about four minutes when someone new joined the conversation asking "How may I help you?" James repeated what he told the first person. The Agent asked "How did you gather this intelligence? James explained "How I got this information isn't really the most important thing. More specifically, it's not something I am willing to tell you." The Agent asked, what can you tell me? How can I help?" James gave the specific location of the storage unit as well as where to retrieve the weapons. He also said "I feel pretty confident that if you arrest these men, this specific attempt on the president will be over. I can't say that for sure, but I feel pretty strongly about that."

After James spoke for about 5 minutes the FBI agent told James "I already have agents in route to retrieve the weapons from the warehouse that you indicated to me. I have another team on the way to capture and detain the potential assassins that you have described at the storage facility. Once we make these arrests, and retrieve the weapons, we will want to debrief you. When are you available to speak to us again?" James answered "Listen, just save the president. Arrest the bad guys. I told you all I know. There is no need for us to ever speak again. Thank you for your help!"

The Agent began to say "We appreciate…" That is all James heard because he pushed end on the cell phone, removed the battery, and threw the phone and the battery out of the window of their SUV. Rachel had her body turned a little in her seat, focusing her attention on James. As James looked up after throwing the phone out of the window, he looked over at Rachel to see her smiling at him. After she kept smiling James replied with a curious "What are you smiling at?" Rachel leaned over and kissed him on his cheek and said "You did good! You did very well! I am so proud of you right now you have no idea! James reacted with "Well, thanks! But you did too! We did! We did a very good thing today!"

They were driving back to the hotel trying to catch their breath. What a roller-coaster day this was! After an exchange of how excited they both were about what they accomplished, there was a few minutes of silence and reflection for both of them. Rachel interrupted by delaring "James, think about it! Just over five hours ago, we were sitting down to breakfast! And now five hours later, we are on our way back to Newport Beach from Los Angeles after having stolen some serious weaponry from some seriously bad guys! We saved the president today! James, I can't plan a day trip in five hours; you know that! But in no time at all; we planned and carried out something so huge today! This is amazing!"

James loved to see Rachel on fire and excited about anything. This was different though. James felt it too! James told Rachel "Well, no doubt we did a great thing today! I have to say, for novice spies, we sure did a great job! However, we both know, the true victory is Gods! I sure hope we made Him proud today! If this is how it's going to be doing the Lords work, sign me up! Talk about an adrenaline rush! I need a nap now! We have been going on pure adrenaline all day! Now all of a sudden, I am hungry, and I am tired! I think I need a rest. How about you?" Rachel answered "I am right there with you, but before we settle in for that rest, I am going to keep you up for a while tonight! I always feel so connected to you, but now, ohhh my, I want to be with you tonight! James answered "if you are going to twist me my arm, okay!"

They returned to the hotel, and went straight to their room. They wanted to see the news on TV. They were interested to see if there were any discussions or hints about the success of their operation. They ordered room service, so they could relax, watch the news and eat without having to leave their room anymore that night. Shortly after their early dinner arrived, a breaking news report indicated that "The president's speech in Los Angeles has been canceled due to a conflict in the Middle East. The president is to return to Washington to meet with Foreign Diplomacy personnel to resolve the matter." Rachel yelled out "Wow! We made that happen! You made that happen with your phone call! What a huge blessing that God allowed us to be apart of this! We were apart of something seriously special today!"

James and Rachel quietly ate their meals while watching the news. They both were flying high after their adventurous day! After a few minutes of quiet Rachel asked "James?" James had to chew the food in his mouth real quick to utter "What's up?" Rachel asked "What do you think God will have us do next?" James gasped and said "Hopefully rest! Actually, I have no idea! I kind of thought you might have a better idea than me!" Rachel asked "Why is that? Ohhh,

I get it, another I have already been to heaven joke!" James laughed at her reaction, and said "You have to admit that is a pretty cool thing to be able to tease you about!"

Rachel said "True Mr. Smarty pants, but I am serious! I can't imagine doing anything more exhilarating or even as important as what we did today!" James agreed, but added "I know, after saving the president, it makes you wonder how anything else can compare! Here is the way I look at it; if that is the toughest and most important thing we do, and then we are already prepared for anything God wants us to do! If there are other things that compare, than thank God for the ride we are about to enjoy! But I think we both already know, that Gods plan is huge, and all encompassing. I'd imagine that to Him every part of the plan that fits together is very important. I just suppose that if our president were killed today that would probably be the start of some things that His plan may not be ready to happen yet. So I guess this had to be done first."

Rachel responded "Ah, I knew my sensible husband was in there! Look at you always knowing the right things to say!" James chuckled and asked, did you think your sensible husband disappeared for a bit?" Rachel grinned and could barely get the words out "Well, when you went all Rambo today with your guns, I wondered!" James shot back, "Hey! You said you were glad we were prepared having those guns...just in case!" Rachel was completely laughing when she countered "I know! And in fact, I am glad we were prepared. But if you are going to tease the dead girl, I get to tease Rambo!" As they were both laughing they quickly quieted when a breaking news report came on the screen.

The newscaster said "We come to you this evening to report that the FBI has interfered and stopped an assassination attempt of the president of the United States. Seven Al Qaeda terrorists were arrested by the FBI when they showed up to a storage facility in Los Angeles, California. They arrived at the facility to load up their weapons that they planned to use to blow up a Los Angeles City Hall building in which the president was prepared to speak. In addition to targeting the president, they had intended to wear jackets loaded with explosives aimed at killing as many innocent people they could.".

"The FBI has released the following statement regarding the arrest of the terror cells:

This concludes a three month investigation and surveillance operation of a terror cell in the Southern California area. There are others they have been working with that we will continue to pursue, but with the threat against the president imminent, we had to stop their plan, and make the arrests. The FBI is proud of the intelligence we gathered, and the swiftness and perfection in which we executed to make the arrests.

"The president is doing well, and is back home at the White House. If there are any further developments in this plot to kill the president, we will keep you informed. Once again, a plan to assassinate the president, and kill numerous other innocent lives was successfully stopped by the FBI, and seven arrests were made."

James said "Wow! They got them! That is awesome!" Rachel was a little annoyed "Yes they got them, but they took all of the credit! They said they had been working on it for three months. Three months? Not even three hours! They didn't mention our helping them at all! They didn't mention any outside help! What a crock!" James laughed at Rachel and her competitiveness "Would you like to go play some racquetball or something?" Rachel looked at James like he was crazy and asked "Why are you laughing at me?" James still laughing said "First, the FBI doesn't even know who we are, remember? Also, they had to put a spin on it, so they don't tip off other terrorists with other plans. They probably want them to think they are watching all of them, all the time!"

James continued "And most importantly, and I know you know this, but this was Gods Victory, not ours. We are just blessed to get to participate!" Rachel said "I know! I just....I just thought that since we did something so cool, and so amazing for how little we are prepared for something like this. Well, I just thought there should be something said to allude to the fact that they did not do this alone, or even some hidden message that only we would understand. But instead, they lie and say they have been working on this for three months. It is just offensive!" James said "I know what you mean, but I have a feeling that we are going to be on the down low side of the credit for a lot of these projects we do! Our rewards will be in heaven!" Rachel said "Oh fine, hit me with a dose of reality while I am pouting; now I really feel bad about how I was feeling!"

James continued to tease her, getting her riled up again, then pulled her close and held her in his arms and whispered in her ear "If you want some sort of reward for what we did today, I can think of some ways to reward you myself!" Rachel's pout turned into a sexy smile as she said "I do! I think I should be rewarded! I can't think of anyone better to reward me than you!" With that she leaned forward and they kissed for several minutes. James slowly pulled away and turned off the TV and the lights and laid her down in bed. He lay down with her, kissing her softly and whispered "I love you Rachel. You are my best friend, and I think you did great today! Thank you, and thank God for you being here!"

CHAPTER 10

The next morning, James was awakened to Rachel pushing her hand into his arm and side. She seemed very insistent; finally he turned towards her and said "What is it babe, are you okay?" Rachel pointed and asked "Do you know him?" Standing at the foot of the bed was a man who was chiseled with muscle, a shield and a sword. Rachel believed this to be an Angel of God, but she was still scared because she did not recall seeing an Angel quite like him in heaven. James immediately recognized him as the Angel in the vision he had at Rachel's parent's house before he left on this trip. He seemed even taller now than he did when James saw him the first time. James sat up quickly and asked "Is everything okay? Are you here to give us our next assignment?"

The Warrior Angel disregarded James questions and pronounced "James, my brother in Christ, and Rachel, Daughter of the Great Lord of Hosts! You have honored the Lord with your obedience and your actions indeed are in line with his great and perfect plan! Praise God today that He is the truth, and all knowing, and even before we experience success, the final victory is already His! Stay prepared and stand ready to continue to do wonderful and mighty works for His Glory! On this day Angels are singing in Heaven praises for the works that you have done and the victory you have brought to glorify the almighty Risen King. This is just the beginning. All of our battles; of the world you reside in, and dimensions in which you cannot see where I fight against the Evil one, are for the purpose of ushering in the end of these final days. Stand ready dear children of God, for all you do, is merely the prelude to Gods final victory! The return of the Risen King is at hand! Fight the good fight! Win the victories that are already Gods!"

James and Rachel looked at each other in astonishment! As they looked back towards him, he was gone. Rachel looked towards James and said "I have seen Angels, I have spoken to them, and eaten with them, and even sang songs with them. But never have I seen an Angel like that! He was absolutely amazing! James, in Heaven the Angels I saw, were so soft and everything about them was love. This Angel was love through strength! He was powerful! I can't imagine the demons not falling at his feet in fear! You wouldn't think anyone; even Satan himself would have the courage to fight someone like that! I don't know if I have ever felt so safe and so incredibly intimidated at the same time!"

Rachel took a breath and continued "In all of your visions have you ever been visited by an Angel like him?" James was still trying to figure this out in his mind when he said, actually, I have met him once before! Next time, I will remember not to ask him anything, he does not seem to like me asking him questions! Rachel, he was there with us! He promised me that we will be fighting these fights together! He told me there are powers at work against us that we cannot see, and that he battles and defeats them so they can not stop us from fulfilling Gods plan! I now remember he said that, but to be honest, I forgot about that while we were hiding those weapons. We truly have nothing to fear but our own limitations that we put on ourselves! We have God on our side, and whomever he sends to us to make sure we accomplish what He wants!"

Rachel interjected "James, you know what you just said about forces working against you. Well it's true! It's so true, and so dark and evil, that from Heaven, those things are not even viewable! That is a strange, but awesome fact about Heaven. You know, each victory as it happens. You know what is happening here on Earth, and in the places the Angel spoke of. But you only see the good! You only experience the victories. It's like God shields our hearts from the enemy, and anything having to do with the enemy! In fact, when I was in Heaven, there was so little that I knew about what you were going through, I barely had glimpses of understanding that you were okay. Now I know, that I was not permitted to know your sadness or pain, and I am guessing that you must have had a lot since my entire time there I can think of very little that was revealed to me about what you were experiencing."

Rachel now had tears streaming down her face, as the depths of Gods love, and how amazing Heaven is, was becoming clearer to her. Aside from the words, and clarification she had from James about the warrior Angel, she also felt like God was speaking directly to her heart and giving her more insight and understanding that she seemed to just intuitively begin to understand. James moved towards her and began to wipe the tears from her face and said "Raech, please don't let that bother you anymore! I know I also couldn't bare the thought of causing you any pain, but that said, I am not in pain anymore! And in truth, even right now, thinking about it, I can't remember what it felt like! All I know is that I have you here now, and I love you more now, than ever before!"

"Think about how amazing all of this is! Last night, I made love to the only woman I have ever loved, shortly after going on the most incredible adventure a person could dream up; interfering with a terrorists plan to kill the president of the most amazing country in the world that I was blessed to be born into! On top of that, I wake up to see the prettiest face I have ever seen because she is prodding me to wake up because there is the most powerful Angel, quite possibly in the entire Universe, standing at the foot of my bed informing me that he shared in a victorious fight against evil! Then, he lets me know that my wife and I, who are children of God, brought Glory to God by our actions. Additionally, we find out that indeed, we have more adventures ahead of us; and if that wasn't enough, Angels are singing in heaven because of what we did!"

"Sweetie, if you are crying right now, let them be tears of joy! As much as I hated losing you, and as sad and painful as it was! Honestly, I wouldn't change a thing at this point! This is entirely too amazing to be true! We have always known that God has an amazing plan, and that all of this fits into eternity and our place in Heaven. But now, we are actually apart of it! I cannot wait to meet Paul! I cannot wait to meet others too, like David, and Peter. What if by the time this is all said and done, as I am looking around Heaven for them, they are looking for us too? What if they are as excited to meet us as we are them? I mean, we are actually doing things specifically for God, assigned by God! Does it get any better than this?"

Rachel had a much more optimistic expression on her face when she said "You are totally right! I know I shouldn't worry about before, but sometimes it's hard! Even having been to heaven, I am not perfect, not by any stretch! You are such a gift; there isn't a person on this planet I love more than you! I shouldn't let my mind wander back to places like that. But I did! That said; you are right! We are right where we want to be, and I am more excited today, than I was yesterday to see what God has in store for us! That must have been amazing for you before you knew what was going on to have visions like that!"

James gasped and said "No kidding! At first, it was very confusing! But that is something I still haven't even told you about. It is just weird to be doing whatever you're doing, and then all of a sudden, you blink, or get sleepy, or seemingly wake up somewhere else. Then out of nowhere, some spectacular Angel is standing there giving me instruction. Rarely do they just come out and say exactly what is expected either. It's always in some bold proclamation or almost coded conversation that I needed to figure out. However, now I think I understand. I think I was given pieces so that I could acclimate and begin to believe what was happening. Things did become clearer as time passed and as I went in the direction I felt I was being led."

"Now there was one Angel, Kaleb, he was different! He was the Angel I met right before you showed up. He reminded me of my Grandpa. He was strong, but soft. He didn't really speak in code either. He said it like it was, but very reassuring, and he let me ask questions too." Rachel said "I love Kaleb!" James was a little surprise, and asked "Do you know him?" Rachel said, "Oh yes, we spoke many times in the short time I was in Heaven. He was the one who began to prepare me for what was to come. Everyone in Heaven is so amazing, so it's hard to say that I like or enjoy someone more than another. That said; Kaleb always seemed different. Such a loving man! Every word he said just sank into my soul! What a sweet, sweet Angel!

James wondered aloud "I hope we get to see him again!" Rachel said, "I have no doubt about that! I am sure he will visit us multiple times!" James then asked her, "So, what do you want to do today?" Rachel said, "I am not sure yet, but I am going to jump in the shower real quick, and then we can figure it out!" While Rachel was in the shower James was straightening up some things, clearing up their food mess from the night before. His cell phone rang, and much to his surprise, it was Rachel's parents. He answered the phone "Hello" Rachel's mom was the first to speak "James, Dear! It's Rebecca and John! We wanted to check in on you!" Before James could say anything, John Said "Hello son, how are you?" James said "Wow, its great to hear from you two! Hey, can you hang on one second, I have the shower running, and need to stop it, be right back, okay?"

John said "Absolutely, if this is a bad time we can talk later. We don't want to interrupt!" James replied "Oh, no, not at all. In fact, I am glad you called, I miss you both; just give me a minute, okay?" Rebecca and John both replied "Okay". James pressed mute on his phone and tossed it on the bed. As he opened the bathroom door to Rachel, she heard him and asked "Hey babe, did you come to join me in here?" James kind of laughed, and said "How about a little later? I need you to turn off the water if you can?" She did and asked "Why?" James said "Your parents on the phone!" Rachel quickly reacted "I can't talk to them!" James laughed even more and said "I know that silly! I thought you might like to listen in, hear their voices! She shot of the shower, and grabbed a robe and a towel for her hair and said "Yes! Thank you!"

Rachel followed James to the bed where he picked up the phone, and turned off mute. Rachel put her head against the side of James face where he had the phone. James said "Okay, I am back, sorry about that! John said "No problem at all! I hope we aren't slowing you down, getting ready for your day!" James said "Nope, just a lazy morning so far, not even sure what the plan is for the day yet. How are you two doing?" Rebecca said "James, we are doing fine, but we really want to know how you are doing?" James kind of paused, not sure of what to say. He could not tell the truth, but he did not want to lie to them either.

James said "You know, I am actually doing very well, considering. I feel like I am recharging, and am definitely more optimistic than I have been in a while. "Rebecca said "that is good! How much longer do you plan to stay?" James answered "I really don't know yet. I have some friends over here that I am expecting to come visit me. So for now, I am going to play it by ear!" Rebecca added "I think Rock misses you too, but he is doing well too! Some of Rachel's friends have come by to visit. That was really sweet of them, but sad too if you know what I mean." James answered, "Yeah, I know exactly what you mean."

Rachel had tears streaming down her face again. The sound of their voice almost put her over the edge but hearing them speak of her in the past tense and knowing they were sad just crushed her! John interjected "We are worried about you James. We know how sad this time is for you; we miss our baby girl so much too. But we have each other, and

Rachel's brother, but you are alone. Are you sure you are doing okay?" This was tough for James! He wanted to tell them Rachel was right there. At the very least he wanted to explain that he gained peace because he spoke to her through a vision or something, but he knew he was not supposed to.

Instead James said "Really, I am okay, and I don't feel alone. I want Rachel here, I want her with me every day, you know that! That said, I am getting along okay, and having a chance to get away from work, and everything that was a reminder of our lives the way they were. I am doing some different things, and I feel like she is with me. I feel like we are on a new different adventure, I talk to her everyday; you know?" Rebecca responded "I know sweetie, and I hope you are adjusting well. We miss you!" James said "I miss you too, and I look forward to seeing you again soon, I am just not sure exactly when." John said "We want you home, but take your time…do what you need to do. Rock can stay as long as you like, in fact, by the time you get home, he may not want to leave the way we are spoiling him!"

James laughed and said "I have no doubt about that! With Rachel and me working all day, it must be nice for him to have you two to see all the time and shower him with attention!" John followed up with "James, I don't mean to pry, but I was wondering if you have had any more visions?" James hesitated, then said "Actually, I have!" As he said that, Rachel lightly slapped him on the arm wondering what he was doing telling them this. James looked at her giving her a reassuring look that he knew what he was doing. Rebecca chimed in "Well is there anything about Rachel?" James knew he had to be very careful how he answered this question.

James said "This is very difficult for me to say, so I have to tell you, I have to choose my words very carefully!" Now Rachel was getting nervous! James continued "I told you before, that I am not supposed to talk about what I have seen, and that is still true. Look, you know where she is! Her whole life was about Christ, and her faith, right?" John and Rebecca at the same time quietly said "Yes" James went on to say "Well, there is nothing in any visions I have seen that would suggest she is anything less than happier than she has ever been! I know for a fact, that she went to Heaven, to be with our Savior! I also believe in my heart, that we will see her again soon! Please take solace in that!"

"You see, I am so reluctant to even say anything too positive because I don't want to give you the impression that I have stopped grieving. I am so scared if you think that, you will think my love for her has lessened, or wasn't as deep as you thought. I also worry there is no way for you to relate to how I feel because obviously, as it pertains to what we are talking about, you haven't experienced it. But at the risk of hurting your feelings, or giving you the wrong idea, let me say, that because of what I have experienced, and what I know to be true; I am not experiencing the same pain I was when I left! I truly know that Rachel is happy, and I feel more connected to her than I have ever, and I love her more today, then I ever did!"

James could hear Rebecca crying on the other end of the phone and she began to speak "James, you have answered our prayers! That is all we wanted to hear!" John interjected "We may not know the details of what you are experiencing, but I think we have a better idea than you think. Whatever the details are, we have been praying, and indeed, I think God just offered us a little relief of the pain that we have been feeling. What you said gives us a great deal of peace!" James responded by saying "Well, I am not really sure what I said, but I am so glad! I think the world of you two, and

I don't want you to be in pain. And I know that as much as we all miss her, we don't have to be heartbroken, and in fact, we should rejoice for her!"

John responded "Amen to that! James, I don't want to push this, but I don't get the feeling you are coming home real soon…" Before he could continue James said "That's right, probably not real soon" and John continued his thought "Does your staying there and not coming home right away have anything to do with your visions?" James simply answered "Yes." John began to stutter over his words a bit as he said to James "Okay, well listen. I hope you know you have always felt like you were part of our family. We have always thought of you like a Son. You and Rachel always seemed to be doing well, you know, financially."

"I guess I never felt like money was too big of a deal for you two. You seemed to have most of what you needed and wanted. Anyway, I never wanted to pry into your business, especially seeing how happy Rachel was; never felt like I needed to, I am rambling…I am sorry!" James said "That's okay! You can ask me anything." John continued "What I am getting at is this; I don't know what kind of savings you have. But Becca and I feel that whatever you are doing is hugely important. So, if you need any money; please just say so! I will send it to wherever you are at. I don't know if we ever went into great detail and the specifics about our finances, but after we sold our business years ago, just know, we have more money than we could spend in this lifetime."

"So if you are out there doing Gods work, and if this somehow connects you to Rachel, you just call if you need anything, okay?" James was stunned, and Rachel had to walk away because her crying was about to get too loud to be near the phone! James replied "Thank you. You two never cease to amaze me! The truth is, financially Rachel and I were doing great. These last two years were amazing for both of us. Combine that with the life insurance policy I still haven't even been able to think about, I think I am going to be okay in that department for quite some time. But thank you! Just so you know, I promise, if there are any details I am able to share, you know I will!"

Rebecca chimed in "We know that! Ever since you left, we have wanted to ask you for more details about what you are experiencing. We have held off calling because we didn't want to put you on the spot, but the more we talked about it, the more we just had to ask you. We already feel so much better, and anything you tell us is only going to be extra blessings at this point! We love you James, take care, and call us when you can!" James said "goodbye, I love you too" as he hit end on his cell phone Rachel sadly said "Goodbye" aloud and fell on the bed crying. James sat down and put his arms around her not knowing what exactly to say.

Rachel finally sat up a little bit, and James wiped the tears from her face as she said "That was so strange! I mean, I feel so relieved that you made them feel better, but I feel so sad at the same time! I so badly wanted to blurt out "I love you two so much!" everything in me had to bite my tongue and just listen. That was so strange; James, my whole life my parents have had all the answers. You know? My entire life they knew God, so they had eternity figured out. My dad ran a successful company my entire childhood, so they had business and money figured out. They raised good children, so they had parenting figured out."

"They always seemed to have the answers. To hear them like they were, searching for answers, about me, was just crushing! Yet, at the same time, this whole thing is such a blessing! I am so confused all of a sudden!" James kissed her face, and tried to reassure her "You know Hun, no parent is supposed to lose a kid. No matter how prepared you are for things to happen in life, nobody is prepared for that! When you do, even as a believer, that is it. You mourn, and you move on with your own life knowing that you will reunite in Heaven! Well, in this instance, they knew a little bit about my visions. Before I knew what was going on, I told them a little about what was happening. They know something is going on! I don't know if it's their own intuition, or God putting it on their heart, they kind of pieced things together a little."

"So now, just like us, they are very much in uncharted territory! Lying to or misleading your parents is not something I would ever want to do! Knowing that the tiniest of details I was aloud to give them, gave them even the tiniest measure of peace, has been something that gives me a great deal of relief! Raech, something I haven't told you yet, and maybe I shouldn't now… is about the pain your parents felt, especially your mom when I told them what happened to you. Your mom knew before I even got the words out. She literally fell to the ground! It was like her legs just quit on her. The pain she felt was literally heartbreaking. When I didn't think I had any more pain to experience, my heart broke even more seeing her."

"Your dad, this big tough guy who I have always respected, was practically speechless. He looked like he lost four inches off his height, and was fifty pounds lighter. To top it off he was pale and his tan was gone, white as can be. Your dad looked so small to me; like part of him was missing. He tried so hard to console your mom, and I could see the intensity of his pain, by the dullness of his appearance. He looked completely spent. The three of us literally held each other for a while. Through this whole thing, I think they have dealt with your loss by focusing on me. They have put their attention and concern on me and how I am getting along!"

"However, when I left, first they had my visions to think about and consider. But after that, I think the focus naturally turned to themselves. I can only imagine the thoughts that went through their head. I am sure that is when they finally, came to terms with this and personally grieved. So to hear them say our conversation today has brought them relief, and a sense of peace; I cannot begin to tell you how happy I am to hear that! What a relief! They are truly special people, and I want them to be happy! You know something else Raech?"

Rachel was quiet, but she sheepishly asked "What is that?" James said "With the insight they have, I wonder if God has revealed something to them as well. At the very least, it seems he has revealed something directly to their hearts to give them a sense of peace!" Rachel perked up a little and said "I think you are right! You could definitely tell a difference in their tone after you said what you said. It's like you gave them some sort of confirmation! They definitely sounded more optimistic." James said, "I think so too! And again, that just makes me so happy, and relieved to hear!" Rachel then asked "Do you think He…well, do you think God might ever let us tell them the truth about all of this?"

James responded "I don't know. I seriously doubt that, but you never know! I would have never imagined any of this, so God allowing us tell your parents is not completely out the question I suppose. Let's stay focused, and keep having victories for God, and maybe He will bless us in that way!" Rachel said "Wow that is fun to think about! That would be wonderful! Okay, now that I have cried three times today already, I am going to go take my shower now and try to scrub away these tears!" Rachel walked into the bathroom and disappeared around the corner. She poked her head out of the bathroom back into the room, and said to James "You may feel free to join me if you like!" "Absolutely!" Was James response to Rachel's invitation.

CHAPTER 11

After their shower, while Rachel was still getting ready, James went out on to the balcony to get some air and to pray. The temperature was seemingly perfect as it was nearing Noon. James sat down in one of the patio chairs to relax and enjoy the Sun. He began to pray "Lord, I cannot stop thanking you for sending Rachel back to me! Thank you so much for what we did yesterday! That was incredibly thrilling, but to know that we were fulfilling your will and doing your work is so special. Thank you for Reach's parents! It is truly a blessing to have them in my life! I am so thankful you are helping them with their pain. Thank you so much for that! I pray that you will continue to use us to accomplish your will! We truly want to serve you however you choose to use us! In Jesus' name I pray, Amen!"

When James opened his eyes and lifted his head, he found he was not alone on the balcony. He started to stand when the visitor on his balcony said "Please, stay seated! I am Elomone, sent by the creator of all to deliver a message of most importance! There is a man in this very city, very devoted to our Lord and Savior. He earnestly preaches Gods word with all of his heart. His deepest desire is to preach the word of God to the four corners of the Earth! You must go to him, and give him clear vision to execute the desires of his heart; that were put there by the Creator of everything living, and not living!

James responded "Where should I tell him to preach? May I know his assignment so that I can be able to give him the direction so that he clearly knows what to do?" Elomone very softly said "My dear child of God! Do you not have faith? Do you not by now believe that God is in control of all things and that His will be done? Child of God, you are to go, and walk by faith. Your mission is simple, give this man the means to see Gods vision clearly and to go forth! He already has it in his heart; he just needs to see it and believe that it is Gods plan for him!"

James was hoping for more details "How will I get him to listen to me? What should I say?" Elomone said "Tell him I sent you! He is expecting you as a matter of fact! You are to go forth on this very day! Do not delay! He is anticipating your visit, and he has a very important ministry to begin to bring the Lord of all a great victory! He will begin his work the very minute you part ways. Rejoice! For his preparations are among the final details before Jesus returns for his faithful children! Oh happy day! The Choir of Angels in heaven will rise as one singing praise to the Father for the continued growth of the most incredible Kingdom ever created; a kingdom that God will preside over for all of eternity!"

"My brother, and fellow follower of our Risen Lord Jesus Christ, the one who is the lover of your soul; I say to you, go into this city, and find the Church of Calvary, that resides on the hill! Go there, and find the Pastor of this wonderful church that has been so blessed, and give this man of God the clear vision he needs to depart and spread the Gospels to so many around the world that crave this message of hope, love, and ultimately, salvation! My dear James, when you depart from each other, you will meet again! Your paths will cross again, even before Jesus returns to take his children home! James, Go! Take Rachel, your helper, and wife, and go in the name above all names, Jesus Christ! Amen!"

With that, Elomone was gone! James did not even see him leave. He just was not there anymore! He did not even see him disappear. But in the blink of an eye, James was by himself. Although James felt like he knew what he was supposed to do, he still felt very uncomfortable! He had to wonder why he was not just given an exact address, and told exactly where to go. He wondered why he needed to figure things out for himself. He kept thinking in his head, "Church of Calvary, on a hill...what hill?" He wondered if that meant Beverly Hills but then realized "No, he said in this very city. We are in Newport Beach, so it has to be here."

James walked through the sliding patio doors and into the room. Rachel was seated reading her bible, and casually looked up and asked "Who's your friend?" James was caught off guard and replied "You knew I was out there with someone?" Rachel said "Yes, I was going to come out and sit with you, but I heard you two talking as I walked to the door, and I saw him through the drapes." James asked "Why didn't you come out?

Rachel laughed and responded "Well, I just felt kind of weird about interrupting you and an Angel sent by God!" With a smirk on her face she continued "I am just kind of weird that way! Actually, I figured if he wanted me part of the conversation, he would have visited us when we were together!"

"So? What did he say?" James laughed and said "Well, it looks like we have our next mission! We need to leave! We are supposed to go meet a Pastor to confirm for him that his desires to reach lost people in other parts of the world were put there by God. We are supposed to encourage him to go do that!" Rachel sarcastically asked "We? Are you sure its okay for me to go? I wasn't part of your big private meeting!" She loved teasing James! Even having been to heaven and back and having a whole new perspective on things, she had not changed! James said "Absolutely, he told me to take my wench and go!" Rachel gasped "Wench? He called me a wench? "Actually I think he called you my wife and helper; but wench sounded more fun!" Rachel said "You are so going to get it!"

Before they left, James signed on to the internet to search for Calvary churches in Newport Beach. When James scrolled through the list of Calvary's in Newport Beach, CA, He laughed at himself for questioning why God's messengers would not just give him an address; especially when he found the listing for Calvary Church of Newport Beach, California on Hill St. He knew it had to be it, and minutes later he and Rachel were in the SUV heading to the church which was just 15 minutes from their Hotel. James and Rachel were excited to be doing Gods work again so quickly!

On the way over Rachel asked James "What are you going to say to him?" James chuckled and said "I don't know! I know I am going to encourage him, and I know that he is expecting us; which is pretty cool! Elomone told me that the Pastor is expecting us. That should be interesting in and of its self!" Rachel countered "No kidding! That is going to be amazing, we are there to see him because an Angel sent us, and he is expecting us! I suppose an Angel visited him too! This is getting very exciting! God is truly amazing!" James said "No doubt about that!"

When they arrived at the church, they found the main office and parked. They walked in and were greeted by a receptionist. James asked "Is the Pastor available?" She responded by asking "Is he expecting you?" James looked sheepishly at Rachel and back to the lady and said "I think he is expecting us to come in, but perhaps not today". She picked up her phone and said "Pastor Rhodes, you have someone here to see you" She hung up the phone and said "please have a seat, he will with you in a few minutes." A few minutes later they were shocked to see a man in his mid-thirties with dark sunglasses and a walking stick come out to the lobby.

As James stood up, the man stopped in the middle of the room and said "Hello, I am Pastor Jeremiah Rhodes. How may I help you?" James walked towards the Pastor and said "Hello, my name is James, and I was told to come here and visit with you for a bit. Is there some place we can talk?" Pastor Rhodes said "Sure! Follow me and we can sit and chat in my office" As they walked down the hallway, with the Pastor slowly leading the way he asked "Is there any chance you are from Phoenix?" James was surprised at the question, and said "Yes, how did you know?" The Pastor then asked "Does that mean you have a wife that you haven't introduced me to yet?"

James said "Oh, I am sorry, yes, my wife is with us, her name is Rachel" As they walked into the Pastors office he said "Hello Rachel, it is nice to meet both of you!" Pastor Rhodes worked his way around to his side of the desk and invited the two to sit. Immediately after sitting down, he stood again and extended his hand towards James and said "I apologize, I do this backwards sometimes, but we should be formerly introduced! I am Pastor Jeremiah Rhodes" James shook his hand and said "Pastor Rhodes, this is my wife Rachel" As she shook his hand the Pastor said "Oh, I'll have none of that, please, friends, call me Jeremiah"

After everyone was seated, James asked "Jeremiah; how did you know we are from Phoenix?" Jeremiah responded "I assume in much the same way I was told to expect you, you were told to come here! This morning, shortly after waking up, I had what I at first thought was a dream. I was being held by an Angel, encouraging me to stay strong for the Lord. He was holding me, protecting me. He informed me that the Lord has plans for me, and that I should expect visitors. I was told to expect a man, and his wife, from the city that rose from the ashes! I think everyone knows that is a reference to Phoenix. Having lived in Phoenix, Arizona myself, I knew right away."

Rachel said "God is amazing! This is truly incredible!"

Jeremiah said "Amen to that! So, James and Rachel, what brings you here? Why did God send you to me?" James said "Well, Jeremiah, It's about your ministry" Jeremiah interjected "Really? Is everything okay with it?" James replied "Yes, in fact, I think God wants you to expand it! Let me ask you a question. What ministry desires do you have now, that you aren't currently doing? How have you thought about expanding your church or ministry outreach?" Jeremiah said "I want to do whatever God wants me to do! My ministry is for him, so whatever he leads me to do, I will do!"

James responded with "Well, I have no doubt about that! What I am asking though…Well, what God put on my heart is that you have some desires to expand your ministry. Please tell me about those desires! Well, I preach a lot about the book of Revelation and end time events. When you look at the world, and what we are experiencing, I think it's just a matter of time before Jesus returns. I believe we are in the 'last days'. There are prophecies being fulfilled right in front of us!"

"Take things like Israel becoming a nation for the third time! When you see that the bible says that a coalition of countries led by Russia and Iran are going to attempt to attack Israel. Combined with Iran and Russia now getting more and more involved with each other; add to that Iran's seemingly weekly threat of 'wiping Israel from the map, or chasing them into the ocean'. I am sure you have read in Revelation about the two hundred million man army? "James said, yes, I know about that" Jeremiah continued "Well, when that was written, there weren't even two hundred million people on the planet! So the thought of such an army was unfathomable. Now China's army is growing faster than that of any military in the world despite not being involved in any conflicts! Any guess as to the size of their army?" Rachel answered "Around two hundred million?" Jeremiah said "Yes! I wonder what they are preparing for? I think one of the last few things that have to happen before the return of our savior is that the Gospel makes its way to the entire globe! There are still places on the Earth that have not received this good news yet!"

"I would love to be part of that! That is the desire in my heart to be able to expand my ministry in this way! I have it in my heart to go to these parts of the world, and spread the word of God! It's something I have longed for, for so long! In my condition though, I just keep putting off the idea. It would be such an undertaking! That said, I have also thought about organizing teams of people that could do this, and I would stay here, and "oversee" it so to speak. Wait! Is that why you are here? Am I to send you as part of the first team of this ministry?" James responded "Actually, no, I don't think we are here for that! In fact, I think that it is you that is supposed to go! God wants you to go! He wants you to know that these desires you have, are from Him, and that he will bless your ministry!"

Jeremiah seemed a little confused but added "I have no doubt that this ministry will be successful! Obviously God knows what He is doing! I haven't moved forward on this dream of mine, just because for me, such an undertaking has seemed so overwhelming, but if this what God wants me to do, I will do it!" James responded "Well, I kind of felt like we were sent here to convince you that your ideas for this expanded ministry was something you need to pursue. Clearly though, this is not a new revelation to you." Jeremiah said "No, I am ready. I have had these thoughts and plans for years, I just always felt that it would be very challenging for me! However, if God thinks, I mean knows I am the man for this; then I am ready to go for him! I always thought I would probably be better served focusing on this ministry where people come to me here in the confines of my office at the church; but now I am learning that God wants me to go in a different direction."

James interjected "Well, like I said, I really thought our meeting was to convince you that you need to expand your ministry, but now, I am pretty certain we are here for a completely different reason! Jeremiah, may we pray for you please?" Jeremiah was a little surprised and was more than happy to have anyone pray for him, and he said "Absolutely! Thank you!" James asked Jeremiah "Do you have any doubts that we were instructed by God to come visit you?" Jeremiah seemed a little puzzled by the line of questions but said "No, I have no doubts!" James followed up by asking him "Well, are you ready to witness a mighty miracle and the power of God?"

Now Jeremiah was completely caught off guard by James questions, and his boldness that suddenly seemed to overtake him. Rachel was equally surprised and was wondering where James was going with this! James asked Jeremiah "Do you mind if we lay our hands on you while we pray?" Jeremiah was used to being the one taking charge like this and leading his congregation in prayer; this was something else. There seemed to be an energy and a momentum building in the room. Jeremiah and Rachel were both were somewhat in the dark as to what was happening, and even James was getting excited about what was about to happen, now that he had figured out why they were there in first place.

James had one more request for the pastor "Jeremiah, would you mind removing your sunglasses for our prayer?" Again, Jeremiah had no idea where this was going, but he kept reminding himself, that even though this was a very unusual situation taking place, that God had set up this incredible meeting; so the pastor was going to go along with whatever his guests suggested! Jeremiah replied "I suppose that would be okay if my eyes do not offend you and your wife." James said "No sir, not at all" and with that he removed his glasses. James walked Rachel behind the pastor and while positioning her hands, he asked her if she would place her hands over the pastor's eyes. James then put one of his hands on Rachel's shoulder, and the other hand on Jeremiah's shoulder and he began to pray.

"Father God, Thank you for this amazing day! Thank you for bringing us here to meet an incredible man that desires to serve You! We ask that you bless us while we are together. We ask that everything that has been discussed so far and what is still to come is of You, and that your presence fills this room and our hearts so that we only say and speak what you want of us! Lord thank you for blessing Rachel and I in the ways that you have! Thank you for making us part of your incredible plan, and sending us on this fantastic journey! What was fear has turned into complete excitement and enthusiasm to see what You will do next! We want to be used by you in any ways that you choose!"

"Lord we thank you for Pastor Jeremiah. We are in awe of how your plans work together to accomplish Your specific will! We ask today, that as You send this man of faith to the corners of the Earth to grow a ministry designed to spread Your word to those that have never heard it before that you will protect him and bless him! Please give him guidance and direction as he makes his way across land and sea to proclaim the wonderful news of salvation through faith in Jesus Christ, our Risen Lord and savior! We pray today that Jeremiah's plans are indeed Your plans!

"Lord we know that your second coming is near, we enthusiastically want to be a part of growing your ever expanding kingdom of heaven! Lord, our brother in Christ, is ready to leave here, and travel this world teaching the truth of your Son, and Your word! Before he departs on this most incredible journey that will indeed be part of historic events leading to your return, I want to call on the almighty power of You, Lord. I want to ask you, in the name of Your son, and Risen Savior, Jesus Christ, that today you will heal Jeremiah's eyes! Please lay your healing touch upon the damaged part of his eyes, and give him sight! Lord, in the name of your precious Son, Jesus Christ I ask you to impart your tremendous power to give him sight!"

With that the three said "Amen!" at the same time, and James and Rachel removed their hands from the Pastor, and took a step to the side to look at him. Jeremiah had his eyes closed but already knew that his eyes were working. He felt it! He was also scared to open his eyes; he just did not know what to expect! Rachel quietly said "Jeremiah, please, have faith, and open your eyes!" Jeremiah with eyes still closed tightly said "Rachel, I do have faith! It's not for lack of faith that my eyes remain closed! It's just….Gods power is so great, and so amazing, I am afraid to open my eyes and actually fully, and completely experience it!"

James patted the pastor on his back and whispered "Jeremiah, if your story, is anything like ours, this is just the beginning of your experiencing Gods amazing power! It all glorifies him, so please, open your eyes, and enjoy it, and praise the Lord!" Jeremiah opened his eyes and he could not believe the clarity with which he could see! "This is truly amazing! Praise God! Praise God! I can see! How did you know? When did you know that God was going to use you to heal my damaged eyes?" James responded "Just a few minutes ago! When I knew that your plans were already in line with God's plan, and your desires for this ministry seemed so strong, and real, and we didn't have to talk you into it; I realized that we weren't here to talk you into anything."

"Then I remembered what Elomone said." Jeremiah interjected "Who is Elomone?" James responded "I am sorry! I assumed the same Angel that told us to come here, was the one who told you to expect us! Elomone is the Angel who visited me just over an hour ago, and told me to take Rachel and immediately come here. I remembered that he said a couple of times that I was to give you the means to see the vision that God has for your ministry so that you could depart and do the Lords work. I realized while we were talking that you already had the same plans and desires for this Ministry that God has for you."

"What you didn't have was the vision, to actually see it through. At that moment, I had a feeling so strongly that God wanted you to see again! I quickly asked God to bless what I was about to do, and wow, there you go!" Rachel added "Jeremiah, I am so thankful that God allowed us to be part of this! Jesus second coming is close! We all have so much work to do! May I ask how did you lose your eyesight to begin with?" Jeremiah said "I will tell you what, allow me to take you folks to lunch, and I will tell you everything you want to know. Okay?"

As they walked out of the hallway into the lobby area, Jeremiah turned to his receptionist, and with a wink said "Marta, I am going to lunch, I will be back in an hour or so" With a look of shock on her face, and not able to utter a word as the three of them walked out the door. Once outside James asked the pastor if he should say something to Marta, explaining "Her mind must be racing!" He spoke those words, when the glass doors flew open and Marta raced out with tears streaming down her face! Marta asked "What happened? How are you all of a sudden able to see?"

Jeremiah gave her a hug and said "It's God! It's a miracle!"

Marta was crying at this point as she said "Praise God! Jerry, I have been praying for years that God would let you see again! Praise God!" Jeremiah seemed a little embarrassed to get this kind of attention from her, but he responded "Thank you Marta! You have always looked out for me more than anyone else! I will give you all the details, but I have to go with my new friends for a little while, and I will be back later. Do me a favor; as tough as this will be, please don't tell anyone yet. I need to pray about that, and probably will have to make a proper announcement to the congregation." Marta was wiping her tears away when she said "I won't say anything. Although every time I answer that phone that is all I am going to want to tell people!"

As they were getting in the car Rachel said "Marta seems like a really sweet lady!" Jeremiah barely let her get the words out when he responded "Oh, she is! She has absolutely been a life saver for me! She looks out for me, will literally help me in anyway I need, and she is really the one that makes the church run! She's like a second mother to me as well! She and her husband both are just incredible people! They are so strong in their faith as well!" James drove the three to an area a few miles away that he figured would have a nice selection of restaurants to choose from. Once inside, they sat down, ordered some drinks, and James eagerly asked to hear the Pastors story.

Jeremiah began "Well, growing up was fairly normal. I was a big kid, so I kind of bullied my way around sometimes. I was finally maturing in High School, outgrowing some of that mean behavior and was starting to become active in sports and other activities. There was a girl I was interested in. We were in chemistry class together, and she agreed to be my partner. I teased her a lot, in a good way! We had a lot of fun. I had really been teasing her on one particular day. Shortly after, we started our project. I mixed some chemicals, and moved closer to her to grab something. Well, she thought I was messing around with her some more, and she turned real quick with her hands out, and knocked the glass right into my face, burning my eyes."

"The thing is, they said I was going to be fine. They said I had some minor burns under my eye lids. There was some burned skin in there that was expected to cause some irritation to my eye balls as the burned spots healed. They had a new technology though that would allow them to use a laser and burn off the extra skin parts that were touching my eyes. So I went in for this procedure, and came out unable to see. All I have been able to see ever since then are shadows and 100% blur. The girl went away for college, and I never saw her again." James thought this story sounded awfully familiar, and then he remembered!

James asked "Wait a second! Are you Jerry? The Jerry Rhodes from Roadrunner High School in Phoenix?" Jeremiah was a little surprised but answered "Yes, did we go to school together?" James responded "Yes! I can't believe this! We barely knew each other. In fact, I don't know if we have spoken more than a time or two, but I remember what happened to you. This is amazing that God has brought us together like this!" Jeremiah asked James "What is your last name?" He answered "James Mahody. Always went by James. Rachel calls me babe sometimes, but I would prefer if you didn't!"

After they all stopped laughing, Jeremiah apologized "I am sorry, but I don't remember you at all. I can't believe I would forget like that!" James reassured him "No worries! It was a big school, I am sure I don't remember a tenth of the people that went to our school! Jeremiah was excited to know that he and James had a history together, but there were more important things on his mind. Jeremiah asked "James, Rachel, what is the deal with the visits from Angels, what is that like? Do you know what's happening?"

James took a sip of his iced tea and said "Jeremiah, to be honest with you, I don't know what we are allowed to say, and what we aren't. I was told that I could tell you that we were told by an Angel to visit you. I would assume we can tell you everything, since it appears that you are about to start your own journey, assigned by God himself! That said, if you don't mind…would it be okay if Rachel and I stepped away for a moment to discuss this?" Jeremiah reassured them "Please, by all means! I would encourage that! I am not going anywhere!"

James and Rachel walked outside and Rachel spoke up "James, I feel completely okay sharing with Jeremiah what we have been through. I mean, how could we explain the part about being told by an Angel to visit him, without at least inferring some of the other things that are going on?" James agreed and said "Listen, I think that makes sense, and I feel that way too; but to play it safe, do you mind if we pray real quick, just to make sure God doesn't want to tell us otherwise?" Rachel laughed a little because she always finds it funny when James asks her if it is all right to do something he should already know she agrees with!

After holding hands and bowing their heads James began to pray "Lord, thank you once again for our new friend and brother Jeremiah and bringing us into each others lives! Thank you for your incredible display of your power, and strength by giving him his sight back! I pray that you use him for incredible things! We are about to sit down together and enjoy a meal, and conversation. We feel that it's okay for us to reveal the truth to him about what we have experienced. However, if you do not want us to do this, please speak to our hearts, or send a messenger to tell us what you want! In Jesus' name we pray. Amen!"

They walked back in, and as they were sitting Rachel looked at Jeremiah and said "Sorry, God said we can't tell you anything." Jeremiah looked shocked to hear that, and as Rachel started to laugh James said "She is joking! She thinks her part time job should be comedian at the Improv!" Jeremiah wore a relieved expression as he said "Thank God! I thought I was out of the club before I even got started!" James was ready to get a little more serious, and asked their

new friend "So, are you ready to hear a story that will absolutely blow your mind and most likely change your life?"
Jeremiah sat up, extremely excited and said "Absolutely, but
lets not forget, that until about thirty minutes ago, for the
last eighteen years, I was legally blind! I think I am ready to
hear this!"

James was excited to be able to tell their story! This was
the first time that he was able to tell another person his best
friend and wife had died, but there she was seated next to
him! For the first time since her accident, James realized that
it did not hurt to say the words anymore. She had only been
back a few days, but those days were so action packed, it
was already starting to feel like she never left! Despite the
miracle they had all witnessed, James and Rachel were a little worried that Jeremiah might think they were crazy, and
not believe them. Instead Jeremiah responded with "This
day just keeps getting better! You know Paul was stoned to
death, and God brought him back to life! I wouldn't have
thought we would experience those types of things again; at
least not until after Jesus returns. This is incredible!"

James continued with his story explaining the visions,
and visitors he had received. Jeremiah interjected with "I

hope I am as blessed as you two that Angels will visit me like that, so that I may experience them for myself! If I may, let me tell you something real quick; I had the most vivid dream last night, and was told simply by a voice that you two were coming. When I awoke this morning, the dream still felt so vivid and real, it hardly felt like a dream! The feeling of this message was so strong, that it resonated with me through the morning. I truly anticipated your arrival. I didn't wonder if you were coming; I wondered when! I would have been surprised if it was just simply a dream!"

"Also, while I am thinking about it, the voice I heard, told me to give you a message too. I was told, you are to depart on the fifth day of this week for the capital city of the Lion in which our homeland sprouted its Eagles wings. Do you know what this means?" James responded "I have no idea." Rachel answered with a look of satisfaction on her face "We are to leave for London on Friday." James asked "How in the world did you come up with that?" Rachel responded "Well, obviously the fifth day of the week is Friday, if we assume that Monday is the start of the week. England is often referred to as a Lion. In the Bible there is a reference to kings and kingdoms. In one instance it is believed to be the United States when there is mention of a Lion with Eagles wings. Obviously the Eagle is symbolic of the United States. We came from England, so I suppose that is what the message meant when the voice told Jeremiah we sprouted our Eagles wings."

Jeremiah and James were both impressed and Jeremiah added "And obviously, London is the capital city of England! You two have a big trip ahead of you! That said, I am sorry I interrupted and got us off track, please, continue with your story of being visited by Angels!" James continued explaining how he had various encounters, some through dreams and visions, and some in person. Rachel explained her perspective of meeting some of the very Angels in heaven that visited James, and also told him of some of others she had met as well.

James told their new friend of how the visions did not make sense to him at first. He went on to explain they kept building and his understanding slowly but surely grew. As his own understanding and faith grew, he received an in person visit that led to Rachel's return to him. James was reluctant to speak of the pain he had experienced, especially with Rachel sitting next to him. He felt it was necessary for the perspective of helping Jeremiah to completely understanding the healing and peace that God brought to him. James knew that this in and of itself was a miracle.

James explained "You know, I know there are plenty of good marriages out there, and I know there are other people that are in love like Rachel and I. But to me, our marriage was, is, truly perfect! She has always been my life. But it was deeper than just us being friends and connected in that way. Although we were both growing every single day in our faith, our life and marriage truly was built on a foundation of God. That made a huge difference in every way as it pertained to our lives together. I never realized until she was gone, the impact she had on our spiritual lives! Without even trying, Rachel encouraged me to be the best Christian I could be, and that clearly impacted our relationship as well!"

"However, when she was gone; I never felt so alone. I never felt so incomplete. It was at that time that I realized my entire day and planning revolved around us together, doing everything we did. It's hard to put into words, but without her, I didn't how to be me anymore. From what I was told by an Angel, God truly enjoyed our relationship. I am sure people have had pain even greater than what I experienced; but praise God for truly having sympathy regarding my pain. I am sure this was part of His great plan to begin with, but I am amazed and feel so incredibly blessed that he allowed us to be apart of this amazing plan of His!"

Jeremiah asked "What is His plan? What is the point of all that is happening?" Rachel spoke up to answer "These are the last days! I know you know this, but everything that is happening right now, is leading up to the return of our risen Lord and Savior, the rise of the antichrist, and the great tribulation! For whatever reason, God has chosen us, and people like us, to fulfill his Will for the end times!" James jumped in "God has already given us some incredible assignments, you being one of them! God is quietly building up His own army so to speak! God is positioning His own people to spread the word to unbelievers and to set a path that will mark His triumphant return!"

"Jeremiah, I am so excited for you! Your mission represents one of the final pieces in prophecy! You are going to proclaim the good news to the parts of the world that never have heard the gospels and the message of Jesus Christ! I would imagine, that soon after your ministry is complete, that Jesus will return! Also, my dear brother, maintain your enthusiasm and know that you are not alone! While you and others like us do the will of God here on Earth, and prepare the hearts and minds for his return, there are other forces working on our behalf!"

"I was recently told by an Angel that while we are working here, there are forces working against us in a dimension or something like that we cannot see. While they are working against us, we have Angels fighting, and defeating them! Have joy, and receive peace knowing that no matter the trials or obstacles you face on your incredible journey for God, that the victory is already His! It is already yours as well because God has already secured it! We are to stay strong, faithful, and ready to act, and God will make our paths straight! He will lead us to victory through our obedience."

Jeremiah felt like he was losing his breath just from the enthusiasm of James and Rachel! He said "I have been blind for eighteen years! It has forced me to move slowly, and deliberately. For the first time since my youth, and I am ready to run! For the first time since my teenage years, I feel like I am ready to jump into something with both feet; and for once, I will actually see where my feet are landing before they land! What a blessing! I have had these dreams and desires for a ministry to reach those that have never heard the Gospels, and yet the enthusiasm for those desires was so tempered! But now, I feel like the enthusiasm that was sort of reigned in, has just been unleashed! I am ready for this! I am ready to be Gods vessel in a way that I have always dreamed of!"

Rachel felt like she wanted to caution Jeremiah "I am so excited for you, and I look forward to our paths crossing again! I want to encourage you though, stay deliberate! Don't get ahead of God, there is no reason to! Indeed, jump in with both feet, but make sure that everything you do, is what God truly wants you to do! I don't know for sure, but I am guessing you are going to have Angels and messengers leading you along the way. Wait for them! Go for it when you know for sure, but wait when you don't! Think about it! If we are tools for God, then surely he won't use us in a way that won't bring victory! And if we make ourselves available for His use and his purposes, I would also think he wouldn't use us any less than what His perfect will calls for!"

Jeremiah was about to jump out of his chair when he loudly proclaimed "Amen to that!" He drew attention from the other people in the restaurant, and the three of them laughed at the strange looks their table was receiving. No one in the restaurant heard the specifics of their conversation. However, the three of them knew that what they were speaking of, one way or another would affect every person inside and outside of that restaurant! Much to their surprise, their hour lunch had been going on for well over four hours. They felt like they had just sat down, but now because of time, and their assignments they believed that they needed to wrap up and get to work!

They were back in the parking lot of Jeremiah's church exchanging hugs and well wishes! They each knew a new bond had been formed that would last for all eternity! They also knew they would see each other again before Jesus returns. Jeremiah realized that he was going to need to prepare his associate pastor to take over his church ministry when he left. James added "You have so much to do to be prepared to go! Rachel and I have a lot to accomplish as well if we are to leave by Friday!" Rachel inquired, "Like what?"

James could not help but laugh, saying "I am pretty sure that we are going to have a difficult time flying into London using the passport of a girl who died a few weeks ago! I think we need to make some calls and find someone who can provide false documents like that." Jeremiah spoke up saying "Hey, I have a friend who might be able to help with that. He works for the CIA, and is also an incredibly faithful Christian. I am sure he could help us out, or at least direct us where to go." James asked "I know you said he is a Christian, but are you sure we can truly trust him. I thought usually you try to avoid federal agencies when doing things that might not be kosher within our laws?"

"Jeremiah responded "Usually, yes! However, when it comes to my friend Clint, normal doesn't always apply! Entirely too many politicians and government officials figure out ways to abuse their power for personal gain. Clint figured out long ago, that he could use the power that comes with his job for good!" Jeremiah assured James and Rachel that when it comes to his friend, trust is not an issue, and added "Also, he trusts me! So I won't even have to give him a lot of details for him to help us!" I will call him when I get back in my office. Well, I will call him right after Marta attacks me when I walk in the door! She is going to want a detailed explanation about my new eyesight and my expanding ministry. As soon as I hear anything though, I will call you on your cell phone, okay?" James and Rachel simultaneously said "Okay!" They then parted ways! Jeremiah walked into the church to a very excited Marta, and James and Rachel were back in the Navigator heading to the hotel.

CHAPTER 12

On the way to the hotel they stopped at a shopping mall to get Rachel some new clothes. They began to understand that this was just the beginning, and they were going to be serving the Lord in this way for some time to come. With that understanding, they needed some clothes and other supplies as they were preparing to travel to various parts of the world. Rachel joked as she selected some clothes "This is fun! This might be my first time I have ever been able to shop completely guilt free!" James laughed and replied "Well, have at it! It's obvious we are going to be doing this for a little while so get what you need! But remember, we have to pack all this stuff and take it with us!" Rachel said "Don't worry! I will only get what I need!" James laughed again, saying "I have heard that before!"

On the way to the Hotel James mentioned that it might be nice to just stay in for the night, cuddle, and relax, explaining "We have a big trip ahead of us, and lots of work to do, we should rest up a bit!" Rachel teased James saying "Sure, relax huh? I know what you are up to!" James laughed, and said "Well, I am not saying that it is going to happen, but I am not saying that it isn't going to happen either! But either way, I figured it might be nice to have a quiet night." Rachel laughed at James. The truth is, she always made fun of him for his "subtleties" when it came to romance, but she wanted to be with him every bit as much as he wanted to be with her.

As they were driving, Rachel had an idea "Oh, James, lets stop at a video store! If we are going to stay in anyway, let's buy our favorite movie! We haven't watched that in a while!" Even though they had watched this movie together well over a hundred times, it was always as enjoyable as the first time. After settling in for the night, Rachel was excited as anything to wear her new pajamas. When she came out of the bathroom James looked up and said "Wow! You are very cute! Have I told you how happy you make me?" Rachel had a sly look on her face and said "Yes, a few thousand times, but feel free to tell me again."

After ordering some dinner from room service, they settled in, close together with their movie on. James could never forget Rachel's enthusiastic gut laughs, but he started to realize how much he had missed hearing her laugh. When Rachel found something funny, she would completely let go laughing and enjoy whatever she found funny. Her laugh was incredibly contagious that anyone around would always find themselves drawn into whatever she found so funny. On this night, James had her all to himself. He quickly remembered why doing something for the millionth time with her always seemed fresh and brand new.

It was easy for James to stay so in love with her, because she did things in a way that were so uniquely her, he was constantly falling in love with her over and over. That night they enjoyed many laughs together, good food, a nice dessert, and some nice conversations. They spoke of their excitement and their upcoming trip to London. This time together was very special to both them as they thoroughly enjoyed talking with each other. They finished off their nice evening together by making love before they peacefully fell asleep for a restful night's sleep.

James awoke first the next morning. As he was laying there in bed thinking about the errands they had to do that day, his phone rang. It was Jeremiah's voice on the other end of the phone "James, I have some good news, and bad news." James inquired "uh oh, that sounds scary! What's up?" Jeremiah said "My buddy called. He can get Rachel's passport, no problem. He can even acquiesce to your need for a speedy rush." James interjected "This all sounds like good news to me!" Jeremiah continued "Well, because of the time frame involved; it's very expensive!" James asked "How much?" Jeremiah said "Ten thousand dollars." James exclaimed "Wow! Are you serious?"

Jeremiah explained that because of the rush on the project, and how illegal it is and the process to do such a thing, it requires a higher price. James said "Well, to be honest, I was expecting this to cost a thousand dollars or so; but it is what it is, right?" "Jeremiah said "Yeah, that's for sure!" James replied "Well, see if you can get me a discount, but whatever, it has to be done, so order it or whatever you need to do" Jeremiah said "No problem! I need a few things from you. Go by the mall, to one of those picture booths, and have

Rachel take a picture. Have several taken so my friend has plenty to choose from. Also, I need a list of her attributes; height, weight, hair and eye color, age; we'll fill in the rest."

James agreed and thanked Jeremiah for his help. They made a plan to meet in one hour with all the things that Jeremiah requested. James started to say goodbye when Jeremiah said "James, sorry, one more thing though, you need to bring cash. We can't have any paper trails, okay?" James said "If that is the case, better make it two hours because the banks don't even open for another hour." Jeremiah said "Good thinking, see you in two hours." James and Rachel left the hotel within 20 minutes and hurried to the mall to get the pictures taken. After they left the bank with the cash in hand, they headed to the meeting place with the Jeremiah.

As they greeted each other with a hug Jeremiah said to James "Whole new world isn't it?" James replied "More like the end of the world!" Jeremiah chuckled saying "You know, never in my wildest dreams would I have imagined meeting in an empty parking garage to exchange materials for cash for the purpose of an illegal transaction!" James laughed and said "No kidding! It's kind of fun though, isn't it?" With

Rachel smirking at the two newfound adventurers Jeremiah answered "So true! That said, it's only fun because we know what we are doing is for the cause of Christ, and God isn't disappointed with us for doing this!" Rachel spoke up "I sure hope He's not!"

Jeremiah said "I should have the passport by midnight; let's plan to meet back here at 8:00 a.m. tomorrow morning." James said "That sounds perfect, well, we better get going; we need to reserve our plane tickets and run some other errands today in preparation. Is there anything you need?" Jeremiah said "I think I am okay! If something comes up, I'll let you know!" James thanked his new black market pastor, and they went their separate ways. Rachel marveled at how life was so suddenly different.

They found a Travel Agency and decided to explore their options there before they went all the way to an airport to check out airfare. They were delighted to find that the Travel Agent who offered to help them spent three years traveling Europe and knows London well. They were not prepared to have a back story when Sandy the Travel Agent asked "What are you going to London for?" As James was searching for an appropriate answer Rachel spoke up and said "Our Honeymoon!" Sandy acted excited to hear this and said "Then I have the perfect place for you to stay!"

They booked a one week stay in the Landmark London Hotel. Sandy described it has very romantic as well as being a landmark that must be seen if you are visiting the area. They had no idea how long God would keep them in London. They figured a week would be reasonable. Sandy found a good rate on a flight that left the next evening. She was very helpful and spent over an hour telling them of the many attractions they should enjoy while they stay in London. She provided them with a pass that was included with their hotel stay that would let them roam in and out of more than 25 London attractions at their leisure. They weren't sure if there would be time for that kind of fun or not, but they certainly weren't going to turn it down.

James and Rachel were so appreciative of the help and assistance that Sandy offered. They thanked her profusely on the way out the door. They headed to another store for some more supplies. On the way Rachel said to James "That was a lot of fun! I hope we have time to actually enjoy the sights a little, and to enjoy our time there, in addition to whatever our next mission is!" James said "I totally feel the same!

We've always talked about leaving the country to see places like Europe and Australia; this is exciting! It's like God is creating a path for us that includes some of the very things we always dreamed of doing ourselves! This is so cool!"

Rachel asked James "What do you think God has in mind for us to do in London?" James answered "I can't imagine. I have been wondering that ever since Jeremiah told us. I hope we do have at least a few days to stay there; I am thinking that booking a week there might be too much, because to be honest, part of me thinks that we are going to London, waiting further instruction as to where we are going next." Rachel interrupted "You think London is a lay-over? Do you think God is getting us closer to Israel for some reason?" James said "The thought crossed my mind! We will be a lot closer to the Middle East from Europe than we are from here!"

The two soon to be world travelers finished up there errands and returned to the hotel, so they could straighten up the room, get their stuff together and be prepared to check out in the morning. They set aside what they needed for their trip. Once they had everything packed and ready to go, they realized it was still plenty early. They went out for dinner and returned to the hotel and went to bed to get a good nights rest in preparation for their big day. Rachel lay down in bed while James was in the bathroom brushing his teeth and getting ready for bed.

As James was about to leave the bathroom he began to feel light headed. This time he started to get excited knowing what was coming next, but he felt like he was about to collapse. He sat down, to regain his bearings. When he looked up, he realized he was not in the bathroom of his hotel room anymore. He saw bright colors, and what seemed like flashing shooting stars flying by. He had never seen anything like this before, and had no idea where he was. As the lights and flashes flew by, changing their appearance constantly someone grabbed him by the shoulder. He turned around to see a man as big as he is, but with a face like a child. The Angel wore a long white robe with sandals on his feet. His robe had a cloth belt that tied around his waste. His hair was extremely short, and James had a difficult time getting a read on this Angels face.

The Angel, whose face had an amazing child like quality to it yet also appeared to be a man in his twenties, began to speak "James faithful servant of God. Your father in Heaven is pleased with you, and loves you dearly. My name is Jamarda, servant Angel of the creator of the Heavens and the Earth! Your destination is known, your mission is not. I am here to give you some of the details pertaining to the next leg of your journey. In the Last days, there will be antichrists', and other cults and demonic powers to lead the world astray. The religion that worships the false god allah is the primary hater of the one true God, his Son and Savior to all people, and his children."

"Followers of this imaginary and false god kill in the name of their fictitious leader. They justify the persecution and death of believers and followers of Jesus Christ, the true Risen Lord. The devil is well aware of this religion, and uses trickery to continue to deceive and encourage behavior to hinder the truth, and reality of the one true God of all things, living and not living. This religion has but a handful of true leaders, and many brainwashed followers herded through their evil doing existence. There in the capital city of England is the breeding ground and recruitment center for people of this evil doing Islamic faith."

"Their religious actions are evil and their desire is to bring such intense violence to the people, and the region surrounding Jerusalem that a world war ensues, engineering what they call Jihad! Oh there will be a powerful destructive war. Indeed this war will cause the rise and ascension of a leader so evil, and so destructive that he was banished from heaven! His greed, deceit and self promotion was and is so great that it has caused him to have to endure eternal separation from his very own Creator that he now denies even created him! Oh the day comes where every knee shall bow, and every tongue shall confess Jesus Christ is the true risen Son of the Lord, and God of all! The great I Am already has this victory assured. What a happy day that will be!"

"Until that time, many sad days lie ahead. This religion and its followers will cause entirely too much destruction! This religion and its followers will cause premature death to many who might have otherwise chosen the gift that our Lord and creator has offered to them. This religion and its followers will prevent even their own from knowing the truth, and as a result prevent their own from receiving the eternals gifts that God so desperately wants each of them to enjoy! There is a leader amongst their ranks who is following the path of our beloved Paul. He has committed so many atrocities against the risen Christ's believers!"

"However, this man has been exposed to the truths and the gospels of salvation and of our Risen Lord and King Jesus Christ! This man currently has a troubled heart. He is walking two paths. He has many under his command in this evil doing religion, and is currently instructing his followers to kill and persecute anyone who does not accept the teachings of their false doctrines and the worship of their impotent false god, Allah. While executing these plans of death and destruction the doubt in his heart is growing. He studies the word of the one true God, reading the good news, in his study at night as he retreats by himself. With each living word of scripture he reads, his heart is tormented even more! His heart is tormented because the light is illuminating the darkness in which he now lives!"

"He already knows the truth, but needs to receive this most incredible gift ever offered to him or anyone! When this man will reject the demonic teachings he has filled his head and heart with since he was barely a toddler, and accept the gift of Salvation and the affection of a Loving God, who wants nothing more to than to love his soul for all of eternity; oh what a happy day that will be! Once he accepts the true and living God, the beginning and the end, that Alpha and Omega, the Holy Spirit will indwell him and allow him to be used by the all merciful and all powerful God. Like Paul, he can go from one of the most fearful persecutors of Christ, to a bold and powerful vessel used to thwart the enemy, and add large numbers to Gods kingdom of heaven that will reign forever and ever, Amen!"

"Go! Make yourself ready, and be prepared to see and know this man who God is seeking to be one of his children. This man aches to receive the truth he already knows; he just doesn't know how to do it. He fears! He fears that the acceptance of Christ and rejecting of his evil doing religion means the abandonment of the only life he has ever known! James, dear follower of the God of Abraham, Isaac, and Jacob, help him to understand that those who hold on to their own life too closely will lose it! However, those who give their life, offer it to the living God, will keep their life, and the love of their Savior for all eternity! Amen!"

James simply blinked his eyes and found himself fully conscious in the bathroom once again. Although he was used to having the visions, and visits by now, their boldness and the way their words and truth penetrated him always surprised him. He turned off the light and headed for bed to tell Rachel what he just experienced. When he crawled into bed he realized that Rachel was already asleep and did not see any reason to wake her. He decided he could wait until the next morning to fill her in on the details. Within 10 seconds of his head hitting the pillow James was fast asleep.

The next morning while they were on their way to meet Jeremiah, James told Rachel "I had another vision last night." Rachel was very excited to hear this "Oh really? What did you learn?" James told her they will probably be spending some time in London. He added "There is an extreme Islamic terrorist that is on the verge of accepting Christ's truth, and it is our job to help him to accept Christ." Rachel asked "How are we going to do that?" James laughed and said "Who knows! Maybe we will ask him nicely! Seriously, it sounds like somehow we are going to have to get to know him, and gain his trust. I don't even know who he is, or where he is yet."

"I am sure that once we get there, we are going to have to befriend him, or some how gain his confidence. The way I understood it in the vision; he is already torn, already trying to figure out the truth, he just needs the courage to commit and trust in Jesus." Rachel said "This is wild! We are going to travel halfway across the world, to become friends with a terrorist, so that he can find the strength he needs to know God. This is so romantic!" James laughed and said "Ha ha funny girl; on that note, I think we might have time to spend in London, and should get to see some sights, and enjoy our time together as well!"

They arrived to meet Jeremiah. Jeremiah handed James and envelope and James looked inside. James was impressed saying "Jeremiah, your buddy did great work! This looks so real! It's so perfect!" Jeremiah said "Except for her name, it is completely real, and valid. You will not have any trouble with it at all." Rachel spoke up saying "Wow, this looks great, I am even happy with the way the picture looks!" Jeremiah sarcastically said to James "Yeah, I can see where she would be worried about whether her picture looks good or not!" Rachel responded "Stop that! But thank you!"

The three began saying there goodbyes not knowing when they were going to see each other again. Jeremiah said "Listen, you two travel safe! I know you know this, but this is Gods plan, so just hear Him all the time and everything should work out perfectly!" Rachel said "Thank you! We are so excited for you too! You have a big task ahead of you too;

this is so exciting!" Jeremiah added "I will forever be indebted to you! I am so thankful that God brought you two into my life. Even apart from getting my eye sight back, in such a short period of time, we have bonded as friends, in a way that I have never experienced before!"

James interjected "Well…Jeremiah, we are so happy to have gotten to know you as well! We will be praying for you and for God to use you in mighty ways!" Jeremiah said "Well, with that in mind, do you mind if I pray for us all right now?" Of course they agreed and Jeremiah prayed "Lord, Father God, thank you for everything! Thank you for these friendships and for trusting us to carry out the details of Your plan. Please guide us, direct us, and protect us as we travel out of our own country doing Your work. Please keep us focused, and humble before You, and help us to feel Your love every step of the way. We love You Lord, and we are so incredibly thankful that we are being used by You for this fantastic journey. Thank you for letting us be apart of these end times events! In the precious name of all who saves, Jesus Christ, Amen!"

James and Rachel thanked their friend for the prayer. They gave each other more hugs, and then parted ways. Rachel and James had some time before they needed to be at the airport, so they decided to stop and eat and make some last minute plans. While seated at their table Rachel asked "Are we going to just leave the car at the airport?" James said "I hate doing that, but I think that makes the most sense. At least it should be somewhat safe there. In fact, we should get going. It is a bit of a drive to Los Angeles; we can talk more on the road."

On the way to the airport they discussed their excitement about what lies ahead! They were extremely excited about seeing London and knowing they were going to make a difference to the entire world by convincing a terrorist to change his ways, and to accept Christ. James said "I just realized we are going to be on a plane for 12 hours; we aren't going to be able to discuss this anymore for a while! So if we have any thoughts about what we will be doing for God, we better discuss them now!" Rachel followed that up by saying "Well, I was wondering, do you have any idea who this guy is, or where he hangs out? Is there anything that we do know about him yet?"

James answered "No, nothing at all. I was not given a name, a place or anything. I just know we will figure that out when we get there. "Rachel said "Well then! I guess there is nothing to plan then! We will just wait for God to tell us what to do next. So, what sites do you want to see first?" James said "I want to see the Tower of London, and Buckingham Palace! There is so much history there, but those are the two that jump out at me as the most interesting." Rachel added "Me too! But I have to say, there are like eight more things on my must see list, and another five that I'd like to if we can!"

Rachel had wanted to travel with James to other parts of the world their entire marriage. With work and schedules and family events, it just never seemed like a good time to get away. Rachel was on cloud nine at this point knowing that she was serving God, spending time with James and getting to travel with him. They decided that they would rent a car at the airport upon their arrival, and immediately check in to their hotel and get settled in.

When they arrived, they were tired, and did not want to deal with the hassle of trying to find a car rental agency open that late. They took a cab to the hotel and decided to rent a car in the morning. Upon settling in at the hotel Rachel declared "This is so beautiful! Everything is amazing!

I am blown away by the city, the buildings, and the hotel too!" James agreed saying "No kidding! It's hard to believe we are really here! We should get some rest though, so we can pick up a car in the morning and try to get in as many sites as possible before God puts us back to work!" Rachel laughed at that the thought of God putting them to work, but agreed.

The next morning Rachel could hardly contain herself! She yanked the covers off of James and yelled "Good Morning! Get up! Let's go!" James tried to reach for the covers, but she had already thrown them across the room; there was no deterring her! A few minutes later James was showering and getting ready for the day. Rachel surprised James by joining him in the shower. While they were leaving their room he said to her "Don't dead people suffer from jet lag?" Rachel laughed and said "I am not dead babe! I have never felt more alive! Let's go have some fun today!"

James was always interested in whatever she was excited about. This was no different. He was more than ready to see the city himself. They rented a car, and began to travel the city seeing the various sites. They started in the morning by seeing Saint Paul's Cathedral, the Tower of London, and a museum noting the history of the area including the quests of William the Conqueror. In the afternoon they made their way to Westminster where they went to the most famous church in Great Britain, Westminster Abbey. From there they continued on to the Houses of Parliament, and Buckingham Palace.

Rachel tried her hardest to get the Palace guards to change their facial expressions and acknowledge her. They would not budge! She even suggested to James, loud enough for one of the guards to hear "You ought to take off your shirt and do your sexy dance! You know the one you do for me!" Of course she embarrassed James, and much to her surprise, the guard stared straight ahead! Once they were back in their rental car Rachel was laughing hysterically and telling James "I had a great time today! This city is amazing!" James responded "That was a lot of fun! You are crazy!" Rachel gave him a funny look and leaned over and kissed him on his cheek. James smiled and added "But in a good way!"

Combining the fact that they had been on a plane for so long, covering several time zones, and all the sight seeing they did; they were exhausted! They decided to turn in early, and relax in the room for the night. They wanted to rest up, hoping to see more the next day. James awoke in the middle of night to a dream that felt incredibly real. He knew it was just a dream. The dream did not appear to be anything of great importance; it was just he and Rachel sitting in a café while in London. What stood out to him was the detail of the dream, and just the impression that was left on him from having the dream.

James went back to sleep and suddenly awoke again, this time after the Sun had already come up. He sat up quickly realizing that he just had the same exact dream again. Rachel felt him move, and noticed he was sitting up and asked "Are you okay?" James responded "I am fine, but I just had the exact same dream for the second time tonight! Rachel sat up and said "That is weird! What was the dream?" James said "It really wasn't a big deal, just you and I sitting at a café watching people and drinking coffee. I don't know if it means anything or not." Rachel casually said "I am sure it does; I'd keep it mind today while we are out."

They opted to leave the car that day, and do more walking and taking in some tour buses. They saw much of the city. They were able to see some more terrific sites, but enjoyed the day meandering in and out of streets and shopping areas. They did not have any specific places they planned to visit that day; they just wanted to get out and enjoy London. As they were walking down a street James stopped, reaching his arm to stop Rachel and said "This feels very familiar!" Rachel asked "Do you think the café is in this area?" James said "I don't know, might be."

As they continued walking down the street hand-in-hand, James pointed ahead, and said "There it is!" They continued ahead and crossed the street to the Café that was on the corner of a four way intersection that was at the end of this shopping district. They walked in, and Rachel grabbed a table while James stood in line and ordered them some coffee. "They sat for a while, enjoying their drinks hardly saying anything to each other." James softly spoke "All of the details are the same as they were in my dream, this is definitely the place, but I don't know what we are supposed to do."

Rachel said "Maybe we are supposed to wait for another visitor to tell us what to do next." More than two hours went by and they were still wondering why they were there. After a while, their focus turned from what was inside, to outside across the street. Rachel noticed something "James?"

She said, continuing "Look over there, across the street. I keep seeing foreigners going in and out of there. They don't look like the rest of the people around here!" James looked and said "Raech, you are right! They look a lot like the guys I saw in my vision of the storage shed!"

Rachel exclaimed "Really? Do you think it's them?" James could not help but laugh, and even struggled to speak for a few seconds, then finally said "No, those guys were arrested, remember?" Rachel became a little shy and said "Oh yeah." James continued "They look like the same kind of people, Middle Easterners" Still speaking very softly James said "Remember, the Angel told me that London hosts one of the biggest training and recruitment centers for Islamic terrorists. I wonder if we are about to see the guy we are supposed to help. He is probably in that building right now!"

A few more hours went by and it was getting dark. James was a little discouraged, and suggested they head back to the hotel. Rachel held on to James arm as they walked and said "Honey, remember, God is in control! So far, everything has been revealed to you in pieces, right?" James agreed, and Rachel continued "Well, this was a piece! Perhaps we didn't need to spend seven hours in a London Café today, but we had a good time being together, right?" James said "Of course! I love being with you wherever we are! I just worry that sometimes I misunderstand God. This all seems so important! What if I had the wrong café? What if were supposed to be sitting somewhere else tonight?"

Rachel laughed at James this time and said "Babe, I am sure if we were supposed to be somewhere else, we would have been! Besides how many cafés could match all of the details from your dream and happen to be right across the street from a building where a bunch of terrorist looking dudes go in and out all day! I'd say we were right where we were supposed to be!" James knew she was right and said "I know! You are totally right! I am sure tomorrow the rest of the details we need will be revealed! You know me! I am details guy, I don't like to be in the dark." Rachel said "Well, Mr. in control, something tells me God is the one in control of this one!"

They waved down a taxi, and rode quietly back to the hotel. Once in the elevator James pulled Rachel towards him and said "You are the best thing that ever happened to me, I hope you know that!" Rachel smiled at him and leaned toward him and let him wrap his arms around her. When

they walked into the room they were startled to find someone in there. As James flipped on the lights Rachel yelled
"Tobiah!" She then ran to her fairly new friend and hugged
him! She looked towards James and said "This is Tobiah! He
is a guardian Angel. I met him in heaven! He was assigned
to protect over my grandfather!

Tobiah looked at James and said "James, my brother!
This sweet child Rachel, your lovely wife, spent a lot of time
telling me of the great man she was married to before her
time in heaven. I am delighted to personally be able to speak
to you on this day! Take joy dear brother, you are one of a
special few allowed to enjoy such a privilege." James said
"Thank you! I think I already knew that though!" Tobiah
said "No need to thank me! For it was your Father in Heav-
en that blessed you with such a miracle! I just hope you both
stay focused and realize that this blessing is highly unusual
and that you can place a great deal of importance as to the
insight that the Lord is showing you in terms of how much
He loves you!"

Rachel asked "Tobiah, do I have to go? Are you here to
take me back?" Tobiah said "Dear child, on the contrary! Do
you not know by now that if your Father wants you back in

Heaven that he would simply think it and it shall be? He hardly needs to send me to deliver you to Him again! I am here to give you a message. You know Rachel, the Angels are singing more now, than they were before." Rachel asked "Why is that?" Tobiah followed up with "Because these are the end of days! The return of the Savior is near! People are accepting Christ more today, than at anytime before!"

"However, on this Earth, where good indeed abounds, we also know that pain is close by. While the count of believers is adding up, the count of the lost souls accumulates as well. Every day people are trusting and turning to the one who paid the price so they wouldn't have to! That said the enemies of the Lord are lining up too! Satan and his demonic little followers are cursing the people of this land, and leading them astray! Satan has put the thought of so many false gods in the minds and hearts of the lost of this world. They kill and persecute the very children who love the one and true creator of all things! Sadly, they do this killing and persecuting in the name of gods, which they think they are serving!"

"Know this! They are only serving the anti-Christ & their own flesh.! I want you to know that your job is very important and that God will use you to save so many people. The man you are here to show the way, and the truth to, is plotting at this very moment with his evil followers to poison a city. If not for the success that your mission will have, 546,982 people will die within forty hours of now. 311,522 will suffer not only a physical death, but an eternal death as well; for they do not know the Lord, and will be eternally separated from God! Because of your willingness to be used as a tool for the Lord almighty, heaven will grow by another 197,777 people by the time the final tribulation is completed as a result of helping this one man to change his ways and accept Jesus Christ as his Lord and Savior!"

"I could go on and on giving you the numbers this one act of service and obedience will yield. How many of the saved will be used by God to go on and save others that might not otherwise be saved? How many more babies will be born during this time that will go on to know our Lord and Risen Savior and spend eternity in heaven as well? Not to mention, how many other senseless acts this man would have led his evil followers into committing, thus preventing more untold numbers of souls eternally separated from their creator because they refused to see the light, refused to see the truth! This one victory; a victory for God mind you! This one victory will assure that Gods kingdom will be greater by more than a million more souls in heaven, with their creator for all of eternity!"

James said "That is amazing! Talk about a domino effect. I had no idea. Can you tell us how many people were saved as a result of not allowing the president to be killed?" Tobiah said James, brother and lover of the God of all, know this! If your president had been killed; it would have set in motion a chain of events that would have given the evil one multiple victories. These victories would have brought on events which were not meant to happen yet. Additionally, the amount of people who would have died, or never had their chance to accept Christ's gifts is staggering! The numerical answers are complete; the final tally is Gods to know! You need to know that your work is important, and that God loves you and will see these good works completed through you."

Turning to Rachel, Tobiah said "My sweet sister in Christ! Take care of this man! Love him like you always have! Continue your battle for your Father in heaven! Soon God's final victory will be had, and we will spend all of eternity celebrating and toasting these stories of adventure and victory! Remember, the outcome is already known! You stay true, and trust in the Lord with all of your heart! Please, brother and sister do not lean on your own understanding. If you do this, trust me, your God will make your paths so clear, and very straight! You are in Gods arms of protection. Hold true to that!"

Tobiah told them goodbye and literally disappeared right in front of them. James marveled to Rachel "Things are so different now! I grew up reading the Bible praying to see little glimpses of God. Now, I am getting huge doses, and loving it! This rocks!" Rachel was enjoying his enthusiasm and added "You haven't seen anything yet! It's so strange, in some ways heaven is a like a faded memory to me. But I can tell you, walking around with the insight that God gives you while in heaven, is indeed amazing! Perspective is so different and enlightening there!"

CHAPTER 13

Rachel asked "Do you think they have a pool in this hotel? I am in the mood to for a swim before we go to sleep." James answered "Actually, I know they do! I saw a sign in the lobby to the pool and Jacuzzi area." They changed, grabbed some towels and headed to the pool area. They swam some laps enjoying the water. James decided to get in the Jacuzzi and Rachel followed. They were in the pool area by themselves as most people were probably at dinner. After they soaked for a while James went under water to soak his face and hair.

When he came up he was not in the Jacuzzi anymore! He was sitting at the café once again! While sitting there a man approached and said "James my brother, I am Shoamer, friend of our brother Paul. I looked after and protected him many times, and now in a very different way, I will be assisting you! Every morning at the ninth hour a man comes to this very café and sits right over there at the table by that plant. You will recognize him because of the large birth mark that is on his forehead. Currently he does work for the evil one. James you and your helper must give him the courage to trust his heart, and his studies!"

"This will not be an easy task as he will have to turn from a lifetime of false teachings, and evil practices that he believed were serving a god that he doesn't even know does not even exist! His very conversion and acceptance of Jesus will be a huge victory for the kingdom of heaven. Here he comes now! See him, and begin to get to know him! You can see the lost look in his eyes! He has a hole in his heart, and he is just beginning to figure out that the hole can only be filled by the true and living God and creator of all things! James meet him, and help him!"

James stood to go speak to the man, and instead realized he was standing up out of the water, and Rachel asked him "Are you ready to get out and go back the room?" James responded with a question of his own "How long was I under water?" Rachel laughed and said "oh, three seconds, might have been four though! I lost track at three and a half!" Now she made herself laugh even harder! James replied "Well, as far I was concerned, that was about five minutes ago!" Rachel asked "What are you talking about?" James told her of the vision as stepped out of the hot tub and toweled off.

As they were settling in for the night and getting ready for bed, Rachel asked "How are we going to approach him?" James responded "I was wondering the same thing. I am not sure what we should assume and what we shouldn't. It seems to me, that the more public our discussion is, the more likely that we are to chase him away. I also worry, if we don't do it right the first time, he may not return again if he thinks we will be there to greet him a second time. We need to somehow invite him to meet us in a place that he won't feel vulnerable. I assume he speaks English as well" Rachel inquired "Why do you assume that?"

"I think most of the world speaks more than one language, and English is one of them. Besides, I wouldn't think that God would choose us for this mission if there were a language barrier." Rachel agreed "Okay that makes sense, but why do you think he would feel less secure in a public place?" James answered "I don't think it's a matter of him feeling safe or protected like we would be a threat to him. I think he would feel vulnerable sitting in a café in the same area where he basically works. He might feel very concerned that while sitting there chatting with a couple of Americans, some of the people he works with might walk in and that would look bad for him."

Rachel understood but asked "Okay, so how are we going to get him to meet two strangers somewhere else? What could we possibly say to him that would give him the willingness to do such a thing?" James answered "I am not sure, but I am guessing its going to be as simple as trusting that God will make our approach work. Let's get to sleep, and perhaps God will send someone to tell me, or you what our plan should be." Rachel said "That works for me, I am exhausted anyway! I am ready to sleep."

The next morning they woke up earlier than they wanted to because they had to be to the café by 9:00 AM. When they first woke up, Rachel asked James "So, did you get any answers in your sleep?" James replied "Nope, afraid not! But I do have a sense of peace about it. I don't feel nervous, or stressed at all. I truly know God is going to work this out for us." Rachel told James "I hope you don't mind, but I have a plan!" James chuckled and said "Mind? Why would I mind? I welcome it! What is it?"

Rachel told James "I was thinking about what you said last night, about not wanting to make him uncomfortable talking to a couple of Americans in public like that. I think you are right, the more we are around the guy in public, the less he will listen to our message. The more he will pull away, and that reduces our chance to be able to share the good news with him." James obviously agreed but asked "Okay, I agree with that, but what is your plan for getting him to a place where we can chat with him?" Rachel answered "Okay, this is going to sound so high school, but I think the best thing to do is to give him a note"

James was a little surprised "A note? Should we put two boxes on it, and ask him to check yes or no?" Rachel laughed "Ha ha funny guy! You're a riot! Okay! I think we prepare a note, letting him know that the one and true God knows his heart, loves him, and instructions on where to meet us to find out more." James questioned "Do you really think he is going to follow the instructions on a note handed to him by a couple of strangers in a café?" Rachel replied "At first thought, no I didn't think so. But I think if we hand him a note, with a brief greeting, and walk away; walk completely out of the café and leave. I think that he will study the note, and the words will resonate with him. I think God will work through the note to not only make him curious, but to encourage him that the answers he has been seeking await him in the meeting place that we provide!"

James said "I can't think of anything better! Besides that, you are right! If this is of God, and we are doing Gods will, then it has to work! I can't imagine that he doesn't show up because the note is a bad idea. I just hope he doesn't check the "no" box! Just kidding! You are right, he will show up!" Rachel said "You are just too funny! Then she got serious and asked "Where should we have him meet us?" James answered "I think we should have him meet us right here! It's private, nobody would know or care why he is here, and on top of that, I think it provides the most convenient way for you and I to provide him a window of time, rather than a specific time to meet."

Rachel said "I don't understand, why do you care about that?" "Well we are going to give him a note right around 9:00 AM. If we tell him to meet us at 10:00 AM, or even

2:00 PM, there is always the possibility for schedule conflicts. What if he has meetings or something planned that would make him worry that his people would catch on if he didn't show up? So instead, if we say, to meet us here, between 10:00 AM, and 10:00 PM, he can choose when to show up. This way if he doesn't immediately choose to accept our invitation, he has all day to think about it, and change his mind. Additionally, I am thinking if you and I have to wait around somewhere all day long for a meeting that may happen anytime in a twelve hour time window, we will be more comfortable waiting here than anywhere else."

Rachel agreed and suggested they prepare the note before they leave. James agreed and said to Rachel "Okay, why don't you write the note since you have much better handwriting than I do." James told her what to write and Rachel jotted down the following on a piece of paper:

The true God of Abraham, Isaac, and Jacob knows your heart! He knows the inner turmoil you have experienced and wants to offer you peace! We know you are agonizing over some tough choices and we can help! Trust God at this time, like you never have before! Please come to the Land-

mark, London Hotel, Room 244, anytime between 10:00 a.m. and 10:00 p.m.

today for the answers and encouragement you desire!

After they finished the note, they immediately left the hotel and flagged a taxi to take them to the café. They arrived about 10 minutes before 9:00 a.m., so they went in and sat down at a table. Sure enough, about five minutes later, the man with the birthmark that James had seen in his vision walked in, and found his familiar table. Immediately James walked over to the man, handed him the note and said "The true God of all creation loves you!" With that, he walked away, and Rachel followed behind. Their taxi was still waiting for them, and they returned to the hotel.

They arrived back in their room around 9:30 a.m., and knew this could be a long day in their hotel room. They decided to order room service and have some breakfast since they did not have a chance to order anything at the Café. Around 9:45 a.m. they received a knock at the door, expecting it to be their breakfast. Instead it was the man from the café. James was surprised to see him there, and invited him in. The man said "My name is Ahmed. I apologize for being early, but I have plans the rest of the day. In fact, my plans conflict with your note, and I think it's time I make a choice one way or the other."

James introduced himself, and Rachel, and said "To be honest, we didn't expect you this soon, and we just ordered breakfast for ourselves, may I call and order something for you?" Ahmed very politely responded "No sir, I really do not have an appetite right now. I would like to discuss this with you though. How did you know that I have tough choices to be made? How did you know that I so badly yearn to hear that God loves me? How do you know these things?" James invited him to walk out on the balcony and sit where they would all be comfortable. James cautioned Ahmed "What I am about to tell you, may seem very unbelievable, but I can assure you that it is real!"

Ahmed interjected and said "You may find that I am not at all surprised. I have been a devout Muslim my entire life. I have followed the principles and ideologies that have been taught for thousands of years. I have served and worship allah for as long as I can remember. Lately, more out of curiosity I began to study the God of your Bible. The things I have read, have resonated with me more, and seemed more truthful than any of my studies of the Koran."

"It has indeed, caused great confusion in my heart. What confuses me even more is that it seems the more I read your Bible, the more confused I get about the scriptures I read in my Koran. It seems now, that when I read your Bible, all of a sudden the teachings of the Koran that I have been reading since I was a small child mean something different than they ever have before." James asked "Do you mean that you have a better understanding of your Koran than you did before because of what the Bible says?" Ahmed answered "Sort of, but in a very different way than what I think you are thinking. For the first time, when I read some of the scripture verses in my Koran, I see some things that seem evil, conflicting, confusing, and inaccurate. I am very confused! The very things I read 6 months ago that felt so right and true to me, and brought forth the best intentions, now all of a sudden read very different to me. Things that I read in the Koran that I believed to be allah, now seem evil, and wrong to me. How could the same thing I read before mean something completely different today?" He quickly continued "What I have come to understand is that it's possible because of false scriptures, my brain has influenced my heart. Reading your Bible has caused a change in my heart that is affecting my brain. I am terribly conflicted!"

James responded "Ahmed, I really do not even know where to begin! I can assure you that the studies you have experienced that are reaching your heart, and for the first time teaching you and showing you the truth about the one true God and creator of everything is very, very real! The changes you are experiencing are real, the reason you feel the way you feel is because God is truly speaking to your heart, He wants you! He wants to love you for your all of eternity! Ahmed, we know you have plans to cause a great deal of harm later today. We know that you are training others to execute an attack that is intended to kill hundreds of thousands!"

Ahmed replied "How do you know these things? How do you know what's in my heart? Nobody knows of my studies of the Bible! I have not told a soul! I study late at night in my own apartment under the light of a candle! Nobody knows! How do you know of my plans? I know of no breach in those in my charge?" James said "Ahmed, God told us to come to you! I saw you in a vision, before I ever saw you in person for the first time this morning! The true God of all creation knows the beginning and the end! He knows your heart! He knows your actions! He even has plans to prosper you and use you for his Glory! He knows that as you prepare others to do these evil deeds that you are reconsidering your own participation. He knows that you no longer want to participate! He wants you to do what you have been putting off, and give your heart to him, and accept the gift of salvation that he is offering to you!"

"The Lord wants you to choose him! He wants you to turn from the evil doers you are associating with, and help to build the kingdom of God, the very kingdom He is offering you to live in, for all of eternity! Ahmed, the end of days is near! The savior that your people are waiting for, is indeed about to rise to power, but he is not a Savior! He is the antichrist! He is the true enemy of God! Your people will celebrate him, and worship him, and he will be the cause of so many you care about going to hell! The end of days is here! God is about to reveal Himself to his people! Jesus is about to return for a second time, to claim his faithful children!"

"My friend, please understand, that this will usher in a great tribulation that will result in Gods wrath, as well as the antichrist that will lead so many astray! Your people consider this to be the Jihad. The Jihad will happen, but it's not going to be the great thing that most Muslims expect it to be! God is personally seeking you! He sent us to meet you! He sent us to talk with you, to confirm that the desires in your heart are real, and true! You need to turn from your sins, and accept the gift offering in the form of Jesus Christ as your Savior! Acknowledge that have sin that separates you from God and that he died for your sins, recognize that he truly raised Himself from the dead three days later and then ascended into heaven! Ahmed, I know for you, this decision cannot be made lightly!"

"I know you feel you would be turning your back on traditions and beliefs that date back thousands of years. I know that you feel you would be turning your back on your family, and your nation! But what matters more? Is it more important to please people? Are you to consider certain people that may or may not even survive the evil and destruction that is coming of greater importance? Or is it more important to choose the one Living God, who created you to be with him in heaven for all of eternity? Nothing matters more than Him! Ahmed, this is not about them, it's about you!"

"Your creator, and lover of your soul, is asking you right

now, to choose Him! He loves you so much, that he didn't leave you to your own studies and conclusions! He actually sent us, as messengers to convey to you the importance of your choice to accept his gift offering. This is important, not only for the sake of your own soul, but if you choose to continue on the path that you are on right now, not only will you end up eternally separated from God, but you will be sentencing to death, prematurely so many innocent people that will no longer have their chance to learn of, and accept Jesus Christ as their Lord and Savior!"

James then asked "What more do you need to know?" Ahmed began to cry, and with tears streaming down his face he dropped to his knees and begged for forgiveness saying "Father God, true God, oh please forgive me! I have known for so long that I was on the wrong path, but continued because of traditions. I have attacked you, and persecuted you! I have killed your children! Oh God, I beg you to forgive me. I am so sorry. I do not deserve this. If you tell me no, I will understand! I need your truths to resonate in my heart! I have learned of, and come to Love you Jesus, the Savior for the whole world! I am so bad, so terrible! You came to save everyone, and yet it was you, and your people that I made the choice to war with, and attack, and hurt, and kill!"

"My Lord, and my Savior, I want to spend the rest of my days serving you! I want to be used by you to help others to see the error of their ways, to see their destructive and evil actions, the same ones I am guilty of, as the abominations that they are! I have failed you my Lord. I hurt you. I am so sorry. Thank you for sending these people to me to convey this truthful message you have been showing me. I am so undeserving but you sought me out, I will never know why, but will spend the rest of my days serving you! I accept your gift of salvation, a gift I am so unworthy to receive! Thank you for dying for me Lord! Thank you for being the all powerful God that you are!

"I have spent a lifetime serving a fake god, a god whose name has been used to justify so many murders for thousands of years. Thank you for revealing yourself to me! Thank you for letting me love You! And thank You for loving me! Amen! Amen! Amen!" James helped Ahmed to his feet, and back to his chair. All three of them had been crying and overwhelmed by what they had just experienced. They just sat there, for at least 10 minutes without saying a word.

Each of them was praying to themselves. Rachel was

praying to God, thanking him for the amazing power that he continues to demonstrate, and thanked him for allowing her return to be with James, and to participate and witness the amazing plans and power of God! James was praying, completely numb from what had just happened. He thanked God for the amazing power He has, and how incredible it was to experience that powerful presence so clearly on that balcony. Ahmed was literally shaking while he was praying. He thanked God for finally being able to truly feel Him, and experience Him for the first time in your whole life! He was so sorrowful for the things he had done. He asked God over and over to forgive him.

Ahmed spoke up saying "My entire life, I thought I knew God, but as it turns out, I didn't know anything! I have been angry, and hateful my entire life, because I thought I needed to be, to serve god. Oh how off I was. It pains me to know that all I have done, persecuting others who didn't believe how my people believe. I thought I was killing and scheming in the name of god, but as it turns out, I was serving Satan. What a bittersweet day this is. I learn the truth, and start my life new, but I will never be able to forget the evilness of what I have done. How could I not instinctively know that a God who loves me would never condone, much less encourage such activities!"

Rachel who had been mostly silent until now spoke up saying "You not only have a fresh new outlook on your own life, but you have a wonderful opportunity to reach others who you know think how you have always thought! You are in a unique position to both help others who need help, and you can also stop the efforts of your people from causing more harm. You know their plans, and you know their intentions of the extremist who want to hurt the cause of Christ, and are so willing to unknowingly help Satan! He is using them, and they don't even know it! You can be such a difference maker!"

Ahmed was surprised and asked "Are you suggesting that I stay with these people? That I continue to work with them, and not run away, as far as I can?" Rachel said "Maybe. I think you need to really pray about this, and see where God leads you. I think at least for the time being, you can stop some things that are in progress. God's Angel told us that you are planning an attack for later today; you must stop this!" Ahmed said "Fortunately, that is not a problem, I know an easy way to stop that from happening; but, after that, I don't know what I can do. How do I train and encourage these actions, while at the same time stopping it?"

James spoke up "I think only you know that. We have no idea how you have operated. We don't know the ins and outs of how your leaders conduct things and those that follow. Obviously you do. I know for a fact, based on what we were told, that you have to stop today's attack. We also know that you are to help others to know Christ, and his gift of salvation. Seems to me that if God wants you to share your knowledge of Christ with those you have worked under you, then you have to stay with them, at least for a while. Again, Rachel is right; you need to pray about this! You now have the Holy Spirit inside you! You have the spirit of God inside you that will lead you and guide through your life."

"That said, beyond that, I would stay, at least for a bit. See how it goes. See if you are able to gain the confidence in a personal way with those that worked for you. They may open up to you. For all you know, there are others who have had the same struggles that are begging for someone to know the truth. You are their commanding leader, if you find that someone in your charge has been having doubts, and they find out that you made this life changing commitment, it will free them to do the same!" Rachel agreed and added "Ahmed, remember something; you have never truly experienced God before! He will lead you! For the first time in your life, you have God on your side!"

"This is a very big deal! In the past, you did things, things you thought made sense based on your own understanding or beliefs. You had people; family and friends that shaped your belief system. They convinced you of things that you held on to as truth, and that was your guiding force! Now you have the Truth, inside you! You have the living God inside you! He will direct you, He will speak to your heart and mind letting you know when you are doing His will, and convict you when you step outside of it! These are things that in many ways you probably, simply can't relate to!"

"But things are different! Now you have to walk by faith! Also, understand, this is happening today, at this time, because things must happen to set the stage for Jesus to return! Christ is returning soon, for all of His believers, including you! Once the Christians of this world leave, and go to heaven, literally, all hell will break loose! The antichrist will rise to power; he is absolutely the most significant enemy of God! Evil will spread through this world even more than it is today! This will take place during the tribulation! This is the seven year period in which God will unleash his wrath on the world in a final attempt to reach the lost."

"Ahmed, I know this is a lot to take in! My point is, nothing can be a more significant instruction to you right now than to study Gods Word, and lean on him for understanding. He will speak to your heart in ways you have never experienced before! This will be a new way for you to live and operate! You are not on your own anymore! You do not have to fight these battles on your own. Because for once, you will be fighting on the side of God, the creator of everything! He won't let you mess up His plan! So trust in him; your faith and understanding of God are just beginning to grow, and you will be amazed at the rapid growth in your relationship with God, in a very short period of time!"

Ahmed said "I don't know if I have ever heard a woman speak with such boldness before! I believe everything you are saying. The truth is, in the last few weeks God has been speaking to my heart, but I didn't know it was Him! I was scared! This visit with you today answered so many questions; and gives me the courage I need to commit to God once and for all. I don't know how I am going to do all of this, but I trust that God will show me that way! I trust that God will keep me protected, and that I will be able to do good for Him. I don't know how, right now, but I am guessing that He will speak to my heart when He wants me to do something"

"This is so different! My people would commit to a plan, which they drew up, and then expect it to work as we would say "allah willing". If it worked, we figured we accomplished allah's will. If it did not, we figured it was not what he wanted. Now we are speaking of walking hand-in-hand with God, step-by-step, accomplishing only what He wants us to accomplish, and not even attempting what we know He does not want us to do. If someone died executing one of these plans for allah, we thought it to be an exceptional honor. Now I realize that if God wants me to do his will, he will protect me and see it through to the end, for his benefit! How do I suddenly understand these truths? I am no different today, than I was yesterday! I am exactly as intelligent as I was yesterday. This is so fascinating!"

James said "Ahmed, my new brother in Christ, you are different! You did not have the Holy Spirit of God living in you yesterday! You were left up to your own accord. God reveals his word to those that believe in Him! You do! So now He is working through you at this very minute! His word and His message is absorbing into your heart at this very minute. Your life is truly different, as is your focus, and your mission! You are hearing God for the first time, and I have no doubt, that the closer you draw to Him, and the more you accomplish for him, the louder He will speak to your heart! He has already sent us personally to speak to you! Imagine how much greater His impact and involvement in your life you can expect to experience!"

Ahmed stood up and said "Thank you! Thank you for allowing yourselves to be used by God. How I have benefited today because of that! I must leave. I have a weapon to destroy! My window of opportunity for stopping this destruction today is closing soon. If I leave now, it will be a very easy task. I will forever be indebted to you!" James said "No, actually, you are not! As you will learn, it's all for God, by God! We simply did what was asked of us! Without God, we would have never known anything about you! God chose you Himself, for Himself! Never forget, it's all for Him! He created you, and loves you, and wants you joined with Him in heaven, forever and ever! Amen!"

Ahmed shook hands with his new friends, then left the hotel to go destroy a suitcase that contained nerve gas. James and Rachel again were in awe of being in the presence of the Lord. Rachel had experienced it so strongly in heaven, but here, it was so amazing to see Him work such mighty miracles among such ordinary people and Earthly surroundings. Rachel said "James, you know that God just used us to make an evil enemy a friend, and to save hundreds of thousands of lives! I feel like I could literally explode crying. My gratitude and Love for God is truly overflowing!"

James remarked "That was phenomenal! I don't remember what I said; in fact, I am not sure I even said most of it! My lips were moving, but words were just flying out of me! I felt like God was completely in control! What an amazing occurrence!" Rachel said "Well, you did good sweetie! I was in awe of hearing you say all of that!" James said "Thanks, but that was definitely God! That said, a few times I felt like I was cutting you out a bit, and not giving you a chance to say anything" Rachel said "Actually, I felt God tell me to keep quiet. I think that in Ahmed's culture; well, you know, women aren't exactly respected. I think that message needed to come from a man!"

"I think this also shows we truly have nothing to worry about! I mean, everything fell into place! Ahmed even showed up fifteen minutes before we invited him to be here! We weren't even expecting him to show up for at least a few hours from now! God is so much in control! We have nothing to worry about!" James added "You are so right about that! To think we wasted even a minute stressing about how this will play out! If God tells us to go, we need to just go and not worry! Like Elomen said, these victories are already Gods!" Rachel asked James "Do you mind if I pray for us right now?" James answered "please!"

Rachel prayed "Father God, thank you! Thank you once again for showing us your mighty power, and how true and real your plans are! We cannot thank you enough for allowing us to be used the way we are. This is exhilarating, and truly spectacular! Thank you for sending me back to the man I love, to do Your work! Thank You for letting me see You work through this incredible man of faith! Please keep him strong, and ready to follow you at every turn! We are finding ourselves loving you more each and every day. You are an awesome God, and all of this is entirely too good to be true! Thank you Lord! Please keep your hands on us as we continue to do your work! Amen!"

CHAPTER 14

They spent the rest of the day traveling the city, enjoying the sites. They continually marveled at what they had experienced. They kept reminding themselves to be quiet just in case they were overheard. Serving God in this way was becoming so exciting; they anxiously waited to hear what their next assignment would be! As it turned out, they did not hear from an Angel for another week. At the end of their booked stay at the Landmark London, they still had not heard from an Angel as to where to go next. They figured it might be an indication it was time to return home, but for now they decided to extend there stay another few days, and check out some of the neighboring countries.

The end of another fun filled day was their ninth in

London. While enjoying dinner in a nice restaurant, James suggested it was time to leave. He said to Rachel "Let's get around in the morning, and take the next flight we can, and go back to L.A. and get the car." Rachel asked "Then what?" James said "I am not totally sure but I think it's time to go home. Or maybe we will stay in the L.A. area and wait for our next instructions. Maybe we are done for a while. It's hard to say. I'd just assume go home, but that might be too risky. If your parents find out I am home, they will stop in to visit; such a risk for whomever else may just happen to see you. That is not worth the risk to me! The Angel told me that nobody can know about you or it's over. I am not ready to let you go again!"

They returned to their hotel room to prepare their things to leave the following day. As they were packing their things Rachel tapped James on the shoulder and pointed towards the balcony. He looked to the balcony and noticed someone standing outside overlooking the city. He took Rachel by the hand and walked to the balcony and stepped outside. "Hello" James said to their visitor. The visitor replied "The end of days are near! The evil one is lying to the Nations and attempting to the thwart the promises of God at every turn.

He has failed, continues to fail, and his ultimate failure is already guaranteed! The Lord has a gift for his believers, and to all who are close to accepting his gracious plan and gift for Salvation!"

Rachel asked "What is the gift?" The man, who was dressed in a long canvas looking robe, had long white hair, and carried a large walking stick that is taller then he is answered "Silence, dear daughter of the most high God! I will tell you all you need to know. The world shall rejoice in a great historical find! One of histories biggest mysteries you shall unveil! This find will cause so many followers of Christ to be strengthened and emboldened in their faith to serve God more and more! This find will cause those that have been reluctant for one reason or another to accept the precious gift of He who died on the cross for all of the sins of the world! So many people remain eternally separated from Him because they are too prideful to accept their need for a redeemer."

"Others like Thomas, who is in heaven because of his faith in Christ the Savior that fully resulted from putting his fingers into the wounds that those who crucified our Lord inflicted on Him needed more physical proof. This gift is for them! Blessed are those who have not seen, and yet have believed. Our God is an awesome God! He will move heaven and Earth to give everyone a chance to know that the scriptures, the very Word of God, were divinely inspired, by Him! There were events which were started thousands of years ago, that are just now being completed!"

"The World is about to see both the love, and the wrath of the One who created everything! Despite the continued rejection of the God who loves all of His people, He is willing to do everything possible to reach those who reject his gift offering. The people of this world will see miracles, signs of love, and wrath. Both should be insights into the very realness of God, and his divine Word, and promises! My dear brother and sister, chosen by the almighty God to do good works for His benefit! Children of God, you are chosen to be witnesses, and to be part of the most spectacular climax the world has ever seen!"

"Before this final chapter is concluded and the second return of Jesus Christ, Savior to all who accept his plan of redemption ushers in the tribulation, some work remains! So few prophecies are left to be fulfilled; and until this time of completion, and the return of Jesus to gather up those who love him, and while Satan continues to distract Gods creation from the truth; our loving God will continue to allow certain revelations to occur to strengthen the faith of those who believe, and to spark faith in those that do not!"

As the man turned around, Rachel immediately recognized him as the Noah from the Old Testament, a man she had met in heaven. He said "My friends, and fellow servants of the God of all creation, we have a unique bond between us that is starting at this very moment! Thousands of years ago before you were even a glimmer of a thought to anyone but God himself; I was given a very unique task! I was given an undertaking that many considered me to be a crazy old man! I received no accolades; there was no praise or cheers to me, but the satisfaction that came from pleasing the lover of my soul, the one who created me!"

"This task epitomized the Great Tribulation that is to come! It embodied God's love, as well as his sense of justice and discipline, and demonstrations of forgiveness! At that point in time, man had reached depths of depravity and sin, that God was no longer pleased with his creation. His first inclination was to destroy everything! Upon second thought, and despite much destruction, humanity was given a second chance! In the end, many perished, and suffered for their rejection of the Almighty God! But this also stood as evidence of a God willing to give his people another chance. It was a testament to his power and might, grace and love, and begged those who rejected Him to choose Him once again!"

"Now, thousands of years later, we are at another crossroads! This time, this age is coming to a close! After this final choice is made, no further chances will be given! The savior of this world was God born into the fragile body of a human baby. He would experience the same temptations that we all have experienced as he grew and taught the multitudes His message of love. He showed the world He was their Savior! He showed them he was the very Savior they had been anticipating for more than a millennium! He showed them the one and true way to the Father was through Him!"

"Some accepted him as their Lord and Savior; some rejected him, even unto His own death! They crucified him in an effort to make him go away, so they could return to being the gods of their own lives! They didn't like the reflection of themselves they saw when they looked at Him! They crucified him and buried him away in a tomb, to forever be forgotten! Lo, there He was, raised and living again, on the third day just like He promised! Many saw Him, many felt Him, many loved Him, and many still feared Him!"

"Now, God, who came in the human flesh known as Jesus Christ of Nazareth, will come again! Hear me! I say, He will come again! He will come for all those that believe in Him, and his message! In the twinkling of an eye, like a thief in the night He will return and gather up His faithful to live in heaven and reign with him for all of eternity! At this point, many will fall to their knees and beg forgiveness! Some indeed will repent, and at long last, they will accept the precious gift of salvation! Sadly, some will still reject Jesus as the Savior of the world!"

"The worst enemy of God will rise to power reassuring those rejecters of God that they do not need him! He will even go as far as trying to convince them that he is god! But no! He is not god; he is a false weak imitator of the one and only God! He is not a god of any kind! He is a pretender; he is the serpent, the great deceiver, weak, and desperate! Although he knows he has no other outcome other than defeat at the hands of the almighty Savior, he will still put up a frivolous fight."

"God sent his Word to the people. He sent his chosen Son whom he is proud of to save the world from its sins! He has blessed those people and nations who have honored him, and he has delivered his punishment to those who have sinned and turned their back on his precious Word. He has revealed himself to the world over and over. Now, after he once again proves to the world His Truth and returns to retrieve His faithful followers; returning to the very world that He offered salvation to, and ultimately was crucified for saving; many will still reject him. They will intentionally choose to believe that the followers of Jesus did not leave to be united with him for all of eternity."

"During this time many will see the wrath of God! They will see the reality of a world that has turned their back on Him!" Will he do this because He hates them? Will He do this for revenge? No! I say unto you, He will do this, as a last effort to reach the lost. He has tried to love them into His eternal kingdom! He has given them so many chances and the freedom to make their own choice! Now His last efforts will be through a series of judgments foretold by John in a revelation given to him, by an Angel sent by God Himself! These judgments will indeed turn some to God! But some will choose to turn even further away!"

"This is where our bond to each other begins! As it pertains to me, I was told to build an Ark, for the purpose of demonstrating my faith, and my trust in the almighty Lord of all; as well as preserving some of the creation that God was still pleased with. I still continually thank God, that He included me and my family among those that were faithful servants to Him! Again, the purpose of my mission was to demonstrate Gods power, justice, and love, and forgiveness to the world!"

"You my dear brother and sister in Christ are going to be tied to the history of the Ark for all of eternity just like me! No, you will not be building an ark in preparation for a great flood like I did! You will not have to persevere on a one hundred year project while others ridicule you like I experienced! You will find the ark! You will go to where I left it, and you will show the world this great masterpiece! You will prove to the world, another of Gods great truths! You will remind people of Gods love, his forgiveness, and if they don't repent, his prophesied wrath! You will give the people of this world hope, another reason to believe that God's living Word, as written in the scriptures is true!"

"Sadly some will choose to harden their hearts even further against the one true God, just like they did when I built the Ark; even when it began to rain! They would not believe! Woe to them! The creator of all knows that this world is full of evil! In a time of evil, and with what is to come; the great Lord of all, is choosing you to reveal this gift, as a way to fight through the evil, and give something physically tangible for them to let their hearts grab on to. My brother and sister, it is time for you to depart! Go West of where I disembarked the Ark. Go to Turkey, the town of Sanliurfa. Our ancestor, and chosen servant of God, Abraham was born in a cave there. Go to this cave!"

"There will be a helper awaiting you there! He will direct your next steps. Children of God, go prepare! Ultimately you will enter into one of the most treacherous mountain ranges in the world! You must take proper care, and proper equipment. Additionally you need to be prepared to show the world of your findings. Take what is necessary to record this event for the entire world to see! My dear sister, to the world, you are no longer here. You are to accompany James and be a great helper to him on this most important adventure! Remember, when the event is to be shown to the world, you may not be present for that."

"Remember, as I told you, I suffered many insults and ridicule for my efforts. Although you will not receive credit and accolades here in this time, your rewards will await you in heaven! Your trip will be tiring, and physically demanding. But remember, God has brought you both this far! He will not depart from you! He remains with you, and as always, the victory is already His! Trust in Him as you always have, and you will find yourself standing before an incredible historical structure that I and my family toiled for nearly one hundred years to build. You will be able to step foot on the very masterpiece that God himself revealed to me how to construct! You will walk the floors of the Ark that my family and I, and so many animals, that God created floated on. You will see and experience the very Ark that was used to carry us through the waters of a great flood that was never before or since seen by mankind."

"My dear young ones! This is a great honor bestowed upon you! You need rest! Although victory has already been determined, this will demand much of your mental and physical energy! Please return inside to your temporary dwelling so you can rest for the night! I will pray for your journey before I depart. Go in peace knowing the hand of God is upon you!" Noah turned to face the city the way he was when James and Rachel walked out of the room onto the balcony. They went inside and shut the door; James turned to Rachel and said "Did we just get sent to bed by Noah?"

Rachel laughed and said "Shush! I am sure he can hear you!" James laughed too and said "I know, but I already felt young compared to him, but I can't remember the last time someone told me it was past my bedtime! Seriously, this is unreal. Noah is on our balcony praying, and we are going to find Noah's Ark!" Rachel said "No kidding, huh? This is really too good to be true!" When I was in heaven, one of the coolest things was when Noah sat and told everyone of the story of building the ark, the animals, the intensity of when the flood first started and how everywhere he looked for miles and miles was water."

"James, I don't know what we did to deserve all of this, but I am pretty ecstatic!" James replied "This is like living someone else's life! This is all so unbelievable! We just had Noah visit us in London of all places! The thing is, that everything we have seen and done this last week or so and what I have experienced over the last few weeks has been so intense, and such a whirlwind that it's easy to lose track of what's really happening here!" Rachel asked "What do you mean?" James answered "I am talking about the fact that Jesus is obviously coming soon! I think we both grew up knowing it could happen in our lifetime, but it's obvious, he's coming back very soon! We have friends who still are not saved. I get to meet Jesus! I am standing here loving a woman who has already been to heaven and met Him!"

"Sometimes it's hard to get a grasp on what's happening! Now your death seems like a distant memory, like it didn't happen. I don't want to take all of this for granted. I mean, God is working in our lives, first hand. As fantastic and amazing as it is, I am scared it's already becoming normal. I don't want to lose the perspective and gratitude to God for all of this. Raech, it's so weird but as much as it hurt when you died; I am now feeling guilty that I don't feel the intensity of that loss. The thing is, through the Angels; I was told that God would lessen my pain."

"I don't know, maybe I am babbling. I am just trying to say, I am so thankful that you are here, and I so thankful that God is letting us do these things, and witness his mighty power and miracles. I am just scared that I am not being as reverent as I should be about it. It's all become so matter of fact, like we expect it now." Rachel put her hand on his shoulder and said "Sweetie, I don't think that is a bad thing! I think God wants us to rely on Him. I think He wants us to expect His involvement in our lives day to day. I know how special you think all of this is, so I can't imagine that God would be disappointed with you getting used to this. I don't think getting used to this means it's no big deal if it stopped. In fact, if this stopped, I am sure you'd be really disappointed at that point, and desiring more, right?"

James said "For sure! Now not only do I want it, I do expect it! I'd feel lost without it and without God's daily physical impact in my life!" Rachel countered "Exactly! Kind of like the last few days traveling around, waiting to hear from God again. Each day that passed, the more we missed it, and worried that maybe our part of his plan was complete. I don't think there is anything wrong with getting used to his involvement like we have. In some ways, that's very much how it was in heaven. Of course perspective was different, but you didn't wonder, or hope, you just knew. We expected his loving whispers in our ear. We expected that feeling of closeness to Him."

"Right now, here, where we are, having these experiences; we are feeling the direct hand of God on us in a way, which maybe only a handful of people are experiencing! To expect that every day, is a good thing! Trust me sweetie!" James said "I know. Obviously you are right. I just hope that I am making Him happy. That is all I want! I know I can't mess things up. That said, things are just too important, and it's God! It's just important that he is pleased with my attitude. I sure hope He is!" Rachel said "I don't think you have anything to worry about! If you did, I doubt I would be here right now, or any of this would be happening to us, or to you!"

Rachel looked out the window on the balcony and continued "Look. He's gone." James looked outside as well, and felt a little sad that Noah had left. James tried to lighten the mood by saying "Well, we better get to bed like we were told!" Rachel laughed and said "No kidding! I'd hate to get grounded for disobeying! Actually, I am sleepy! We have a lot to do, and a lot to plan. Let's go to sleep, and figure it out in the morning. Sound good?" James replied "Yeah, definitely. Let's not worry about the alarm. Let's just get up when we have slept enough!" Rachel agreed.

CHAPTER 15

The next morning, they woke up feeling very rested, and very motivated! Rachel said "Any ideas where we should start?" James said "I had some dreams last night." Rachel interjected "Oh? More details?" James said "Not exactly. They weren't like the visions I have had, and not quite as detailed, although very real. It seemed like I dreamt most of the night that you and I were looking for the Ark, in a very thick mountainous area. We were doing a lot of rock climbing. There were no trails. We had to really hike these mountains. There was a third person with us, but I don't remember him having any equipment or climbing. He just seemed to be there with us."

"Anyway, I am thinking that factoring in my dream,

with what Noah said about this being physically demanding; we probably need to buy some serious rock climbing gear." Rachel said "Yeah, I already figured that! I assumed we were going to have to work our way to wherever the Ark is, and figured the thought of a helicopter flying us in wasn't realistic!" James knew she was serious but making fun of him at the same time "Okay funny girl! I am just saying, we need to get some supplies. We have to get full rock climbing gear, as well as whatever we will need to survive for days out there. I am sure we will be somewhere in the area of Mt, Ararat or the region of mountains that it rests in, and if I remember correctly there are at least fifteen peaks out there over 14,000 feet high."

Rachel was impressed "How do you know that?" James chuckled and said "Actually, I have done a little studying on this! I have always dreamed of finding the Ark! Never thought I would actually ever try to find it, but I always thought it would be fun to try, plus it was a good excuse to use some of these rock climbing skills we have! Originally I heard they guessed the Ark settled in the mountainous region of Eastern Turkey. Then I learned that although there is a Mt. Ararat; that Ararat is also a region of mountains that extends across the border into Iran. So, based on some things that I read, I kind of believed that the Ark was rested in a huge mountain range in Iran. However, we are being told to go to Turkey, so I guess I have my answer to that one!"

Rachel teased "Well Mr. Smarty pants, not quite as brilliant as you thought huh!" James said "Actually, I am surprised! I mean, Turkey is a much friendlier place to travel than Iran. Seems to me if it was in Turkey, well, I am surprised someone hasn't found it by now. I know there are a few who have claimed to have found it, but nobody has really proved they found it. If it were in Iran that would be a lot scarier place to go exploring and looking without an army to back you up. Iran is a Muslim nation, so not only do they hate Christians and Americans, but they absolutely don't want anyone to discover something that makes the Bible look more reliable and accurate. Turkey has Muslims, but they have Christians, Roman Catholics, and have a lot more tourism as well."

Rachel could not resist the opportunity to tease James saying "I didn't know I was married to such a worldly man!" James laughed and said "Yeah right! All book smart! You know me; I have few real life experiences!" Rachel rolled towards James and said to him "Well, truth be told, I am impressed! I am also completely in love with you, and am so thankful I am here with you!" She leaned into him and kissed him. They kissed and held each other for some time enjoying the touch of each other. After they finally were ready for the day, they went to a nearby restaurant for brunch and to make some plans.

James asked Rachel "Do you think we should load up on supplies before we leave or do you think we can get what we need in Turkey?" Rachel answered "I know they have everything here; what kind of shopping do you think they have in Turkey?" James answered "I don't know. I would assume they have plenty of shopping there, but I don't know anything about it. I hate lugging a whole bunch of stuff across the world if we can just buy it there, but I hate taking a chance on not getting something or not getting exactly what we want" Rachel responded "Well there is your answer! Why take a chance? Let's do our shopping here where we feel free to move around the city, and make sure we get what we need!"

They decided they would spend the day shopping for

supplies and researching Turkey, and fly out the next morning. James said "I have never heard of Sanliurfa, so we are going to have to see if it's a major city, or a town. I am guessing we can't fly from London to Sanliurfa, so we will have to figure out the best way to get there. I am sure that will be easy enough to figure out at the airport." Rachel agreed "So to record this, I suppose we need to get a camcorder and camera?" James said "Yes, I can't think of any other way to really record the event. Too bad I didn't think to bring our cameras from home when I left. We should take lots of pictures, and record various parts of the hike and then of course as much as we can, the ark itself. I think videoing some of the surrounding area and the trek to where the Ark is a smart idea so nobody can refute what we claim or say we staged it or something like that!"

They spent the rest of day buying all the supplies they need for an intense mountain climbing adventure. They bought two digital cameras, a camcorder and camping supplies in case they stay out longer than they planned. They were concerned about being weighed down by their supplies. They packed as light as they could, but they took what they needed. The rocking climbing equipment, cameras, clothes, sleeping gear, and food were all necessities. They were very excited for the next day to arrive! Rachel said "This is so cool, in such a short period of time we have gone from America, to Europe, and now to the Middle East! I can't wait to get going tomorrow!"

"Actually, I am excited to go rock climbing! As you know my last experience on a mountain wasn't such a good one, so I am looking forward to making amends!" James groaned and said "Raech! You are killing me! That is the last thing I want to think of!" Rachel laughed and said "Don't worry babe, it's not like I am going to die again!" James groaned again and said "You are torturing me!" Rachel followed with "I thought you said it was becoming a distant memory!" James shot back "Yeah, and I would like to keep it that way!" Rachel countered "Apparently you can dish it, but you can't take it!"

They had an early dinner and gathered everything together, so they could get up at a decent time and check out of the hotel, and head to the airport. Once at the airport they learned they were going to have to fly into Istanbul, Turkey, which is the upper Northwest part of Turkey. From there they would have to fly a local airline to the Southeast region to an airport about 35 miles from Sanliurfa. After some grueling flights, they found they were unable to rent a car, and had to pile into a bus that operated as a taxi service taking groups from the airport to various towns and cities in the area. They were exhausted but delighted that Sanliurfa surprisingly resembled some sort of modern civilization.

They discovered a very Americanized hotel and they immediately checked in. They had no idea how long they would be staying in the area but they figured it would be nice to have a base and to not have to lug around their stuff all day. Just before dark they decided to head back to the hotel. They had no idea what to expect from the locals, so thought playing it safe made sense. They decided to get some sleep, and go exploring the next day, including finding the cave where Abraham was born. They had some dinner, before lying down in bed to watch some TV and relax. Rachel laid her head on James' chest, and both were asleep within two minutes.

James awoke in the middle of the night and reached for the control to turn off the TV. As he started to click the TV off; he noticed someone was standing in front of the bed. His eyes were blurry, so it was hard to make it out who was in the room when he heard "Brother James, it is me Elemone! I apologize for startling you! I bring you good tidings! "James whispered back "It is good to see you again!" Elemone responded "Your works are delighting the Lord! Your faithfulness brings honor and glory to the God of all creation, and He loves you very much! James, my brother, and friend, you are not alone in this journey! In addition to the help of your wife, you have Angels like me to guide you; you have the hand of God upon you! Goodnight dear James!"

James turned off the TV, and kissed Rachel's forehead. She was still lying with her head on his chest. He quickly prayed to God "Lord, thank you! I do not deserve any of this, but you keep blessing me! I know this is so wrong to say, but I can't imagine heaven being much better. My life is perfect. You are amazing, and I love you so much! Goodnight Lord. Thank you! In your Son's perfect name, Amen! James kissed Rachel one more time, and immediately fell asleep.

When they were getting around in the morning James told Rachel of the visit from Elemone. Rachel said "That is really cool! There is no doubt God has his hand on us right now! These are exciting times! I know we have an advantage, but can you believe there are people who continually reject God?" James responded "I sort of get it with people like Ahmed. I mean, he has been raised his whole life where that belief system is more important than air and water. What surprises me though, are the people who really don't choose anything; either rejecting the notion of a creator, or thinking that any sort of belief in God is okay. There are so many fulfilled prophecies and proof of the God of the Bible. I am just so thankful that God has blessed us the way he has!"

Rachel said "Amen to that! So, are you ready? Ready to go see the cave where Abraham was born, and to find out what where we go from here?" James responded "Absolutely! I am very excited! I think this is going to be by far, our most exciting assignment yet! Saving the president rocked! But this…this is Noah's Ark!" Rachel agreed "I look forward to when we go to heaven, for good this time; finding out how many people accept Christ as a result of this historical find! I wonder how many people will literally just drop to their knees realizing that the God of the bible is true and His word is true!"

James said "No kidding! You know, there are people that

to this day still believe that the story of the Ark was simply a parable or some symbolic story! Imagine the surprise they are in for! In a matter of days, or a week, this story is going to be all over the place!" Rachel countered "Think about this! Whether its days or months or years after the Ark is found by us, Jesus will come back for his faithful believers. You would think those two things alone would be more than enough to convince every single person on the planet of God's divine plan!"

James said "That is going to be a lot for the world to digest! That is just the beginning! The Tribulation sounds like a scary time! I am guessing you and I will be leaving with Jesus when he returns, but I wonder if that will be it for us here, or if God will send us back to keep fighting for him?" Rachel answered "I seriously doubt we would be coming back! I think God's wrath should be enough to get their attention! But you never know! I hope to serve God here until the very end, or as long as he will let us!" James said "Me too! For sure!"

James and Rachel left their hotel room and went down stairs to the front counter in the lobby to find out if anyone knew the directions to the cave Abraham was born in. They were happy to find out that they were only 10 minutes from the cave. They decided to walk, so they could get a feel for the area. When they arrived at the cave they did not know what to expect. Abraham's birthplace had been made into a tourist area, for all to come and see where Abraham was born. They found the history fascinating but were getting discouraged after wandering around for over an hour before they heard an excited voice exclaim "James....Rachel!"

They turned around to see their new friend Jeremiah greeting them! James yelled "Jeremiah! What are you doing here?" Jeremiah laughed and said "The same thing you are! I was told to greet you here!" Rachel greeted Jeremiah with a hug and said "Hello Jeremiah!" She then suggested to the guys "Do you guys think we should get out of here and go somewhere private to talk?" They agreed with Rachel and went back to the hotel where they could have some privacy.

When they arrived inside their room, Rachel asked "So God told you to come visit us?" Jeremiah responded "Well, actually, an Angel of the Lord came to visit me. First he told me that I was to go to some tribes in Africa that you probably have never even heard of to spread the Gospels to the four corners of the Earth. It was incredible the power and conviction with which he spoke!" James interjected "Yeah, I will never get used to hearing them tell me God's plans or intentions with such authority! Talk about intense!"

Jeremiah continued "No kidding! Well, he explained to me where I was to go, and what my assignments are. He told me who I was allowed to tell these details to and of what was happening, and nobody else! He explained that my works are part of fulfilling the prophecy 'But you shall receive power when the Holy Spirit has come upon you; and you shall be witnesses to Me in Jerusalem, and in all of Judea and Samaria, and to the end of the earth'. He explained that I am able to put together a team for this purpose. Obviously outside of you two, the people on my team are the only ones I am able to tell of these details. Anyway, he told me where to go, but that I was supposed to let most of my team go on to the first tribe, to set up, but that I was to stop here in Sanliurfa at the birthplace of Abraham to meet you two!"

"He went on to instruct me to keep one of my team members with me, but to not take him with me to birth-place of Abraham. I really don't understand that part, but needless to say, he is not with me." Rachel asked "Where is he?" Jeremiah answered "Actually, he has family in the area, so he is visiting with them. He is very thankful for our detour so that he can see some brothers and sisters he has not seen in many years. Praise God! Although, his family would probably be very disappointed to know that he became a Christian five years ago. His parents are devout Muslims, so he is torn on what to tell them. He really wants this to be a happy reunion. Perhaps you two can keep him in your prayers?"

They both agreed. Rachel asked "Why are you supposed to meet with us?" Jeremiah chuckled and said "I am kind of hoping you can tell me! I was told you two are going on an historic journey, and that I am supposed to show you the way. He said my expertise will be of great importance to you, as well the experience of Yimad." Together James and Rachel asked "Yimad?" Jeremiah said "Yimad is my friend. He is the one I brought with me who is with his family right now. Anyway, so what are you two up to? Why are you in Turkey?"

James spoke up saying "Well, believe it or not, we are charged with discovering Noah's Ark!" Jeremiah yelled "No way! I am so jealous! That is a dream of mine! I am so excited for you!" Rachel asked "How do you think you are supposed to help us?" Jeremiah said, I am almost certain I know exactly how to help you! I know where the Ark is!" James exclaimed "You do?" Jeremiah clarified his declaration "Well, I have a good idea where it might be. I think I know the area of where it should be! I did a lot of research a few years ago on this. Combining what I read in the Bible, along with some other accounts, I think it's in a Range of Mountains just past the Iranian border.

James gave Rachel a look of satisfaction; she couldn't help smirking back at him! Jeremiah caught there looks and asked "What is it?" Rachel spoke up saying "Mr. Smarty pants here and I were talking earlier and he told me he guessed the Ark to be on the Iran side of the border; but after we were told to come to Turkey, he figured he had guessed wrong." Jeremiah said "I would say it's a certainty that it's in Iran, especially since God knows my conclusions on this, and He has solicited me to help you. This is very exciting! You two have your work cut out for you though!"

"Do you have any idea how treacherous that mountain range is?" James said "We have some idea" Jeremiah said "Well, there are at least fifteen peaks that are over 14,000 feet high! I know the area! But I don't know which mountain! You don't want to get lost out there! If you get lucky, it could be a three or four day trip. If you start searching in the wrong areas, you could be out there for over a month if your supplies will last that long!" Rachel spoke up saying "I have to believe that God will lead us in the right direction! If you don't know specifically where to go, I would think somehow we are going to get the directions we need."

Jeremiah said "I agree; I just want to make sure you both know what you are up against! I seriously doubt there are any hiking trails out there. Rachel, can you handle this kind of a grueling climb?" James spoke up for his wife "Actually, she is a terrific climber! We have all the equipment we need as far as that is concerned. Rachel and I can handle the climb. What scares me is packing light enough that we are not bogged down, but like you said, making sure we have enough supplies to last the duration of the climb." Jeremiah added "Well, you are fortunate, or I guess more appropriately, blessed that you do not have to worry about snow this time of year! In fact, it will probably be very hot during the day!"

Rachel said "I'll take hot over cold any day! Okay, so you know the general area of where the Ark is, but how far inside Iran? How do we get there? Can we just cross the border into Iran? If so, from where? I think those are the questions we need to get answered." James added "Yeah, I agree. I think getting to the mountain range is going to be our biggest challenge. How do we go about that?" Jeremiah answered "Well, I am guessing that is where the expertise of Yimad comes in! This is his home. He knows this region as well as anyone. I am sure that is why God had me bring him. I bet he will be your guide! I will go find him. You want to meet back here this evening? Let's say, after 5:00 p.m.?" James and Rachel agreed to meet just after 5:00 p.m.

Jeremiah left and came back that evening with his friend. Jeremiah had already given Yimad the details of the conversation he had earlier with James and Rachel. Yimad was very excited to be part of this exciting adventure! Before he was even officially introduced in his very heavy accent he said "I know how to get you in to Iran! We leave in the morning!" Everyone laughed at his enthusiasm and James asked "Are you sure it will be easy to get into Iran from here? Aren't the borders protected?" Yimad explained "Much of the border is heavy with mountains! Nobody wanting to go into the heart of Iran would choose to go that way."

"It would take a long time to get through the thick mountain range to get anywhere near civilization. Anyone trying to take that path to get to the main cities of Iran would probably run out of supplies or die of weather conditions long before they could get where they want to go. There are border points, but I know how to get us across." James inquired "Us? You are going too?" Jeremiah spoke up and said "Actually, all of us are going." Rachel asked "Are you sure? You have already been assigned a mission. Your people are waiting for you in Africa."

Jeremiah responded "After I left you two earlier, I went to find Yimad. When I stopped for some food, I had a vision of my own. I was told that Yimad and I are to escort you into the mountains until we are greeted by the guide who will take you to the Ark. Once the guide shows up, Yimad and I are to return the way we came, and go on to Africa to begin our ministry. So yes! We are all going!" Yimad spoke up again saying "If I may, I have a plan?" James said "Yes, please, by all means! What do you have in mind?"

Yimad said "My brother has a bus. He takes people back and forth all the time from Sanliurfa to towns and cities in the Eastern part of Turkey. Nobody would give a second thought seeing his bus go back and forth. He leaves in the morning at 6:00 am. We ride with him, until he drops everyone off that is going from here, to the East. He will then take us to where I instruct him. Do you have money?" James said "Yes, how much does he need?" Yimad said "No; money for horses not for my brother. Once he drops us off, we will rent or buy horses. It's quite a distance before we even get to the mountainous area."

"The horses can go in only so far. Once we get far enough in, we will have to tie the horses and walk or hike until we are greeted by the guide we are expecting to lead you the rest of the way. Jeremiah and I will make our way back to the horses and take them back. My brother will be waiting for us, so we can make our way back to Sanliurfa, and then on to Africa. After you find the Ark, and make your way back, I am afraid you will have to walk the path back that we came in with the horses. We can't leave the horses for you because if you aren't back within a day or two, which is unlikely, the horses are sure to die. Once you return to the town that we picked up the horses, you will need to wait and watch for my brother. I will make sure he waits in the area until at least 2:00 p.m. each day until you return."

"If you arrive after 2:00 p.m. you may as well find lodging and wait to meet up with him the next day. I would not try any other means to get back. If you are detained and it is discovered what you have found, you are sure to be killed." Rachel questioned "Killed?" Yimad answered "Yes, killed! Very few in this region want something that proves biblical events like Noah's Ark to be discovered. They know it's out there, but they worry that its find will have huge benefits for Christianity, and Judaism. Even the Jews do not want it officially discovered because they fear the backlash and retribution on them. Only the Christians would rejoice in such a find!"

Yimad continued "I would think it would be safest for you to make it all the back to America before you announce your findings to the world." James said "That is fine, that was our plan anyway. I have to say though, isn't this so cool? I mean, we are talking about finding Noah's Ark like it's a guarantee and almost like it's already happened! God is amazing! This is so much fun!" The group smiled but Yimad spoke up once again "While I agree that this is exciting, and no question God will be with you! Be prepared, these mountains are very nasty! Many have died in those mountain ranges. In fact, most that have gone in never came out!"

"I have no doubt that God will protect you, but unless God or one his Angles is going to float you to where the Ark is, and gently set you there, I would prepare for something more physically challenging than anything you have ever experienced! During the day you will be so hot you wish you could wear nothing at all and will be desperate to escape the rays of the Sun, and at night it can get so cold that you won't have enough clothes to keep you warm. You must drink lots of water; in fact I would start tonight! You don't want to get dehydrated! You definitely don't want to get sick while you are out there!"

"If you are okay with all of that, be ready with your gear outside of the hotel tomorrow morning at 6:00 am and we will take off. Sound good?" James said "Yeah, I think all of that makes sense. Jeremiah, what about you?" Jeremiah confirmed "I already talked to Yimad about this on the way over, and I think this plan makes the most sense. I think it's a sound plan, and I am very excited for you! Tomorrow you begin an incredible journey to see one of the most incredible things ever built by man, with the help of God! This is truly a mighty blessing from the Creator of all things!"

Yimad and Jeremiah left so James and Rachel could get to bed right away to rest up for a grueling journey. The next morning they walked outside about 10 minutes before six and the bus carrying Jeremiah, Yimad and his brother were already there. They loaded their gear and boarded the bus ready for a bumpy five hour ride. Rachel was relieved that there were not any soldiers or people with weapons on the road. There were people on the road the entire way. They would intently stare at the bus as it would go by, most of them hoping the bus would stop to give them a ride. Yimad's brother Yemish would not even slow down. He kept his focus straight ahead, and stayed to the task at hand.

After they dropped off the few passengers that were picked up in Sanliurfa they arrived in a dusty looking set-tlement town. They grabbed their gear from the bus and hopped out. Yemish drove off without saying a word. Yimad saw the look of surprise on James face and leaned close to James to whisper "It is better if we give the appearance that we are merely passengers on his bus, rather than being to-gether. It keeps him and his business safe and doesn't draw any undue attention to us! Stay here while I go get some horses. The other three quietly chatted while Yimad went off to negotiate a transaction.

James quietly said to Jeremiah "Yimad is quite the leader isn't he?" Jeremiah responded "Actually, this is the first time I have seen him quite like this. I think he is in his element here. Truth be told though, he did serve in the Turkish army, and from what he told me, he was some sort high ranking commanding officer. He is a great guy go though! I trust him implicitly!" James followed up with "Oh, I do too! I think there is no question he is the right guy for this adventure" They saw Yimad returning without horses.

Jeremiah said "No luck?" Yimad said "I had to do some serious negotiating, but I got us four horses. James, I need two thousand dollars." James shot back "Two thousand dollars? It costs two thousand dollars to buy four horses?" Yimad replied "No. It's costing that much to rent four horses. This is a deal actually! They saw us arrive, and knew you and your wife are Americans. They figure you are rich. Originally they wanted five thousand dollars. I was able to convince them you are not rich. Also, if we do not return the horses by tonight, they are going to want another two thousand, but this will not be a problem. But we need to load up and get going!"

The four moved along at a good pace. They only had to go about an hour longer before they reached the base of the mountain range. They were able to keep up a decent pace even while traveling along the base of the mountains. About 45 minutes into the mountain range it became increasingly bumpy and the horses were becoming agitated having to move along the slippery rocks. They could see just ahead it was going to be time to start doing a little hiking by foot. They found a place to secure the horses and began to unload the gear.

As Rachel was putting her gear on her back Yimad said "Rachel, please, let Jeremiah and I carry that. We will carry all the gear until we meet your guide. You two need to preserve your energy and health. You have a big trek ahead of you!" James kept one of the small packs on his back, but Yimad and Jeremiah carried everything else. They were now in the thick of the mountains. There were mountains in every direction; it began to feel like they were in a valley. The sweltering heat was bouncing off the rocks, and they were sweating through their clothes. "James asked "Are you two okay? You are completely loaded down. May I carry something?"

Jeremiah said "I am okay James! Remember, you are going to have to carry all of this for days; we have barely been doing this for an hour. We are fine!" Yimad said "That looks slightly concerning! Look ahead!" Rachel said "It looks like it dead ends up there. We are going to have to climb up!" Jeremiah said "Do you have enough gear for all of us to climb?" James said "We really don't; that may be where we will have to part ways." Jeremiah said "I really don't want to head back until we see whoever it is that God is sending to take you the rest of the way! I was told in my vision that when we meet your guide that will be point we are to part ways and head back. Seems to me; any variation to that is not being obedient!"

Rachel said "I don't think we have to worry about that! Look up there in that crevice to the right. That looks like…." James exclaimed "Noah!" Jeremiah said "For real? Is that really the Noah?" Rachel said "Yes! Is he really to be our guide? This is completely unbelievable! Noah himself is going to guide us to his Ark!" James looked over at Yimad and he had tears streaming down his face. He asked Yimad "Are you okay?" Yimad said "This is a happy day! God is so good! Jeremiah told me of some of his experiences seeing visions, and his one visitor. I prayed to experience something like this myself!"

As they approached Noah, he said to them "My brothers and sister! Today we gather to accomplish a most important part of the Heavenly Fathers plan! Thank you Jeremiah and Yimad for being obedient and guiding our friends out here. You have friends in Africa waiting for you! Your task there is equally important!" Jeremiah said to James and Rachel "This is where we part ways! I will pay close attention to the TV for news of this great discovery!" James said "I am very excited and optimistic about your mission as well! Think about it! You are going to be largely responsible for witnessing to the parts of the world that has not received the good news of the Gospels!"

Jeremiah said "I have not ceased thanking God for including me on this excellent journey since the moment I first found out about it! To think that I could not even see until a couple of weeks ago, and now here I am in mountains with some dear friends, and Noah of the Bible! God is blessing me in ways I never thought were possible!" James turned to Yimad and said "Thank you so much! God obviously knew what He was doing when He told Jeremiah to bring you along! You have truly made what would have been nearly impossible for Rachel and me actually very easy!" Yimad responded "You are more than welcome my brother in Christ! I would do anything that God asks of me, gladly!"

Jeremiah suggested that they pray before he and Yimad turn back. They gathered to pray, and Jeremiah asked if Noah would join them. Noah responded "Anything that brings glory to God would be my honor to participate in!" Noah joined the group and Jeremiah asked Noah if he would like to lead the prayer. Noah said "Again, I would be honored!" Noah bowed his head as did the rest of the group. James and Rachel held hands while they prayed. No one was sure whether they should touch Noah or not, so they just stood there as he began to pray.

"Father in Heaven, we Love You, and seek to bring glory and honor to You in all that we do! You are the creator of all things, the beginning and the end. Oh, how that means so much more today as you are ready to bring an end to this age. We thank you that evil will no longer be present. We thank You that everywhere we turn and look will be other brothers and sisters who love You as much as we do! Lord, Father, I ask for protection for my new friends here. I ask you that you protect and bless them as they do Your work! Their obedience shows that their love of You is genuine! Thank you for allowing me to once again be part of something that is so impactful on this world, and will be known for all eternity!

"Lord, even though Christ came thousands of years after my time; thank you for allowing me to accept him as my Savior as well. You are so powerful and almighty that you have been able to weave people together from different generations for Your good! We love You, and will love You forever and ever! Amen!" Jeremiah thanked Noah for leading the prayer and hugged James and Rachel Goodbye. Yimad shook hands with his new friends, and began to hike back towards the horses.

James and Rachel took the opportunity to drink some water as they prepared, for what looked like a very intense climb. Noah began to speak "Friends...you have a two and half day journey ahead of you. The first leg of your trek begins here. Look up this cliff wall in front of us. You must first climb up and over that wall to get to the point where we can make our way towards the ark. I will be waiting for you there. Do not forget, God is with you at all times! Go in peace and know the victory is already Gods!"

They took out their rock climbing equipment and helped each other getting strapped in. James then helped Rachel with her gear and loaded himself up with the rest of the backpacks and gear. James leaned forward to kiss Rachel on her cheek as he asked "Are you ready? Are you sure you can do this?" Rachel said "I know I can do it! I am nervous though! You know, my last experience on a mountain wasn't such a good one!" James did not like hearing that but had to remind her "Well that said, these mountains make that mountain back home look like a kiddy slide!"

Rachel said "I am teasing….sort of! Actually, I am ready! I am very excited! God didn't bring me out here to fall off of another mountain! We better get going; we aren't doing ourselves any favors by standing around!" They began to secure their equipment into the mountain wall as they climbed up the steep jagged mountain wall. They had climbed together so many times before; they performed great as a team. They alternated their way up the wall giving each other the next belay station to make progress all the way to the top. Just about an hour after they began to climb they made it to the top of the first wall, which was almost three hundred feet high.

As they made their way over the top Noah greeted them "Well done children of God!" James and Rachel looked beyond Noah and for the first time understood what was ahead! They thought they were surrounded by mountains before! James said "Wow! This is scary! I thought being in the ocean made me feel small! These mountains don't end!" Noah said "Fear not! I will guide you! You will not climb a single mountain wall or hill that is not necessary and the most direct path to the Ark!" Noah pointed diagonally from where they were looking and said "See in that direction, count two peaks over. On the other side of that second peak is where the great box is located! From here, you need to make your way towards that first peak."

"You will not make it to that peak before dark, but you can make plenty of progress before you make camp for the night. Head that direction and I will be there waiting for you. Once you get there, I will show you where to rest for the night. For much of the next two hours they felt like they were traveling down a mountain. They did not need to use their equipment very much because they were not climbing many steep walls. They could tell there were plenty of steep walls upcoming, but for now they enjoyed the break from intensity of feeling like they were hanging off the mountain. They had completely soaked through their clothes with sweat, and they were not very comfortable at all.

Fortunately, their excitement and enthusiasm for the task at hand outweighed their discomfort. As they walked up and down the rocks, and hill formations they spoke of what it will be like to find the Ark. Rachel became very quiet in a way that James knew she had something important on her mind. James asked "What is it?" She said "I miss my parents! All of a sudden I just had the weirdest feeling that while I am out here climbing mountains doing something so incredibly special for God, my parents are missing me, sad that I died. It just seems so strange, doesn't it? I mean, why am I thinking about it now?"

James agreed "It does. I know this doesn't compare, but I had a similar feeling." Rachel inquired "Tell me about it!" James said "Well, the truth is, as I told you before, I was lost without you! I think a lot of our friends and family were genuinely worried for me. My boss literally told me to get out of the office. He knew I wasn't ready to go back to my life the way it was; not without you. Well, I haven't really been calling anyone! Nobody has heard from me. They know I left to be alone and get some clarity and get over it so to speak, but I know they are worried about me."

"I am sure they still are, especially having not heard from me. So now, here I am with you again; loving you just like before, even making love to you, so incredibly happy, in fact even happier than before, and to them, you are still dead and I am still mourning your loss. I know how your parents feel is even stronger and more of an issue, but I have a good idea where you are coming from on that." Rachel said "Yeah, and I know we shouldn't feel bad, because this is all of God for God himself! This is an incredible blessing! I just miss them, and I hate knowing that they are so sad."

James tried to reassure her "Raech, they will never stop loving and missing you! But remember, that last time we spoke to them; they seemed very relieved at what I was able to tell them. Another thing too; I don't know if Jesus is coming back in months, or years, or whatever the plan is. Regardless, it's not too far off. Soon Jesus will be back to take them and all of His believers to heaven, and they will see you again! I know you miss them. I miss them too."

There was little the two of them enjoyed more than

spending time together. They never were at a shortage of topics to discuss. As a result it occurred to them how fast the time flew while they were hiking and talking. James pointed out "I don't think the Sun will stay up for another hour! We have made a ton of progress! I bet we see Noah again pretty soon!" Rachel said "We have covered a lot of ground already! This hasn't been nearly as painful as I expected. Actually, it's been fun! I love you so much! You are truly my best friend!" James said "Thanks babe! There isn't a person on this planet I would rather spend time with and talk to like this! I love you too!"

About 45 minutes later as they worked their way up a hilly rock formation, they saw Noah waiting below. They approached Noah after taking about five minutes to work their way down to him. He gave them a very friendly greeting again, and suggested they prepare camp for the night. Noah said "You will want to sleep over there in that rock formation. It's basically a cave and will shield you from the elements." James smirked and said to himself "That is convenient! God is truly awesome!" Noah went on to say "I would avoid any sort of fire if possible; you don't want to attract anyone or any animals to you."

"I will return at sunrise to guide you on the next leg of your journey. You two have done very well, and have earned a restful nights sleep! May you find rest in the comfort and knowledge of He who rules in Heaven and who loves you, and will continue a good work in you!" Rachel said "Goodnight!" Then Noah took a few steps away and disappeared from their sight. James used supplies from one of the backpacks to make a bed for them. It was not the most comfortable bed because they packed so light, but they probably could have slept standing up if they had to!

Seemingly five minutes after they lay down to sleep, they woke up to Noah saying "Children, it is time to rise!" They woke up feeling very refreshed. Neither James nor Rachel felt like the entire night could have already passed, and yet both felt surprisingly refreshed and ready to go! As they gathered there supplies so they could resume their trek, they spoke of how rested they both felt. James said "Rachel this is amazing. I don't know if I ever slept that well before!" Rachel replied "I know! I don't even remember sleeping. I just remember waking up ready to go!" James inquired "Do you suppose God is refreshing us, and giving us extra energy for this?" Rachel answered "I don't know for sure, but it wouldn't surprise me, and it really doesn't make sense for us both to feel as good as we do."

Noah approached and said "It is time! Today, you will actually see the Ark!" James responded "Today? I didn't think we'd get to see it until tomorrow!" Noah answered "You will see it today, but arrive at its location tomorrow. You are making significant progress, and today will be no different!" Noah continued guiding James and Rachel all across the mountain range. At one point while they were marching toward another check point, Rachel said "I sure hope Noah is planning to guide us out of here as well, because I wouldn't have a clue on how to get back!" James said "Yeah, I really thought coming in we would be able to find our own way back; but these mountains are so thick. I think we could find ourselves wondering for days until we couldn't go anymore!"

They followed Noah all day long, up and down mountains and hills; sometimes needing their rock climbing equipment, other times not. They approached yet another spot that Noah had told them to go to, and Noah pointed up, and said "Look! Tomorrow, you will make your way up that mountain! You will go nearly all the way to the peak of that mountain. Can you see it?" James and Rachel both searched and searched with their eyes before James said "No, I don't see anything!" Noah pointed out what looked to be a mark in the mountain that had a slightly different color than the rest of the mountain. Rachel said "I can see that, what it is?"

Noah replied "That my dear friends, is the Ark that I built so many thousands of years ago! It barely sticks out of the mountain. One would not even know to think anything of it unless they were told like I told you; or unless they happened to be up there" James exclaimed "No way! This is amazing! Thank you Lord for this amazing experience!" James immediately took out their camcorder and digital camera. He gave the camera to Rachel and said "Why don't you start taking pictures and I will get some video coverage. We need to make sure that we don't film you or Noah, but let's start documenting this!"

They took pictures of the area, and zoomed in on the blemish up on the mountain side. When it was nearing dark Noah said "It is time to make camp, and prepare for to-morrows climb. Goodnight my friends sleep well!" Rachel commented "You know, Noah really isn't a man of many words is he?" James laughed "I think he is incredible! But you are right; he doesn't say a whole lot. I think he is just making sure we stay focused on the task at hand. I am so tempted to ask him so many questions about heaven, other old testament people, and God himself but I don't think I am supposed to."

Rachel joked "What about me? Noah may have been with God for a few thousand years longer than me, but I have been there too!" James laughed "Oh I know! But I already found out everything you know, you are just a rookie! I just want to ask the veterans from here on out!" Rachel had to laugh when she said "Oh thanks a lot! You know how to make a girl feel good!" James said "I am just teasing! You know that! I could sit here talking to you all night, but what do you say we get to sleep so we can wake up and go see the Ark?" Rachel agreed and the two went to sleep.

Once again, early the next morning they were greeted by Noah "Children, it is time to rise!" Again they felt refreshed and they were also very excited about what they were about to see firsthand, and knowing they were just a few hours from seeing the Ark had them very excited! This day was much more grueling of a climb. There were no trails and they had to use their rock climbing equipment most of the time. Again working as a team they worked their way up the mountainside. They took breaks on this day, so they could take pictures and record their adventure on the way up. They could not even see the Ark or the place it rested as they climbed up because the ridge that it rests on hung over where they were climbing.

They kept moving up the mountain towards the location of the ark; every so often they would hear Noah's voice offering encouragement. They finally reached the underside of the ridge and had to use strength and might to work their way from underneath to the top of the ridge. When they arrived at the top they were absolutely stunned at what they saw! James said "It looks like a lot of it is covered over by the mountain" Noah, who had a look of pride and satisfaction said "Time and weather have changed its appearance a bit from what it looked like when I built it. But this is it! This is the Ark that God instructed me to build! James already had their cameras out, and they began to take pictures and video the Ark and its surrounding area.

Rachel approached and felt it and said "I think it's petrified." Noah replied "Yes, much of it is. There are only parts that will you will able to walk inside but you can still get a feel for how impressive and massive it is! Looking back, I realize now how fantastic this was! So many in my hometown thought my family and I were crazy! Looking at this now makes me realize how out of place it must have seemed to them! God had a plan though, and I followed it!" Rachel said "It's enormous! I cannot see the whole thing, but it looks like it must be five or six stories high! How long is it?" Noah answered "God instructed me to build it 450 feet long."

Much of it was in the mountainside. There were pieces and fragments strewn on the ground where harsh weather had affected it. James found a few small pieces and put them in his bag, then looked to Noah and asked "Is this alright?" Noah said, yes, by all means! Whatever you need to do, to prove to the world that this is real, please do!" James asked "Where can we go inside?" Noah said "This way, I will show you." They found an opening and walked inside. Rachel exclaimed "This is incredible! I cannot believe we are walking inside "Noah's Ark!" Noah stated "I know that is what everyone calls it, but I always thought of it as God's Box."

James filmed as much as he could with the digital camcorder. The Ark was very dark inside and difficult to see but he recorded as much of the inside as possible. The rear of the ark, was sticking out from where they climbed up from the side of the mountain. They made their way around to the other side of the ridge so they could see the front of the ark as well. It looked absolutely magnificent! A gigantic boat on the top of a mountain! Rachel had tears streaming down her face as she said "I remember when I was a little girl in Sunday school hearing the story of Noah's Ark! Here it is, and here you are Noah! These blessings are just too much!"

Noah said "Child, your Father in heaven loves you! The biggest tragedy is missing out on the blessings that God has intended for you. Do not feel guilty for receiving exactly what God wants to give you! To receive blessings such as you are right now is nothing more than exactly what He wants for you! Through this blessing, He also receives glory! So many things are happening now, and will continue to happen because God does love his children, and wants them to choose Him! If the world had not turned their back on the Creator of all things; many more blessings like this would have been experienced by so many more people through the years."

"Now God is using servants like you for His glory to show the world the truth! Additionally, the strong hand of the Lord, because of how just He is, has been, and will continue to be felt in a stronger way! Woe to the inhabitants of the Earth after Jesus comes for his true believers! The judgments that will beseech humanity will be unprecedented. Despite his wrath being felt by so many as a way of getting their attention, and to give them one final chance to choose Him, over the evil ruler of this world; many will curse Him instead. Again, turning their back on Him, and forever cementing their choice to remain apart from God, for all of eternity."

"My brother and sister in Christ Jesus! When I built this Ark with my family, it was a monumental task! It was an occurrence that was seemingly not appropriate for the times. Yet what was accomplished was only accomplished because of God's instruction, and help! Yet people would not believe. We built a structure so big, in the middle of land and nowhere near water that it's very existence defied logic and any form of common sense. God's hand was all over it! Yet people would not believe. This structure was so enormous; in fact too enormous for just a handful of people to accomplish, yet there it stood in all of its magnificence! Yet people would not believe!"

"The rains came, the storm grew stronger, and water levels were rising! I pleaded with them to repent and to turn back to God! They cursed me, and then cursed God, and still, they would not believe! As they were being swept away by flooding waters, and my family and I were safe aboard this incredible structure loaded with two animals of every kind, they still would not believe! In a matter of days, you will show the world your discovery! Many will marvel! People will have to come to terms with a gigantic ship, what they know to be Noah's Ark, in the middle of nowhere, thousands and thousands of feet high in the mountain tops."

"People of this generation have heard of this story since childhood. Some have dismissed it as a story, a myth, maybe even a parable. They have heard stories, sang songs, and enjoyed the great story of Noah's Ark. Yet, many do not believe! Now they will hear this story again, but this time in these modern times! This time they will hear that the Ark is real! In its dimensions, its size, and even its resting place. They will hear that once and for all, the story of the great Ark is true! Because of God working through you, many will be able to see it for themselves. Yet, many will still not believe! God in His infinite power and wisdom has allowed things throughout the corridors of time to happen, that are so much bigger than man can understand or even imagine!"

"He has allowed things to happen that the only explanation could be divine help, guidance, and in some cases intervention. Yet many choose not to believe! Here is another case. Here is another instance of something so monumentally huge that man himself is not capable of, and that truly, the only explanation is God. Yet, many will not believe! Woe to them! Woe to anyone who chooses to reject the one true living God! Thank the Lord though! Many will indeed believe because of these things! Many will choose to finally accept the truths of Jesus Christ, our Savior and Lord of all!"

"Some will wake up to see reports of the great Ark being discovered and they will fall to their knees begging God to forgive them for being blind for so long! The Ark's discovery for some will be a turning point in which they simply can't reject the creator of all things anymore! This event will come and pass! These later generations are so numb to the happenings of the world! The news of this great discovery will be worldwide and monumental, for seven days. Then those who chose not to believe will not worry or think about it anymore! Just like when Jesus will return for his followers! This will be the biggest event in the history of mankind!"

"Yet, after the dust settles on it, many will go be back to their lives as they knew them, not thinking about it anymore! Many will repent, and accept God's offer of grace and salvation! However, many will stay numb, and when the aftermath clears, they will not burden themselves with such thoughts anymore! Woe to them! Because shortly thereafter the wrath of God in the form of bowl judgments will begin, and their chances to continue to reject God will be decreasing by the day! God will not unleash his wrath in a fit of anger, or temper. What they fail to realize, is that He is reaching out to them in ways, even stronger ways, than they have previously seen to open their eyes and change their hearts!"

"This release of judgment and wrath has been foretold! This should not be a surprise! When a parent tells a child they will be punished for committing a certain act of disobedience; and the child commits the act and is punished, the child does not ask where the punishment came from! The Child knows! The Word of God clearly states what is to come! The judgments, the wrath, it has all been foretold!

When it comes, the children of this world will know where the source of it is! That is a loving God following through on His promise. What a happy day it will be for those that finally look up, and accept the gift of eternal salvation from their loving Father in Heaven!"

"My dear brother and sister…Go and reveal to the world this great discovery! At every opportunity speak of it! At every opportunity remind people of the Father that loves them! Witness to everyone about what you know to be true in your heart! For time is running out! The Christ will make his return soon! Amen! Finish recording your account of this discovery, and let us make our way back! It is time that the world knows the truth concerning an event written in the first few pages of God's divinely inspired word!"

CHAPTER 16

James and Rachel were mesmerized by the words of
Noah! He spoke with such conviction and strength; they
only hoped they could hold on to every word he spoke to
them! They resumed taking pictures and filming the Ark.
They wanted to make sure they could provide every possible
detail they could. Much of the Ark was in the mountain.
Although, there was more than enough exposed for them to
prove to the world this was indeed Noah's Ark! Their claims
would not be disputed! Just over two days later, Noah guid-
ed James and Rachel back to the point where he was first
waiting for them.

Noah said "James and Rachel, you have served your God
well! You can go back the way you came. Just follow the

straight path out of here that you came in, and you will have no troubles finding your way!" James said "Noah, I cannot begin to thank you for all of this! It has been an incredible honor to be able to spend time with you, and experience this with you!" Noah interjected "James, my friend; we have no need for extended goodbyes, for we will see each other soon in Gods eternal kingdom! We will be able to speak of these travels together many, many times over! I am as honored as you! Believe me; your travels will be spoken of at many dinner feasts served by God Himself!"

"James, Rachel, we can say goodbye now, knowing that God will allow us to meet again, very soon!" Rachel spoke up saying "Noah, thank you! Thank you for everything, goodbye!" Noah said "Goodbye children of God." He turned around and took a few steps out of their sight. Rachel said "All I can say is, wow! We just hiked more in the last six days, then we did our whole lives, and I am not one bit tired or fatigued!" James said "I know! I feel great! Thank God we do though! Because we still have a long walk ahead of us! Rachel laughed and said "I know, and I am not weary at all thinking about it, but I am so ready to be back! I want to show the world these pictures! I can't wait!"

As they hiked and walked over the small rocky formations James said "I have been thinking about the best way to get this news out to everyone." Rachel interjected and said "I am thinking we should just go straight to the news networks! Let's get back, and call Fox News and tell everyone!" James said "That might be the best way to do it. I just wasn't sure if we should go through a Christian Organization first or not. Rachel said "I don't see why. I think we should go straight to a major news network so that it is sure to be shown all over the world. Then we can call some of the Christian organizations and let them have copies too so they can use them on their websites and in churches and stuff like that."

James agreed that probably made the most sense. They were glad when they reached the point where they had originally tied down the horses with Jeremiah and Yimad. They knew they were going the right way. They also knew that they had reached the final stretch back to where Yimad's brother would be waiting for them. After a long walk across the desert, they would be back to the small town they bussed into. A few hours later as the sun was setting they arrived in the town and found a place to sleep for the night. The next morning they left the small inn and found an outdoor coffee house on the main road where they could sit and wait for Yimad's brother to bus into town.

They were delighted when they saw his green bus pull into town just before noon. They flagged him down, and loaded their gear on the bus. There were people on the bus that he still had to unload. As they boarded the bus he motioned his eyes as if to say "We can talk later." After he unloaded the last person, and started to head back to Sanliurfa he asked them "So? Was your mission a success? Did you find the Ark of Noah?" James moved up towards the front of the bus where Yimesh was driving and said "It was a huge success! We found it! It is absolutely spectacular! Yimesh, it is stunning to look at! I mean, it would be unbelievable if you were looking at it in a museum; but to see it resting on top of, and in a mountain top is truly remarkable!"

Once back in Sanliurfa they went to the hotel, and retrieved the rest of their belongings, and headed for the airport. They were fortunate to find a flight leaving the private airport heading back to Istanbul that afternoon. James asked Rachel "Should we fly to the nearest east coast city and show everyone there, or should we just go back to Los Angeles where we are closer to home?" Rachel answered "Either way is fine with me, but if we get to Los Angeles we can get our own car, and we will feel like we are a little more settled in." James agreed and 18 hours later they were at the Los Angeles International Airport walking to their SUV.

Once in the car James used his cell phone to get the number for Fox News headquarters in New York City. After being transferred several times he told the person on the phone "I just got back from a trip to the Middle East. I have found Noah's Ark, and I have many pictures and video of the Ark, and the surrounding area." James was invited into the studio to show his pictures and if true they would report on the news. James said "Actually, that is not how I want to do this. I want to have a press conference. You can host it, and all of that fun stuff. But I want a live press conference. I will be glad to show you all of my pictures and video in advance so you can verify its true, but I want this to be broadcast to everyone!"

They reluctantly agreed and told him where their studio is in the Los Angeles area. They said once the local affiliate there verified everything, they will put him on Live TV and give him a chance to present his findings to the world. He was asked if he would be willing to take questions and James responded "I will be glad to take questions about everything concerning the Ark, the mountains, the location everything; except about my team. There are members of my team that wish to remain anonymous. I will respect that. Nearly two hours later James was standing in front of a podium with the Fox News logo board behind him.

He and Rachel agreed that she should not go with him to the studio. They had checked into a hotel, and Rachel stayed in the room to watch James on TV. They also used that as an opportunity to save all the pictures and video on to James laptop. A Fox News newscaster said "We interrupt the O'Reilly Factor to bring you breaking news! We have a man in our California studio who claims he has found Noah's Ark and has proof! Before we hear from him, Fox News would like to make it clear that although we have reviewed his pictures and video evidence of the Ark, and even though we do believe it to be real, and authentic, Fox News cannot guarantee the details of this story until further investigating is complete."

"We now take you to Los Angeles to introduce James Mahody of Phoenix, Arizona. James, thank you for being with us tonight!" James responded "Thank you for having me! Let me start by saying that I have been a Christian my entire life. I have always read the stories of the Bible, and things like the Noah's Ark have always fascinated me. I have always had interest in being on some exploration team to find things like the Ark, but time and circumstances never made anything like that a real possibility."

"Recently, some things in my life have happened that made this possible. Combine that with the fact, that according to the Bible things are coming to an end as we know it! Jesus Christ is to return at some point to gather his believers, and that will mark the rise of the Anti Christ and the seven year tribulation that will follow, which will culminate in Jesus defeating Satan. I have always believed that for so many people who refuse to believe in the promises of Jesus Christ, that if only they had something of significance, something tangible to see or feel, they might believe!"

"I believe that God allowed me to find Noah's Ark for this reason! You have to understand, there is a gigantic boat resting near the top of a 15,000 foot mountain in the middle of a huge mountain range east of the Turkish border in Western Iran. That in itself should make one consider the claims about God to be true! Knowing the Biblical story of the Noah and his Ark, and the fact that the Bible tells us that the Ark came to a rest in the mountains, in that general part of the world, and that this is true, only adds to the reliability of the Bible as God's divinely inspired Word!"

"I have many pictures of the Ark, and its surrounding areas! I walked in the Ark! I was not able to walk inside the entire Ark because it was lying on an angle, and it was very dark inside. Additionally, much of the wood is either petrified or little pieces have fallen to the ground because of weather conditions over the last few thousand years. I have video footage of the Ark, and the surrounding area. I know after many tests of the pictures and video, their reliability and authenticity will be confirmed. You will see from the pictures and video that I have, that the dimensions of this huge boat are absolutely in line with the dimensions that God instructed Noah to build.

"People, please understand that the Ark was built so long ago because of a fallen world. Most had turned their back on God. God became disgusted with his creation, and wanted to start over. Here we are now, in a world in which, with so many things the Bible predicted thousands of years ago, are starting to happen like Russia and Iran are teaming up, with Iran threatening to eliminate Israel! We have talks of a one world government. They have invented chips to be inserted in animals and people for identification purposes and so many more things! We have more anti God sentiment than ever before. Once again, God is using the Ark as a way of getting your attention!"

"The Biblical account of the Ark is real, and this proves it! Please, accept Christ as your savior! Go to a church in your area and learn the truth! You probably already know the truth, but have been ignoring it for a long time! You are running out of time, you need to make a choice now! You do not want to be left here when Jesus returns for his faithful believers. I will be launching a web site designed to help you understand who Jesus Christ is, and His message of Salvation. There will also be pictures of the Ark for you to view. This site hasn't even been started yet, but if you do a search online for Noah's Ark, James Mahody, I am sure you will find my newly launched website in a matter of days. Any questions you have about giving your heart to Jesus will be answered there as well!"

"Thank you for giving me this time tonight to tell the

world of this discovery! This is obviously very exciting news, and should have a huge impact on everyone! I am very excited, and feel very blessed that God allowed me to be part of such an experience! A reporter in the room asked "How did you get into Iran? Did you have permission from their government?" James answered "No I did not. We had a guide that took us in from Turkey. It was a grueling hike, but we felt like we were in God's presence the entire time!"

Another reporter asked "Can you tell us what the Ark's condition is, and what it felt like?" James answered "Well, most of it looks completely in tact. But most of the wood has petrified. It is almost slick as you run your hands over it. You can see parts that were destroyed by weather, and there are pieces of wood fragments on the ground. I collected a few, and will turn them over for analysis. It is magnificent though! I wish I thought to take flashlights, so we could see the inside better." Another reporter spoke up asking "How can you make such claims? Even if you found something up there, how can you claim it's a boat! In the middle of mountains? That seems silly to me!"

"They aren't silly claims to me! How do you explain the moss growing on rocks up there? How do you explain what looked like petrified fish skeletons? Clearly there was a flood, and clearly that area was filled with water. That being the case, is it so silly to think a boat could have been in the area? All I know is that the Bible gives us clues. I followed them! With what I know to be guidance from God, I found it! I found a huge boat near the top of a mountain! I would encourage you though, before you are so dismissive about it, to figure out what the real truth is, and not what you have boxed yourself into believing is possible and might be true! Your soul depends on!"

"Thank you for giving me this time tonight! Thank you Fox News for interrupting your normal programming for this. Obviously this is historic and has huge implications for every person alive. Like I said, there will be a website to help people make sense of all of this. I am here for no other reason that to proclaim God's truth! Jesus has given me life, and blessings that truly shouldn't even be possible, if not for the Grace of God! Eternal life in heaven is real. Each and every one of us is going one place or another for eternity! Please, figure out what is real, and what isn't before you make your final decision! Goodnight!"

They wanted him to answer many more questions, but

James felt like God was telling him to excuse himself. James was ready anyway. As he left the studio, the people from Fox News were asking if he would be willing to come back on after he launches his website, and James agreed "I think that would be great! Thank you!" James left the studio and drove to the hotel to be with Rachel. This was the first time since she had come back he left and went somewhere without her. He was anxious to get back to hear what she thought of the press conference.

He walked in the room and she flew at him very excitedly! "James! That was great! You did so well! That was so neat to see you on TV like that! It was incredible, as you were talking, they did a split screen and were showing the pictures and video we took! It looked like a real documentary! It was so exciting! If that doesn't make people believe, I don't know what will! God is great!" James said "It was like a blur to me! I felt like I did okay, but I couldn't be sure! I do have some bad news though" Rachel questioned "Bad? What Happened?"

James said "Well, not bad, but, well anyway I had three missed calls from your parents while I was still at the studio. I am assuming they saw me." Rachel said "Of course they did! They thought you were here the whole time, they had no idea you left the country, let alone went to the Middle East! James, I am so excited. Seeing the Ark was incredible, and experiencing it. Tonight though, it hit home for me how many people are going to accept Christ as a result of this, and their souls will be saved! Babe, we did a good thing! You were terrific!"

Rachel's parents called again. James said "Okay, you need to be quiet, they can't hear you!" Rachel agreed and James answered his phone "Dominos Pizza, may I help you?" Rachel's dad said "If you became a pizza delivery man that would have been a lot less shocking than what we just saw on the TV!" James said "I know. I am sorry I didn't tell you. There has just been so much going on, so much that I have been unable to talk about. When I left, I had no idea I would be holding a press conference on National TV."

Rebecca spoke up and said "James, dear, we are so excited about seeing you on TV. That was some news report! But to go from needing to get away for a while, to leaving the country without saying anything. I know what you did was for God, and we couldn't be prouder of you! But this is really hard to understand, especially since we haven't seen you in a month! Is everything still okay? Can you give us some details yet?" James said "Listen, I know how hard this has been for you both. I am really sorry! I am going to come home tomorrow. How about I come over tomorrow night and we can sit and talk about things?"

John asked "James, how are you doing though? Are you coping any better about…everything?" James said "You know; it's so tough to answer that! I mean, in some ways yes, and in others no. I am not in the funk that I was in before I left, I can tell you that!" John said "I think we understand. After we spoke to you on the phone a few weeks ago, we were walking on clouds for days! But then we started feeling sad again. I am sure you know how it feels! The emotions go high and low. It does not seem like that long ago! I know you needed to get away, so you could escape the familiarity of Rachel; but for us, I think it is the opposite! We lost her, and with you being gone….well son, it just feels like we lost you too."

James said "I know, and I am sorry! You haven't lost me! I promise! I told you before how much you mean to me, and how you are my family, even with what happened. I love you both! Look, I am going to leave first thing in the morning. I will call you when I am getting into town and we can make a plan for me to come over later afternoon or early evening." Rebecca said "James, why don't you plan to have dinner with us, okay?" James said "That sounds nice. I love you both! I will see you tomorrow."

Rachel, of course, was crying. She said "They sound really confused. I have never heard them sound like that! All of this good news, and they are more concerned about how you are doing and handling things." James said "Yeah, I think they might think I have lost my mind a bit. Truth is, my heart isn't even in it keeping them at bay anymore! I feel like I should make them believe I am dwelling on losing you, but I just can't! Well, I will explain as much as I can to them tomorrow! Hopefully seeing me in person will reassure them that I am okay. Rachel said "Will you do me a favor?" James said "Of course, anything!" Rachel said "Make sure my mom packs you some of that dinner for leftovers! I miss her cooking!"

CHAPTER 17

The next morning James and Rachel took their showers and gathered there things together. They were ready to leave the room and check out of the hotel. As they were ready to walk out the door, James looked back at the room one more time, and saw someone sitting on the bed. James said "Rachel, we can't leave yet, we might not be going home!" She turned around and said "Why not…"as she noticed the man in the room. She continued "oh" and set her stuff down and walked with James toward the bed. The man just sat there looking at them seemingly very lovingly.

He finally spoke up saying "My name is Shaleem. I bring you good tidings today from the Lord! The Lord continues to be impressed with your servitude. You have brought him much Glory with your good works on his behalf!" Rachel said "Thank you Shaleem! We love God, more than anything! We are so blessed that he keeps looking to us to serve him! We are very grateful for everything!" Shaleem said "Yes and the Lord knows this! Your latest endeavor brought forth a beautiful song from the Angels! You will be able to hear this beautiful song yourself when your work here is complete!"

"I am here to present you with a blessing from your Father in Heaven. When you started on these missions, you were instructed that nobody could know of the details. Then at the appropriate time, the truth was revealed to his servant Jeremiah and eventually to Yimad. Nobody else was permitted to know! The Father has spoken, and now is the appropriate time for the daughters' parents to know the truth, and receive this blessing as well. James asked "Are you saying we may tell her parents the truth?" Shaleem replied "They may know the truth, and Rachel may enter into their presence!"

Rachel exclaimed "For real? I can see my parents again? They can see me?" Shaleem said "It has been said." Rachel literally fell to her knees crying and said "Lord thank you so much. Thank you so, so much! When I think things couldn't get any better or more exciting, they do! I love you so much Lord! Thank you!" Shaleem said "Your Father in heaven loves you too, very much! Because of your faithfulness and that of your husband many more will be in the kingdom of heaven!"

James knelt down to put his arms around Rachel and whispered in her ear "I love you! Thank God we are experiencing all of this together. God is truly amazing!" James helped her to her feet, and as they looked up, Shaleem was gone. James said "Raech, this is so amazing! This is such a relief! I am not a big fan of misleading your parents! Your mom is going to lose it!" Raech just stood there and finally said "This is too good to be true. Everything in me made myself not say anything when you were on the phone with them. I just wanted to yell out, I love you! It was so hard not to!"

James said "What do you say we get on the road? I think we have another reason to get back to Phoenix now! Rachel said "No kidding! I am so excited, let's go! About four and half hours later they were nearing their home. Rachel hadn't been home since before the accident. She said "Barely into town, and I feel home already!" James decided to call her parents and change the plan a little "Hi mom, it's me"

he said when she answered the phone. Rebecca asked "Are you making it back safely?" James said "Yes I am! I was wondering though if we could change the plan a bit."

Rebecca cautiously agreed asking "When do you want to get together?" James answered "Well, I am tired, and looking forward to settling in a bit. I am wondering, would you and John mind coming over to my house instead?" Rebecca said "Oh absolutely! That would be fine…" She let John know they were going to James house instead. She asked James "Would you like me to bring dinner with me?" James said "That would be great!" John took the phone and asked "James, would you like us to bring Rock?" James said "If you don't mind, can we hold off on that for a day or two?" John said "That would be just fine. He is welcome to stay here as long as you like"

Rebecca was back on the phone and asked "When would you like us to come over?" James said "I just need an hour to get in and get settled, so anytime after that is fine!" Rebecca said "That is perfect; we will plan in about an hour then." They said there goodbyes, and Rachel could hardly contain herself! She asked "Why did you change it our house?"

James said "Well, I am afraid we will give them heart attacks if we both show up at their door! I think it would be best for you to hide out in our room, and I will tell them the story, and let them know you are back, before you show yourself!"

Rachel agreed "I didn't think of that! They still might die when I walk in the room though!" James said "I think we have had enough dying, from you! We don't need anymore!" Rachel shot back "Oh more dead girl humor! You think you are so funny!" James said "Sorry! You know me, I can't help myself!" She said "Yeah, I know you alright! Hey! This is exciting! I get to hug my parents again today! James, it has really made me sad at times knowing their pain! Just to take away their sadness tonight, that is all I care about! God is so amazing. There is no doubt he loves us! Not that there ever was any doubt before! But when you go through what we are experiencing, it sure makes it obvious!"

Just over an hour later James was hiding Rachel away in their bedroom because there was a knock at the door. When he opened the door Rebecca gave him a huge hug, and would not let go! She said "We have really missed you James!" John gave him a big hug too and said "You know, we expected to see you pretty soon, but we weren't expecting to see you on TV!" James said, I know, I have so much to explain, huh?" John and Rebecca said at the same time "Yes you do!" James invited them to sit down.

They brought dinner in cooking dishes and Rebecca asked "Do you want me to prepare dinner now?" James said "Even as hungry as I am, I would rather sit and chat a bit before we have dinner if that is okay with you two?" Rebecca said "That is fine! Let me just put this stuff in the kitchen." They put the food in the kitchen and they all sat down in the living room to talk." James said "I am really not even sure where to begin." John replied "James, we are worried about you. We are not just concerned because you left the country like that, but the truth is we have no idea how you are doing! You lost Rachel, and then shortly after you took off for what turned out to be a long time."

"So we just don't know how you are dealing with things. We want to be here for you, but we don't want to be pushy either." Rebecca asked "Have you had any more visions?" James said "Yes I have. A bunch in fact" John responded "Are you totally sure they are from God?" James said "Yes, they are for sure from God!" John asked "Did God tell you to go find the Ark?" James answered "Well, God sent an

Angel to tell me that, so indirectly, yes, it was God." Rebecca's voice cracked as she said "James, these things just don't happen to people! I know you believe this, and I don't want to question you, but I am really worried about you!"

James said "Okay, listen; I need you to hear me out. Okay?" They both agreed and James went on to say "Okay, well, I mean really hear me out! I have a lot to say, and I need to get it all out!" At the same time they said "Okay." James continued "A lot has happened. I am going to tell you some things and some you are probably not going to initially believe, but I can assure you, I can and will prove everything I am telling you. You really don't need to worry for me, and you don't need to be skeptical! I promise everything is going to be okay and make sense to you!"

"So as I am explaining things to you, that you may not believe or understand at first, rest assured in the next ten minutes it will all make sense! Okay?" John said "Okay, tell us!" James said "After the funeral you know I started seeing visions. Sometimes they were dreams; other times they would happen while I was awake. I might get dizzy, or close my eyes, and sort of just be somewhere else; I would have a vision and then all of a sudden just as fast be right back where I was! At first it was terribly confusing, and then little by little I started to understand. In fact, when I decided to leave to get away to clear my head, I knew I was being told to go somewhere. I just didn't know where yet!"

"In fact I left feeling very confused. I kept getting instructions, and only parts would make sense to me. Before I left, I told you I had a vision and that I was told I couldn't talk about it. Do you remember that?" They both remembered and James went on "Well, I was specifically told that all of this was to remain between me and God, and whoever visited me. On my way towards the coast, I had a vision that led me to believe I was supposed to go to Newport Beach, California." Rebecca interrupted "Where you and Raech went on your honeymoon." James responded "Yes. Everything was very confusing and somewhat overwhelming!"

"Anyway, I am going to skip ahead a bit. I was told to go to many places. Remember when the FBI stopped some terrorists from killing the president a few weeks ago?" "John said, yeah, I remember that." James said "Well this is where it gets weird! I was the one who stopped the terrorists and notified the FBI." John exclaimed "What? Come on! How were you able to do that?" James continued "Well, there is more before I tell you that." Rebecca said "More? Could there possibly be more?" James said "There is."

"God sent Angels to tell me how to stop them. I was told to go to a church in Newport Beach where God used me to help a blind pastor regain his sight. He also sent Angels to tell me to go to London and help a terrorist to understand that accepting Christ is the right thing to do. From there he sent me to Turkey to find Noah's Ark." John in disbelief said "So you are saying that Angels took you to the Ark? That is how you found it?" James replied "No, actually I wasn't led by an Angel to find the Ark" John interrupted "You found the Ark on your own?"

James told them "No, I didn't find it on my own. Actually, it was Noah who led me to the Ark!" Rebecca said "Sweetie, come on, Noah has been dead for thousands of years. You are telling us that Noah came back to lead you to the Ark?" James answered "Actually, yes, I am telling you that! I wouldn't make this stuff up!" John responded "James, we would never think you would lie to us. But all of this is too spectacular to believe. I am sorry. Noah comes back from the dead to help you find the Ark? That is just crazy talk, I am sorry!"

James smirked and said "I know! This is all too good to be true! Listen, God has really blessed me through all of this! I have to tell you though; I was not alone in these endeavors. I had help" Rebecca asked "From other Angels you mean?" James said "No, I had a helper assigned to me. God sent someone to me who had also died, and had been sent back to be with me on these journeys." John asked "Who was your helper?" James said "Rachel!" Rebecca said "That is not funny James!"

James responded "Listen, I would never do anything to cause any pain. I can prove it too. I told you all of this to prepare you for my proof. I didn't want to startle you right off the bat. I am guessing by your reaction thus far you are startled for a completely different reason. But I assure you I am telling you the truth. Are you ready for me to prove this to you?" "John said "James, you need to do something fast to make sense of all this!" James said "Are you sure you are ready? I am very serious? Are you prepared to see a true act and miracle of God?" Rebecca said "James, you are scaring me, but anything to get this over with! I am ready!"

James looked at them, and paused. He was a little nervous. He then called out to Rachel "Rachel, would you please come in here" Obviously her parents were stunned when Rachel walked out of her bedroom to see her parents. She had tears streaming down her face when her dad jumped up and said "Raech is that really you?" Rachel was crying as she went into her dads arms and said "Yes Daddy, it's really me!" Rebecca screamed out "How can this be?" She stood to her feet. She walked over to Rachel and cupped her face in her hands and said "How could this be? I buried you! How can this be?"

Rachel said "I am so sorry to have put you through this! I did die, and I went to heaven. God has a plan, a wonderful plan! Jesus is coming back soon, and for whatever reason, God has blessed us with this is incredible miracle!" Rebecca grabbed Rachel and began to sob as she tried to get out the words "I have missed you so much! I love you so much sweetie. Thank you Lord! Thank you for sending my baby back!" John said "I just can't believe all of this! How did this happen? When did you come back?" James spoke up saying "On my way to the coast, I was instructed to go to a hotel in Newport Beach."

"When I got there, I was visited by an Angel who told me many things. When he left, Rachel was there to greet me! When I spoke to you by phone a few weeks ago, she was listening." Rachel interjected "It took everything I had not to say something. I could hear your sadness, and I wanted so bad to tell you I love you guys! I am so sorry you were hurting because of me!" John said "Rachel, baby girl, you don't...Oh, I am stunned. Don't you be sorry! I cannot believe I am holding on to you again! What happens now? How long are you here for?" Rachel said "I really don't know. I am sure I am here as long as God has a plan for me to continue doing things for him, but I don't know." James said "God is preparing the world for the second coming of Jesus. Things are wrapping up, soon!"

"He has been using us, and it sounds like others for that purpose. The point of finding the Ark was like I said on TV, to do something so bold, so obvious that unbelievers should and would finally give their heart to Jesus. John... Rebecca, I would encourage you to be prepared to have visions or visitors of your own. Maybe not, but so far, it seems like everyone that knows of what is happening, ultimately becomes a tool of God as well. After we went to the Pastor in Newport Beach, and helped him get his vision back, he was sent on his own mission trip to Africa to help spread the

Word of God to the last three percent of the planet that has not heard of Jesus Christ and the message of the Gospels."

Rebecca spoke up "Rachel I can't believe this is really you! You feel, and smell exactly the same! You are really are my baby girl!" Rachel looked to her dad and noticed the big tears streaming down his face. She said "Oh Daddy, are you okay?" John replied "Okay? This is the happiest day of my life! All in one, I get you back, and realize even more how much God loves us! He just wouldn't do this for us if he didn't. You know?" Rachel said "Dad, I have been in heaven, and trust me, you don't have any idea the depths of God's love for you! It's truly spectacular and there aren't words to described how loved you feel in his presence."

Rebecca said "Your Brother is going to be absolutely blown away!" Rachel said "Mom, you can't tell anyone! I am sorry! We were permitted to tell you, that's it. Everyone else must think I am dead. God has a plan, and we can't go against it, not even in the smallest way!" John said "Then we won't say a word!" Rachel said "Dad, I think if you do, I think I go back. That is not so bad for me, but then all of you will have to wait until Jesus returns before you can see me again! For real, you can't even hint to anyone about this."

John asked "What now? How long will you be home?" James said "We don't know! I have no idea when we are going to be given our next assignment. We are going to stay for a few days, but we need to go somewhere else pretty soon. We just can't take a chance that someone sees her. I'd hate to have someone come by and either see Rachel, or see "some woman" here that I have to tell them was someone else, and give them that bad impression. It's just not worth the risks." John asked "James, when you two leave again, may we go with you? We just got her back, we don't want to lose her again. It's going to be tough on us if you two are going to be gone for a long time."

James said "John…Rebecca, you both are welcome wherever we are! You should know that!" Rebecca said "Sweetie, thank you! I am so sorry we couldn't accept everything you were saying! It just seemed so….well, it seemed crazy to be honest with you!" James laughed and said "You don't need to apologize! Rachel and I marvel nearly every day how amazing our experiences are. We are literally blown away by what we see, do, and who we talk to! And yet, we have already experienced so many amazing miracles of God! Still, with each one we are caught off guard! I don't fault you at all! It has been really difficult for me to not share this incredible news with you, I am so thankful that tonight you can hold your daughter once again!"

John and Rebecca were both clutching on to Rachel as if they were afraid to let go! They spent the rest of the night telling of their adventures and how amazing it was to serve God in such an incredible way! Rachel added "It was always neat serving in the church, or donating for a good cause. But for God to give you an instruction and you follow it, and that the outcome is already determined, is such a rush! Can you imagine what it is like to be following Noah around the mountains and to see the very Ark that he built? We prayed with Noah! A group of us prayed and Noah led the prayer! This has been a whole new ball game!"

"James and I often talked about our relationship, and our love for each other. In the past we really talked about whether or not we were pleasing to God as a couple. He has answered us in so many ways! In heaven, I was given insight to the love that James has for me! I was also given insight to how you two feel about me. That is why not telling you crushed me so much! I am so relieved that you know, and that your pain is gone!" John said "They say a parent should never have to bury their own child. Oh, how true that is. But on top of what would be considered normal sadness and grief we lost not only our child, but a friend. Rachel, your mom and I have always cherished such a special relationship with you. To lose that day-to-day interaction with you was the most painful thing for us"

Rachel said "I know. I have always appreciated our relationship, but when I saw things from your perspective through Gods eyes...I completely understood why our bond was so strong! He even let me see how much you love James, and why so much of your love for James comes from how he treats me and makes me feel. The perspective was so amazing. If people could see these things every day walking around, I think there would be less fighting and issues among people. Knowing how the three of you truly feel about me, how could I ever want to have a single misplaced word with any of you? That just seems like such waste where so much love is present!"

It was getting late. They still had not even had dinner yet. Rachel reminded them "You know, it feels like a lifetime ago that I had your cooking! I am ready for some dinner!" Everyone laughed and James said "Rachel thinks the dead girl humor is a lot funnier than it really is!" Rebecca said "I think this is all still too new for me to enjoy jokes about your death! Maybe later I will find that funny. Much later!" The four enjoyed a nice home cooked meal, and caught up on so many things. Rachel had all kinds of questions about the family, and how they were doing. Her parents did not want to leave, but finally sometime after 1:00 a.m. they got up and made themselves go home, but not before making Rachel and James promise they would meet for breakfast in the morning.

The next morning firmed up their plans to meet for breakfast. They picked an out of the way restaurant, so they would not risk running into anyone they knew. While James was in the shower getting ready, Rachel was looking around their home, looking at pictures that she had not seen in a while. While she was looking through an album, she felt someone behind her. She turned to look and it was Kaleb. She immediately stood up and said "Kaleb! It is great to see you again!" Kaleb said "Daughter of God, it is good to see you as well! I come as usual, bearing news!" Rachel asked "What is it?"

Kaleb said "For your entire life you have honored your

parents as He has commanded. This among many other reasons is why God chose you to return for his purposes to fulfill His will. You have brought glory to God through your faith, marriage, and even in death, you continue to honor the Father who sent you. You have another assignment. Further instructions will be given at a later time. For now, you must flee to the East coast of your home country. You will be directed from there. You must flee before the sun sets on this very day! Also, my dear Rachel, you must prepare your parents for service to the Lord"

Rachel said "I don't understand, prepare them for what? They have always served the Lord!" Kaleb responded "They will have their own experiences through visions and dreams, just like your husband has had. Eventually they will have visitors from those like me, perhaps even me! It is time for them to receive their instructions to carry out the will of God. Meet with them this morning as planned, ready them for what is about to come, and then you and James need to depart. Another important victory awaits!" Rachel asked "Just so I understand, we can leave here anytime as long as it is before it gets dark? Kaleb said "As you have said."

When James finished getting ready Rachel told him

of her visit from Kaleb. James said "Your parents are going to be disappointed they can't go with us." Rachel said "I know, but at least it sounds like they are going to get some adventure of their own! Hopefully that keeps them busy and focused." James asked "So we can go anywhere on the East coast?" Rachel said "He wasn't specific. Where are you thinking?" James answered "Either New York City or Florida. Your choice!" Rachel said "Oh aren't I special; I get to choose! I don't get the feeling we are going to have much time in either place, but let's go to New York City. At least we can say we have been there, even if it's only for a day!"

They met Rachel's parents at the restaurant and enjoyed a nice meal together. Rachel wanted to wait until the end of the meal to tell her parents what Kaleb said. However, Rebecca and John wanted to discuss some plans they had for them all to do together. Rachel told her parents "I had a visit this morning from an Angel. James and I have to leave this afternoon." John said "Already? Where are you going?" Rachel said "For now New York, but that is just a stop over until we get further instruction."

Rebecca said "May we go with you?" James spoke up saying "Actually, we don't think you are supposed to." John said

"Why not? Were you told we can't go?" Rachel said "No, but I was told to prepare you and mom to start having your own visions and dreams, and perhaps even visits from Angels." Rebecca asked "Why would that happen to us?" James said "It sounds like you are going to have your own mission to go on!" Rachel said "We think God has a plan for you to go out like we have, and do something for Him! These are indeed the end days, and it doesn't seem like there is much time left before Jesus returns!"

John said "Are we equipped to do such bold things God?" Rachel said "Daddy, you and mom are no less capable than James and me if you have God leading you! God has had us do some incredible things, but after it's over, each one turned out to be pretty easy. It's all God! All you have to do is trust Him, have faith, and do what you know you are supposed to do. Rebecca asked "How will we know?" James said "You remember how confused I was at first?" John spoke up and said "Yes! I remember that very well, and that is what scares me!" "James said "But that is the point. If you don't know what to do, you don't do anything. Or you do exactly as much as you know you should."

"You go as far as God tells you to go. You go only as far

as you know you are supposed to! Trust me on this, God will reveal it all to you! Truly, it is all God too! He won't have you do anything He isn't capable of doing through you!" Rachel interjected "Mom, Dad this is a huge blessing! Really, when you do something for God, that you absolutely know He wants you to do it…Well, it's incredible how that feels! It's one thing to help a cause that you think he might want you to be involved in. It's another to travel from one place to another, meeting and affecting people all because He told you to do it! These are special times we live in! They are scary for some, but incredibly special for us!"

They all walked out to the parking lot, and Rachel promised "Obviously now that you know about me, you can call anytime! We will stay in touch as well! Let us know what you are told to do; I am so curious! I want to know exactly what God sends you two to do!" Rachel's parents hated saying goodbye, but they did. James and Rachel quickly went home to pack some things. They had just finished unpacking everything the night before and now it was time to head back out. While Rachel was getting some things together, James took out his laptop and reserved a pair of tickets from Phoenix to Newark, New Jersey. This was the only flight they could get without a three hour layover somewhere.

CHAPTER 18

Once they arrived in New Jersey they rented a car and drove to New York City. It was not a very long drive and they enjoyed seeing the area. Rachel was very excited when she could see the Statue of Liberty as they drove in. Rachel said "If we have any time at all, I'd like to go see the Statue of Liberty during the day!" James said "I am hoping we have time to see some of the sites before we have to leave. Hopefully we can spend at least tomorrow seeing the area!" They found a nice hotel right in Times Square and checked in.

Once they were settled Rachel said "It's still early, let's get out and see some things!" James was just as excited saying "I think the Empire State Building stays open until eight or nine; we still have time!" The two spent the evening checking out the sites walking around Times Square and visiting one of the seemingly hundreds of TGIF restaurants in the area. They woke up early the next morning somewhat relieved they did not have a new visitor sending them on their way yet. They spent the entire day seeing the tourist spots in the area; Statue of Liberty, Ellis Island, United Nations Building, Central Park, and even had time to go to Bloomingdales.

That evening, they had a visitor waiting for them when they returned to their room. All he said was "Your presence is requested in the land of God's chosen people. Depart tomorrow!" Then he disappeared. James looked at Rachel, and she asked "Did he just tell us to go to Jerusalem?" James said "I think he did!" Rachel said "I think we should pray just to be sure!" They bowed their heads and held hands and James began "Lord, thank you for this incredible journey! We are so grateful for all that you have done for us, and through us, and what you continue to do! We seek your guidance as we believe we are to go to Jerusalem. We are planning to leave in the morning. If this is not your desire for us, please send someone to tell us otherwise! In Your Sons name we pray, Amen!"

Rachel said "And we thought Noah was a man of few words! He didn't tell us his name; maybe we should call him the 'Tornado' because he just blew through here!" James laughed and added "Maybe we are becoming veterans in all of this! We lost our rookie status and the longer messages aren't required for savvy veterans like us anymore!" Rachel laughed and said "Maybe we shouldn't be making jokes about this! We could get cut from the team at any time!" James said "Ah, see, you just couldn't help yourself!" Rachel said "Well, that was a fun short stay! But I have to admit, I have always been fascinated by the thought of going to Israel!"

James replied "Me too! We will get to walk where Jesus has walked! There is so much history there to experience, obviously!" Rachel added "Something tells me we are going to get a front line look at that history! James went into the bathroom to get ready for bed. Rachel said "While you get ready, I am going to call mom and dad and let them know we are not staying in New York" James asked "Are you going to tell them where we are going?" Rachel answered if they ask me, yes I will. I do not think we have to keep secrets from them anymore. Right?" James answered "I think you are right, I am sure they are okay to know!"

A few minutes later James came out of the bathroom and asked Rachel "What did they say?" She responded "They didn't answer. That seems a little unusual for them. The Phoenix Suns are playing tonight too; I can't imagine dad isn't camped in front of the TV right now. Oh well, I left a message. They can call us back later. While Rachel was getting ready for bed, James figured it would be a good time to return the call of a buddy he works with and who goes to the same Church with as well.

When his friend answered the phone he said "Hey Cody! It's James Mahody." Cody exclaimed "Well, if it isn't the man of the hour!" James replied "You know me! I try to make a big impression at all costs!" Cody laughed and said "Well, you certainly succeeded there! So what's up?" James answered "Well, I take it you listened to the entire thing with me on TV?" Cody replied "Of course! Very exciting! Besides that, it seems that is the only way to see you these days!"

James said "Ah, rub it in! For good reason though, right?" Cody said "Yeah, I think so! Finding Noah's Ark, or going to work; yeah that is a real toss up!" James continued "Well, listen, I was wondering if you are open to taking on the building of a website like I explained on TV. Of course I will pay you for your time." Cody said "Well, to be honest, when I heard you say that on TV, I knew you meant that it would be me setting up the website! Of course I will! You don't have to pay me either! This is exciting!"

James told him "I will email you everything you need tonight so you can get started. Obviously you'll need to a get a domain name. Pick whatever you think is best! I am serious about paying you. Feel free to get anyone you think would be beneficial involved in the project. Obviously I want all the information possible about the discovery of the Ark, but I want this to be a witnessing tool as well! Give people a chance to have someone to pray with them, sources and people to contact. You know anything a person needs to learn the truth about Jesus as the only way to salvation."

"I hate to cut this short, but we are in New York, and it's late! We need to get to bed!" Cody responded "Okay world traveler! You be safe! I will take care of the website; don't even worry about it! I can't wait to see the pictures myself! Thanks!" James said "Goodnight!" Rachel walked out of the bathroom and asked "Was that my mom and dad?" James said "No, that was Cody. I asked him to put together the website I promised everyone on TV." Rachel replied "Oh, good idea! He is so good at stuff like that!"

After checking out of the hotel they headed to the airport to catch a 7:30 a.m. flight. They were thankful that James chose to book the flight the night before when he signed online to email the pictures. Flying out on short notice and arranging all the connecting flights proved to be challenging. They were relieved they did not have to stress about making it all work from the airport. Shortly after their plane took off Rachel said to James "We are sure racking up the frequent flyer miles aren't we?" James laughed and said "I have flown more miles in the last week than I have my entire life combined!

They finally made their way to Jerusalem and were shocked by all that they saw! Rachel said "There are so many biblical references here, but it's like its no big deal to them! There is a sign to Bethlehem Square! This is so cool!" James said "Look you can see the Dome of the Rock! I can feel it; God has something really big in store for us here! I love to serve God like this! Nothing could be better! Rachel added "This is very exciting, but honestly, it so much more special doing all of this with you!"

Right after they checked into a hotel, they decided to see the Wailing Wall. They approached the wall, and there were people all around. Some were leaning against the wall in prayer, while others just stood there facing the wall in quiet prayer. Some stood at podiums or tall tables reading from their Bibles. The area was very quiet as everyone wanted to be respectful. James and Rachel each stood facing the wall, and quietly said a private Prayer to God thanking Him for all that He'd done. Rachel was so thankful for being able to see her parents again, and thanked Him over and over. She was also thankful that God allowed them to be part of His plans for ushering in Christ's return.

After they finished praying they walked away from the wall, and soon after they heard familiar voices saying "Raech…James!" They turned around to see Rachel's parents! Rachel tried to be quiet but could not help letting her voice get a little loud because she was so excited as she said "What are you two doing here?" John leaned forward and whispered "We don't know! We were told to come here and help you two! So, what are you two doing here?" James said "We don't know either, we haven't been told yet!"

Again, whispering John said "Beck and I had the same dream telling us to come here to Jerusalem to help you serve the Lord. I woke up yesterday morning telling Beck of the wildest dream I had, and the more I told her, the more her jaw dropped! I finally asked why she was having that reaction" Rebecca spoke up saying "I told him I had the same dream, and finished it by saying that we would find you two at the Wailing Wall." John said "I hadn't even told her that part yet, so I was quite surprised when she told me!"

Rachel said "This is wonderful! This is an answered prayer! I was just praying for the two of you at the Wall! God never ceases to surprise does He?" Rebecca said "No He does not! We just wanted to hang out with you guys, and spend some time with you honey! But if we can help on your assignment! Even better!" James said "If God sent you here to be part of it, then it's our assignment! When we arrived here, I could feel God preparing me mentally for something big. I think you two…I think we are all in store for something huge!"

James asked "Have you two checked into a hotel yet?" John answered "No. We came straight here! The dream said to come to Jerusalem and find you two at the Wailing Wall.

That is what we did!" James said "Well, let's go back to our hotel, and make sure you can get a room there so we are all in the same place." Rebecca responded "That is a good idea!" They were happy to find out there was a room next to James and Rachel's. The plan was for John and Rebecca to get checked in and settled, then to meet in James and Rachel's room.

James and Rachel returned to their room to get cleaned up and wait for Rachel's parents. They were both in the bathroom finishing getting cleaned up; James thought he heard someone in their room. He walked out of the bathroom to see a man standing in the corner of the room. The man said "I am Kolesh, Angel and servant of God the most high!" James called to Rachel "Raech, you need to come here!" Rachel came out and saw the man, and she said "Oh, Hi!" James said "This is Kolesh. He is an Angel of God." Rachel whispered "I kind of figured that." Kolesh let a smirk appear on his face.

James asked "Do you have our next assignment?" Kolesh replied "I do, but you have four assigned to this task. We will wait for the other two." At that moment, there was a knock on the door. Rachel opened the door and it was indeed her parents. When they walked in and saw the man Rebecca said "Oh, I am sorry, you have company!" Rachel said "No, well, yes, we have company, but he is here to see you two as well. His name is Kolesh. God has sent…"

Kolesh interrupted and said "If I may! My name is Kolesh; I am an Angel of God, sent by the Creator of all things to give you instruction on yet another discovery, of great historical significance! Already countless numbers are accepting the Christ Jesus as their Messiah as a result of Noah's Ark being found! This find will see equal numbers of people turning to Christ for Salvation! You are about to discover something lost, that was once so Holy, that if a man merely brushed the back of his hand against it he would die! The Ark of the Covenant was mans connection to the Holy dwelling place of the one true God!"

"Of course, with the crucifixion and blood atonement of Jesus; His subsequent resurrection from deaths grip, ascension into heaven, and the arrival of the Holy spirit such a Tabernacle is no long necessary. Our Father in Heaven dwells in each of his people. The bodies of His believers are his dwelling place! Still, skeptics claim that because such a Holy Ark, of significant historical importance has never been found; many question the Word of God as it relates to the accuracy of such an artifact. Tomorrow during the tenth hour, there will be a great earthquake!"

"The Earthquake will cause the temple that is occupied by enemies of God to be destroyed. Below the temple, are caves and hidden passageways that contain the resting place of the Ark of the Covenant! Tomorrow I will lead you away from the Temple, and to an area that holds the door into the tunnel corridor that leads to and from the Temple, that is known today as the Dome of the Rock. A small earthquake will open the Earth, and by extension the opening leading to this tunnel system. I will then lead you down through the tunnels into the cave that houses the Ark of the Covenant. As we arrive, a large Earthquake will cause the entire temple to crumble above us, and be destroyed!"

"While confusion and chaos ensues, you will take the Ark from its resting place and deliver it to God's chosen people! They will take good care of the Ark until His return! They will then offer it to Him as a gift once he establishes His kingdom on Earth! God's chosen people will show the world that the Ark has been returned to them! Many will see this event as the proof they have needed to allow their stubborn hearts to accept the true Word of God, and His message as their one and only path to salvation!"

"Thank the Lord that many will see this as the evidence they need to change their hearts, to repent, to fully commit to Christ Jesus the Savior! This will spare these people the wrath that is to come! Still, many more will need other evidence and occurrences to change there minds. However, blessed are those that receive the Lord of all things, before the rise of the anti-christ and bowl judgments and wrath of God that will occur following the second coming of Jesus. Lord Jesus is returning soon for his faithful, there are few things left for God to do to reach people who simply don't want to be reached!"

"I will return to this dwelling in the ninth hour tomorrow. Between now and then you must devise a way to transport the Ark of the Covenant to the Synagogue of God's chosen people. You must conceal it so that the enemies of God do not try to the thwart your efforts. Good day to you, and peace to those that that truly seek the true and living God!" The four sat in silence for several minutes. Rebecca was terrified. John was stunned at what he just saw. Rachel continued to be in awe of how incredible God is. James was already thinking of a plan to conceal the Ark once they recover it."

Rebecca spoke saying "How am I supposed to contribute to such a thing? I don't think I can do this!" James reassured her "Mom, trust me on this, okay! The victory is already God's! That is one thing you will learn as you do things for God, he isn't dependent on us" Rachel interjected "We are dependent on Him! The fact that God chose us for this, shows that you can do this! Besides, what gives God more glory than doing things through people who really aren't capable of what they end up accomplishing?" Rebecca answered "I know that makes sense, but I feel so in over my head!"

"I thought leading my bible study was a big deal! The ladies in the study would never believe this!" Rebecca began to laugh, and more boldly she spoke "That is really funny to think about! Those ladies would never bet I could do such a thing! You are right, not only can I do this, we will do this!" John was caught off guard by his wife's newfound boldness as he said "Whoa honey! Where did that come from?" Rebecca said "I don't know, but a sense of peace just overcame me, and I am not worried at all! In fact, I am excited and ready for this!"

"What is the plan" she asked? Everyone seemed to look to James as he said "Okay, here is what I am thinking…All over town are those guys who ride the bikes who have the covered canopy trailers to give people rides here and there. I think we should go offer a couple of those guys some money for their bikes. Then tomorrow John, Rebecca and me will follow Kolesh down into the caves to retrieve and carry the Ark out. Rachel, you will stay behind with the bikes. You are going to need to stay somewhat hidden until the right time, but you need to be where you will be safe from the Earthquake as well"

"When you see the Dome crumble to the ground, you will immediately bring the two bikes over to where we originally entered. We will put the Ark in one of the canopy trailers, and you two ladies will sit in the other one. John will ride one bike, and I will ride the other, until we reach the Synagogue." John said "Perhaps we should also pick up the same kind of clothes that the 'bike taxi drivers' wear. That way we don't stand out as we are racing away from the crumbled Dome of the Rock." Rachel and James simultaneously said "Good idea!"

They decided they should leave right away and find a couple of bikes to buy, and do their clothes shopping before it was too late. Shortly after walking out of the hotel, they found a couple of bike taxi drivers to see if they could buy their bikes. Neither wanted to part with their bikes; but after driving up the price close to what it would cost to buy a motorcycle, they had their bicycles and their plan was underway. They immediately took them back to the hotel, and steered them into James and Rachel's room for safekeeping.

They also took note of the clothing the men wore. The bike taxi drivers wore clothes that were not very different than what most of the locals wore. They found a clothing shop. They bought clothes for all of them so they would blend in. It was getting late, but they found a place they all could sit down to eat. Rebecca surprised everyone when she said "This is kind of like Raiders of the Lost Ark!" John teased her saying "You didn't even like that movie!" She shot back saying "Living it is a lot more fun than watching it!"

After they all stopped laughing and sharing their excitement, for what was to happen the following day, they decided to return to the hotel. They figured it was time to call it a night so they could get enough rest for what was sure to be an eventful day. Before they parted ways, the four held hands and prayed together. Rachel led the prayer saying "Father God! I thank you for allowing us to be servants of yours in this most critical time! Thank you for trusting us to allow You to work through us to complete such amazing tasks for You! Thank you for sending me back to my husband that I love so much, to serve You with him! I also thank you for bringing my parents here to help us with this incredible mission! Lord, we devised a plan, and want to submit it to you right now. We hope and pray that our plan is what you would have us do. If not, please let us know and we will gladly change our plan to be in line with Your perfect will! Amen."

The next morning at 9:00 a.m., John and Rebecca were knocking at James and Rachel's door. They welcomed them in, and they had a friendly greeting expressing excitement for doing God's work! John said "I had a dream last night. I was visited by an Angel! It was so amazing how he conveyed to me that the loving hand of the Lord is on us! The sense of peace I had was overwhelming, and it has carried through until this very moment!"

Out of nowhere Kolesh, who they did not even know

had joined them yet said "The Lord has already seen this victory! Peace is all that you should feel! In fact, your Father in heaven does love you and knows the depths of your love for Him. This task that we will accomplish today is for the sole purpose of adding to God's kingdom! There are people doomed to hell as of this moment that by tonight will have their name written in the Book of Life! Is there any greater victory?" James said "Amen!" And the others followed suit.

The Lord heard your prayers last night and indeed, your plans are His plans. Children, victory is already the Lords! It is nearing the specified time. We must go, and ready ourselves for the appropriate moment. They walked outside following Kolesh. James leaned toward Rachel and whispered in her ear "Do you think these people see him?" She whispered back "I have no idea!" James and John were each pushing one of the bikes. They made their way within two hundred yards of the Dome of the Rock. Kolesh motioned to the area in which the opening will appear.

James suggested to Rachel "Over there by those trees, I think that is where you should wait. I would think that those trees are solid enough that a small quake is not going to unearth them! Be ready though! Let's take the Bikes over there, and then we will follow you Kolesh when you tell us it's time, okay?" Kolesh said "As you have said." They moved the bikes under the trees and waited. James looked at his watch and it was only a few minutes before 10:00 a.m., so he knew it would be anytime! At that point, Kolesh said "Let's go!"

They walked away from the Dome of the rock, in the wide open area towards a ravine. The ground began to shake. They could hear screams from the people in the area. James immediately looked back toward Rachel but it did not appear the ground was shaking where she was at! Right before them, a hole in the ground appeared, and Kolesh immediately went down into it. Following behind him was Rebecca, John, and James. The cave was dark but Kolesh appeared to have a slight glow to him, so they could see where he was going and stayed close behind him!

Two minutes and about seven turns later through the winding corridor, they made another turn into a space that opened up into a room. There in the center of the room was the Ark of the Covenant! Kolesh exclaimed "There it is!" In the center of the room was a golden box that stood about two feet by four feet. The Ark had the most beautiful Cherubim Angles on both sides, with their wings outstretched towards each other, as if they were protecting the Ark! Each corner had a solid gold ring, so that staves could be inserted into the rings so that the Ark could be carried. The staves were lying beside the Ark.

Kolesh told them to insert the Staves and carry it out. John and Rebecca were on one side and James on the other. Just as they lifted the Ark and were stepping out of the room, the ground began to shake and the noise from above was loud and frightening! Kolesh said "Do not worry! You are safe under God's protection! God will keep these tunnels safe until we are out!" They moved as quickly as they could while trying to be as respectful of the Ark as possible. They all knew of the story of the Ark of the Covenant. They knew that the Holiness of the Ark was no longer the same as it was before the crucifixion of Jesus.

They still felt an amazing sense of reverence being around it. All three of them were captivated by it, and yet felt they should not look at it either! When they came out of the tunnel, from where they went in, they found Rachel right there waiting with the bikes. They quickly put the Ark on one of the trailers so no one could see. The ladies quickly sat in the other canopy trailer, and the men quickly pedaled away. James said to John "Nobody even knows we are here! Everyone is so panicked nobody is paying attention to us!"

They biked as quickly as they could to the Synagogue, so they could hand over the Ark of the Covenant to the Church. They were greeted by a Rabbi who was shocked to see what they had. In complete astonishment he asked "Where did you get this?" James answered "This is going to be hard to believe, but we were sent by God to recover this from below the Dome of the Rock and to give it to you!" The rabbi responded "Sent by God? Is this some kind of joke?" John told the Rabbi "Sir, this is certainly not a joke! We were told of the Earthquake before it happened, and were told to be ready to go in and get the Ark at the right time"

James continued "We were instructed to deliver the Ark of the Covenant to God's chosen people and that you would protect it." The Rabbi responded "Well, what are we supposed to do with it?" James said "God wants you to show the world! He wants the world to know that not only is it in Israel, but it is where it belongs with His people, and not being held below His enemy's feet! Rebecca asked "Rabbi, do you believe this to be true?" The Rabbi said "I do, clearly this is the Ark of the Covenant that I have read about in the scriptures; yes I do believe!"

Rebecca continued "Then there is something else you must know! The same God that sent his Angel to tell us of the location of Ark of the Covenant, and to lead us to its resting point, also sent His Son into the world as the Savior of the World! He wants you to know, that the Messiah you are waiting for, already came; Just over two thousand years ago! He was born of the Virgin Mary, shared His message with his people, was crucified, and rose to life again three days later! You have known of the Messiah your entire life, but have rejected Jesus Christ as the true Messiah because you have had your eyes shielded to the truth!"

"The same God, the one and only true God commands the veil be lifted from your eyes, and know that the truth of the Messiah is in the very scriptures you have devoted yourself to studying! He loves you! He died for you! He wants you to accept Him! He is coming again! He is coming again very soon and will take his believers with Him!" The Rabbi looked stunned to hear all that she had to say. Tears began to stream down his face and fell to his knees and began to cry out to God!

"Father God! I am so sorry that I have been blind this whole time! I am so sorry that I held tradition over truth in my heart! I beg you to please forgive me! Forgive me Father, and allow me to receive your gift, your precious Son as my blessed redeemer, my Savior! How could I have not allowed myself to accept this truth that is so clear to me at this moment! For the first time in my life, the scriptures truly are alive in my heart, and I fully comprehend them now! Thank you Father! Thank you for sending these people, and thank you for your continued blessings!"

The Rabbi stood up and said "Thank you for following the will of God! I will pray many blessings for you! I know what to do! I now know what to do in many regards for the first time in my life! But I will take care of God's sacred temple, and make sure that is preserved! They parted ways and Rachel said "Mom! Where did that come from?" Rebecca answered "From God! I was just standing there and as I was looking at the Rabbi I could feel God speaking directly to my heart!"

I felt him say 'Therefore, whoever confesses Me before men, him I will also confess before My Father who is in heaven. But whoever denies Me before men, I will also deny before My Father who is in heaven.' Then I heard Him say 'Confess my name to him Rebecca!' The feeling was so intense! I just knew! I had no reason to hesitate! I knew!" John said "Well, as much as I know that was God speaking through you, I am proud of you! The strength with which you spoke was inspiring! I already accepted Christ as my savior long ago, and I wanted to do it again!" James gave his mother and law a kiss on the cheek and said "That was incredible! Thank you for letting us witness God working through you!"

They biked back to the hotel. They left the bikes outside this time, not caring if they were taken. They all went to James and Rachel's room to sit and talk, and to plan their trip home. John asked if he could lead them in prayer and, of course, they all agreed. He began "Father God, we are truly humbled that you have chosen us to be part of such an exciting, and yet profoundly important event for you! To do what we were able to do today, and witness the things we saw, were nothing short of the miraculous power that You have! You are a mighty and awesome God, the true beginning and the end, and we love you! We are here, to serve you in any capacity that you lead us! We love you Jesus! Amen!"

The other three said Amen, and they also heard another "Amen" from behind them. They looked up to see who Rachel and James recognized as Kaleb! Rachel exclaimed "Kaleb!" Rachel introduced her parents to him. Kaleb said "My friends, and fellow servants of Jesus Christ, the Risen King! You have made your Father in heaven proud once again! Your servitude has included unwavering faith and Trust in He who has sent you! You may be interested in knowing, that already several other Rabbis in the Synagogue have accepted Christ as their Savior!" James said "That is wonderful news!"

Kaleb continued "That is just the beginning! As word spreads about discovery of the Ark, and its new residence, and the destruction of the Temple controlled by enemies of God, many, many more will come to accept Jesus Christ as their Lord and Savior. The serpent devil and his evil demons are squirming and gnashing their teeth at this very moment in time! He is plotting his next move, but as it has always been, he will fail! Soon, the Creator of all things will defeat him! You have done very well! You should be very proud knowing that God has worked his mite through you to bring millions to the kingdom of heaven!"

"For now, you have earned some rest. However, be ready for your next calling, because there is still more work to do before Jesus returns! His return is indeed very close at hand. As you know, he will come like a thief in the night to many! Go in peace my friends! Relax and enjoy the rest you have earned!" Rachel asked "What about me? Am I going back with you until there is more work to do?" Kaleb responded "My Dear daughter of God, you are going to spend eternity in heaven with your Father! You have the choice to return with me now and wait for your loved ones. Or you may stay and enjoy a restful period with them, before you are called to do good works for the Lord again. Then, when the trumpet sounds; you will all join Jesus together in Heaven!

Rachel looked at James and her family and said to Kaleb "I love my family, and I love doing good works for the Lord! That said, nothing is better than heaven! But, I cannot bear to cause my husband and parents another moment of sadness being without me. So if the choice is mine, for as little time as we have left here, I would like to stay to love them, and to serve with them!" Kaleb said "It is as you have requested! Rachel said "Thank you Kaleb! You have been a good friend since I first met you! Kaleb responded "Oh, child, God has blessed me to see you through His eyes. You are so, so special, and mightily loved!

After Kaleb left they made their plans to depart Jerusalem. They knew they could not go back to Phoenix together but they also knew they were not going to live apart! James took Rachel in his arms and said "To think this all started with some visions that made me think I was going crazy! And now, hear I stand holding my best friend, and the only girl I ever loved in my arms! I know you did not give up heaven, but thank you for putting it off for just a little while longer, for us! Rachel's parents approached and put their arms around Rachel and James, and John said "I am glad to have you back baby girl!

They knew they needed to go somewhere that people would not be likely to accidentally discover Rachel. Since John and Rebecca always discussed a retirement home in Hawaii, they believed that made the most sense to be able to explain to the rest of the family. Of course James and Rachel thought living in a Hawaii for a little while would be fun too!

They followed the news closely, listening to stories and

people continuing to speak about the destruction of the temple, and how amazing it was that the two Arks had been discovered. James kept in touch with Cody to monitor the website and was excited to help thousands of people who had visited the website learn about Christ and ultimately accept him as their Savior!

Several months had gone by with the four enjoying most of their time spent in the sun and in bathing suits. During that time they did not have any more visits from Angels, or any visions. They knew that was soon about to change. There had been many discussions in the world news concerning a man rising to power in the European community. They knew it was just a matter of time before Jesus would return. They also knew, before His return, God would have more assignments for them to complete. They returned from dinner one night after enjoying a fun day on the beach. They were greeted by an Angel waiting for them inside their home. He said "Servants of God, I am Shale, and I am here to here to deliver a most important message to you…"

Acts 2:17-18

> *And it shall come to pass after That I will pour out My Spirit on all flesh; You sons and daughters shall prophecy, Your old men shall dream dreams, Your young men shall see visions. And also on My menservants and on Maidservants will I pour out My spirit In those days.*

Mathew 34:36:44

But the day and hour no one knows, not even the Angels of heaven, But my Father only. But as the days of Noah were, so also will The coming of the Son of Man be. For as in the days before the flood They were eating and drinking, marrying and giving in marriage, until The day that Noah entered the ark, and did not know until the flood came And took them all away, so also will the coming of the Son of Man be. Then two men will be in the field: one will be taken, the other left. Two women will be grinding at the mill: one will be taken, and the other left. Watch, therefore, for you do not know what hour your Lord is coming. But know this, that if the master of the house had known what hour the thief would come, he would have watched and not allowed his house to be broken into. Therefore you also be ready, for the Son of Man is coming at an hour you do not expect.